MW00617962

KRISTI COPELAND

KRISTI COPELAND

Twisted Tales Publishing 2023

Heaven Scent

Twisted Tales Publishing 2023

For information contact :

https://kristicopelandwriter.com/

Cover design: Pretty Indie: Book Cover Designs

Editor: Brian Paone

Formatting Template : Derek Murphy

ISBN: 978-1-7376339-9-0 (paperback)
978-1-7376339-8-3 (ebook)

For Jenni:

All our shenanigans could never have happened if you hadn't saved me from getting my ass kicked in eighth grade. For that, I am forever grateful! One day, I'll write that book…

CCHS 4-ever!

SET LIST

Lemonade	1
Cold as Ice	2
Cat Scratch Fever	17
Love Song	27
Hazy Shade of Winter	40
Garage Days	54
I’m not Alright	69
Livin’ on a Prayer	85
Famous in a Small Town	95
It's My Life	103
Stronger	117
Don’t You (Forget About Me)	131
Start of Something Good	142
God Blessed Texas	152
All Star	169
Girl on Fire	180

Heaven Scent

Master of Puppets 192

Paradise City 204

Fallen Angel 222

Party in the USA 230

Girls Just Want to Have Fun 243

Don't Stop Believin' 255

Uptown Funk 268

Who Says You Can't Go Home 282

She's a Big Star 299

Part 1

Callaghan's 12.16.06

Manic Monday

Seek & Destroy

Animals

I hate myself for Loving You

Summertime!

Nothin' But A Good time

Fancy

Love Song

Rock on!

Cowboy

Edge of 17

No Sleep til Brooklyn!

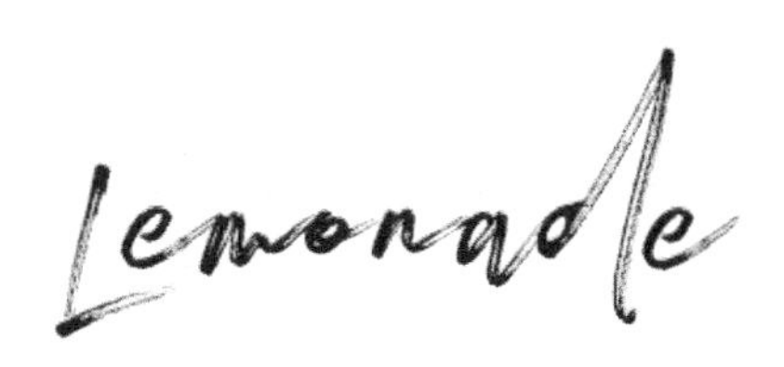

The Interview: January 8, 2015

"THANK YOU, *Dallaaaasss*!"

Pyrotechnics explode behind the stage as streams of white extend from floor to ceiling. Multicolored bursts of fireworks illuminate the rest of the arena as the roar of twenty thousand people drowns out all other sounds.

The band members of Heaven Scent saunter toward the front of the stage to form a line. Lead singer Alli Summer, lead guitarist Charlie Stanley, and bass player Sara Deville arrive to their positions first. In awe of the energy their fans are producing, they join hands and raise them in unison. The girls perform a well-rehearsed end-of-concert bow and blow kisses to their fans in the front row.

The drummer, Tommy Tomac, bounces from his pedestal at the back of the stage and jogs to join his bandmates for another bow. Adrenaline flows through the veins of the foursome as they turn and walk backstage. Even though they have toured for years, nothing compares to this sort of rush. After another spectacular show, the band shares congratulations in the form of hugs and high fives.

Drumsticks beat the air in Tommy's path while he walks behind the bar. Longhorns and barbed wire decorate the wall above a flat-screen TV. In his after-concert routine, he mixes a drink for Alli, pours a glass of wine for Charlie, grabs beers, and pours shots for Sara and himself. A silver tray sits on the bar; he loads it up and carries it to the coffee table.

In the center of the room, two cowhide sofas, with end tables at each side, sit on either edge of a cowhide rug. An eccentric glass-top coffee table is situated between the couches. Overstuffed chairs at each end complete a rectangle of coziness. The scent of barbeque lingers from the meet-and-greet prior to the show.

Unable to sit still, Alli bounces from side to side as her fisted hands punch the air. Brunette curls move in sync as her excitement flows free. Leather pants accentuate her curvy shape, and a loose-fitting see-through purple button-up shirt covers a tank top.

Charlie picks up her glass of wine, sinks into a chair, and rests her head against the cushion as she pushes a howl from her throat. Jeans with holes in the knees cover cowboy boots. Long sleeves on a white gauzy top are rolled up to her elbows.

Sara leans her head back and spins in a circle as her black shoulder-length hair drifts away from her face. Outstretched arms provide balance until she stops to ward off the dizziness and giggles. Her short black skirt and signature calf-high stiletto boots reveal long muscled legs. A sparkly, cheetah-print tank top completes the ensemble.

A security guard opens one of the French doors and

announces a visitor. "Charlie, this nice young lady has a pass and is on the list for an appointment. Says here her name is ..." He pauses to confirm the name on his clipboard. "Jennifer Schneider."

"Thanks, Jack. We're expecting her."

Alli lined up an interview with a fan who is writing a book based on a girl band from a small town. At first, Charlie thought the idea was a little kooky, but Alli and Sara convinced her that it would be fun to reminisce. What perfect timing that Mike Allen surprised the band tonight and introduced them to his family; they wouldn't have made it to the top without him. Four years came and went like a speeding freight train. None of them had any idea how meeting Mike at his bar in LA would be a monumental, life-changing event.

An attractive young lady steps through the doors. Dressed in a black leather jacket over a black sweater with ripped jeans, she looks comfortably classy. Her black cowboy boots create a light thump in her wake.

Before they have a chance to speak, Charlie gets a positive vibe from the woman and instantly approves; she just knows they will be great friends.

Unsure of herself, Jennifer holds a notepad close to her chest with one hand and her purse strap for comfort in the other. "Hi there. I'm here for the interview." She removes her gloves and stuffs them in her purse before she reaches toward Sara to shake hands. "My name is Jennifer Schneider, but everyone calls me Jenni. It's so nice to meet you, Sara."

Jenni shivers from either the cold or nerves; she's not quite sure. She surveys the room, her gaze landing on the rest of the group, individually. "It's just so great to meet everyone. I must tell you that tonight's performance was absolute perfection. I have been to my fair share of concerts, but y'all really have a fantastic presence. I'm a huge fan and, to be honest, a little nervous." A shy smile graces Jenni's face. "This is all surreal. I hope you'll bear with me."

Tommy hands her a bottle of Coors Light and nods. "Welcome. Come, have a seat." He backs toward the bar and lifts himself onto a stool, the bottom rung supporting his feet.

"Thanks, Tommy." Two swigs later, the author exhales and blinks slowly before she settles into a chair. "I needed this."

"Eh, we're all friends here." Alli offers a genuine smile and dismisses any tension with a wave of her hand. She grabs her drink from the tray and relaxes onto a couch, "Tell me, Jenni, what made you want to write this book?"

"Well, I'm from Brooklyn, too, and I love your story. You are such an inspiration to so many; your positive lyrics reassure young girls, and boys too, that they are good enough and to never give up. I want to capture your essence and share it with the world."

"I love that. Thank you." Charlie lifts her eyebrows. "It'll be so much fun to revisit all these memories. Hope you have some time; this might take a while." She nods toward the pen and pad of paper in Jenni's lap and playfully gives her a hard time. "Goin' old school, eh?"

A digital recorder appears in Jenni's hand, and she places it on the coffee table. "Don't worry. I have a voice recorder. This"—Jenni twirls her pen—"is for key words that I want to be sure to find within the recording."

Sara sits in the other chair. A shot of tequila sits beside a bottle of beer. She drinks the shot, grimaces, then chases it with the beer. Even though this drink combination is her after-concert ritual, it makes her shiver every time. She leans back and crosses her ankles on the glass tabletop.

Charlie silently thanks Alli for this opportunity by raising her drink. She admitted to herself that going back in time would be fun and most likely entertaining. Guarding her heart had been a thing of the past; she found it healing, to be honest, unlike when she was growing up in Brooklyn.

Satisfied with the approval, Alli nods. "Let's do this."

"Okay. Let's begin." Jenni presses the record button. "My style of interview is a little different from most. Instead of asking single questions and receiving single answers, I like to ask a series of questions and let a story unfold. Let's start at the beginning. Tell me, how did all this start? How did you know each other? Was one or all of you in the high school band or choir? What did your family think about you forming a band? What was your life like in Brooklyn in two thousand five? What were some of your favorite ways to pass the time?"

Charlie, Alli, and Sara smile and, as if it had been a normal occurrence, sing in unison, "Girls with guitars." Their signature Bill-and-Ted-style air-guitar riff finishes the phrase.

Confused, Jenni squints and shakes her head.

The founding members of Heaven Scent laugh. Charlie explains, "Well, Jenni, it all started when I got a guitar for Christmas ..."

Cold as Ice

Charlie: December 26, 2004

"PUT YOUR fingers like this, then strum the strings." An unlit Marlboro Light hung from my lips.

"Like this?" Alli's fingers on her left hand contorted on the neck of the guitar, and her right hand strummed the strings.

"That's it! See? It sounds just like Deep Purple." The flame from my lighter was barely visible but hot enough to light the end of my cigarette. I sucked on the filter and inhaled the mild smoke, then exhaled three perfectly shaped *O*s and one misshapen oval.

Alli sat beside me on my bed, bent over my new guitar that sat cradled in her lap. Brown eyes, hidden under long brown bangs, darted between her hands. Focused on the placement of her fingers, she completed exactly three repetitions before skipping a beat, the rhythm lost.

With pursed lips and knit eyebrows, she huffed and shook her head, then pushed my Christmas present back into my hands. "I suck."

The snow-white Fender had been my one and only

gift. Honestly, I was more than a little pissed that my sisters each got five gifts. But I guess since the guitar was the only thing I had asked for, it was the only thing my mom thought I deserved.

Whatever. I tried to convince myself it was okay and that my mom was just naturally an asshole. At least now, Alli, Sara, and I could form the next Heart. This guitar symbolized a step in the right direction, one less hurdle for us to jump before becoming a rock band. Sara already had a bass guitar, and with Alli's God-given steely, rustic voice, all we needed was a drummer.

Music was our life; it was all we thought about, besides boys, and most of what we talked about, besides boys. We lusted after rock band members, no matter their position in the band; although everyone knows lead singers are the hottest, followed closely by the lead guitarist.

"Yeah, you do." Sara giggled from the bean bag in the corner of my room. "That's why you should leave the stringed instruments to me and Charlie. You've been tuning your voice for ages so you can just be pretty and sing." The bass guitar she owned had been a gift from her grandmother. Sara's mother refused to buy anything for her other than absolute necessities.

For the past three years, Sara had focused on learning how to play and used her growing talent to escape her daily home life. She had spent most of her free time in her room, with our favorite music pumping through headphones. She had to keep her amp low enough so her parents couldn't hear it in the kitchen, otherwise they would punish her.

Our friendship had transformed from acquaintances to besties during freshman year in high school. Once we'd realized we had interests and life-sized goals in common, we became inseparable. The bond we formed was strong—better than sisters. The differences in our home lives had enticed our curiosity. My mom's snarky, flat-out mean words would hurt more than my sister's punches, and Sara's mom would ridicule her about being too fat.

If we didn't love Alli so much, we would probably hate her. It wasn't fair how much her parents supported everything she and her brother ever attempted. She wasn't perfect, by any means, but her mom and dad thought she hung the moon. The ability to ask any question about each other's home life allowed us to be open and honest. Our love as friends grew with every story we shared.

"Here. Listen." I handed Alli my cigarette to hold, not smoke. It made me feel like the rock star that I would be one day. For two entire days, smiling came easily and often. For once, my mom's words didn't matter.

I sat with the guitar on my knee and expertly strummed the first chords of "Smoke on the Water." I didn't even need to look at my fingers anymore, so I grinned at my new bandmates as I played. Granted, it was the easiest thing on Earth to learn, but I figured since I had only been playing for two days, I was doing pretty damned good. I wasn't concerned in the least that Alli and Sara had more years of perfecting their talent. I was determined to catch up and promised myself that I would practice every day.

With one foot tucked under her, Alli sat next to me on the bed so she could face me as I played. She placed the cigarette between my lips and moved her fingers as she tried to mimic mine.

Air guitar, literally.

"You're really okay if I only sing?"

"Only?" Sara stood and joined us on the bed, the mattress sinking under her weight. "We can't be a band without an incredible lead singer. You'll be one-fourth of the most important positions."

"Being in choir all these years will pay off, I'm sure. My mom always says I have a unique voice. I never really knew if that was a compliment or not, but I'm gonna roll with it."

"Alli, come on. You know your voice is magical. Angelic, even."

Alli rolled her eyes. "Oh, stop it." She batted her eyelashes. "No, really, go on." The way she giggled always made me shake my head.

"I'm serious. Your steely rasp is so sexy. My voice is way too soft. Innocent, almost. I will never understand why. We both know how far from accurate that is." I winked. "The night you came over after the Rob and Bob incident and you sang "Love Song" to me, that was the night I knew, for sure, you will be a star. I couldn't even cry anymore after you looked into my eyes and poured your heart into mine. That wasn't the first time your voice touched my soul, but it was when I knew, for sure, we'll be famous. Every time I hear you sing, I know we will make it big." With raised eyebrows, I nodded at my best friend. "It's true."

Blushing, Alli changed directions. "You've already mastered this guitar, and with Sara's expertise plucking those bass strings, nothing can stop us." She fell backward on the bed and reached for the bottle on the nightstand. "I bet Kevin would agree to be our drummer. He's constantly banging on his set in the basement. There is literally no rhyme or reason when he plays, drives my mom crazy. You've heard him, though. He's pretty good."

"I think that's a great idea. He has some older friends who might have some connections, too." I stopped playing and blew another perfect smoke ring into the center of the room. My beloved guitar gently found its way into the hard-sided padded case before I latched it closed and put it away. It lived under my bed—the hiding place of many treasures.

After Alli took a swig from the bottle of pop, her face puckered, and she took another drink. "I'm not sure

I like this Mountain Dew. Why does it taste weird? It's not stale, but …" She wrinkled her nose and shook her head again.

"Girl, will you never learn?" Sara teased. "You're lucky this time. I only mixed in some Southern. I heard Rick drank someone's chew spit at a party in Adrian last week. He picked up a bottle without knowing what was in it and drank it. Serves him right. Asshole."

"Oh my God, that's disgusting. I bet he tried to make out with Julia after that, too. Nasty!" Another Alli-nose-wrinkle.

A smile tugged at the corner of my mouth.

"Do we have to wait for Kevin to name our band? Or can we choose without him?" Alli wondered out loud.

"Is Kevin here?" With my lips pursed and eyebrows raised, I twitched my head. "Hell, we're nice enough to include him. I say we decide."

"Agree." Sara reached for the bottle.

"Mr. Scary," I said, suggesting my favorite George Lynch piece, then laughed.

"Yeah, because we're guys," Alli said, picking up on my goof.

The three of us went back and forth with ideas until we found a name we all agreed would fit.

"Fine, then. How about It's My Life?"

"Teen Spirit."

"Gypsy Cry."

"Iris."

"Brooklyn."

"Nah, not original enough." Alli shook her head.

"Fuel."

"American Idiot."

"Speak for yourself," Sara said, laughing.

"Sugar."

"Tears in Heaven."

"Heaven Sent."

"Ooh, yeah. That's it." Alli nodded, eyes wide. Her grin spread from ear to ear. "Heaven Sent but spelled like a perfume—s.c.e.n.t."

"Sara?" I asked, and she nodded.

"Deal." I outstretched both pinkies to seal the deal with my two best friends.

We had just named our girl band, Heaven Scent.

Best. Day. Ever.

Charlie: January 3, 2005

THE NEXT WEEK at school, Alli and I walked down the hallway like it was any other Monday. That day was different, though. We were going to be a rock band.

"Okay, so it's official. You're the new lead singer of Heaven Scent. What do you think?" I finally got it through Alli's thick skull that this was seriously going to happen. Because I had gotten a guitar for Christmas, our dream of forming a band and being rock stars had changed from just that—a dream—to reality.

"Pretty fucking cool. Pretty fucking scary." She lowered her chin and gazed at me through her eyelashes. "What if I let you down? What if I'm not good enough?" Her lips tightened, and she sighed.

"You won't. You are." I hoped my simple words would encourage Alli to believe in herself. "Ask your mom if you can take voice lessons if you're worried. The way you sing in the car when we're goofing around, and especially the way you sang "Love Song" to me, dude, you got this."

Alli focused on her hands and picked at her fingernail polish as kids passed us in the hallway. I could almost see the movie playing in her head as she mulled over the concept of being the lead singer in a rock band.

Over a matter of seconds, a smirk spread into a grin and ended in a full-blown smile. Long bangs hung over her eyes as she nodded and gazed at me. Then the toothy smile faded. "I'll have to get new boobs," she said with a straight face.

"Ha!" She totally caught me off guard; I lost my grip on the pile of books in my arms and juggled them before they dropped to the floor. A giggle started in my throat as I visualized double *D*s on Alli's small frame. Backed up to a random locker, I couldn't hold back as the laughter grew into hysterics. I could hardly breathe thanks to my friend's reaction. I had to sit down.

"What? You think I could get on stage wearing a kiddie bra? How would we ever attract groupies?"

Cool fingers wrapped around my arm and tugged me to my feet. My breath caught again and caused me to spurt an unattractive hiccup. At least this made her relax a little.

"Come on, get up. It's not that funny."

"It's kinda funny." Metal rattled behind me as I used the locker to stand. "One of these days, I'll steal one of my mom's bras, put it on you, and stuff watermelons in it. Then you'll know what it feels like to have double *D*s." I hovered both hands a foot from my chest as a visual.

This got her to giggle, then finally laugh at the ridiculous idea.

We pushed through the gymnasium doors with the last of the students. A faint odor lingered from the most recent boys' gym class. I always wondered why they didn't freshen up the place before they herded the entire school into a stinky venue.

Pep rallies always proved to be lame, but at least they got us out of class early. Each grade essentially had assigned seats in the gym bleachers. The rest of our sophomore classmates were at the far end of the gym, and we climbed the steps to our spot behind Sara and her boyfriend, Jeff Bradley.

Sara wore her usual black t-shirt and black jeans, which blended nicely with her black hair and brown eyes. According to her mom, black was slimming. She carried a few extra pounds but wasn't as big as she thought—or as her mom forced her to think she was.

Jeff wore his usual skater swag with ripped jeans. His punk spiked black hair with frosted tips clashed with Sara's look, but they made such a cute couple. She was artsy and passionate, and he was laid back.

The marching band gathered at the corner of the gym floor and played the Columbia Central Fight Song. The vice principal called the names of the basketball players and motioned for them to gather in the center of the gym floor. Each of them wore their game jerseys to school on every game day. Between the crowd of kids, the blares coming from the band, and the speaker squeaking with feedback, I started to get a headache.

"Sara, I would ask what you're wearing to AllSkate on Saturday, but I think I can guess. Black, black, black, and black." Having to yell over the noise annoyed me.

"Yep. Shirt, jeans, shoes, jacket. At least my mom won't have a reason to call me fat." She didn't take her gaze off the cheerleaders. Admiring their thin frames, Sara gawked at every move. She told us that she hoped one day she would be just as skinny and pretty as all the popular girls in class.

"You are aware that a buck thirty is *not* fat, right?" I overheard Jeff say as he raised his eyebrows at Sara to prove his point. Her rail-thin mother had beaten her down throughout her entire life so even with his encouraging words, she still didn't believe it.

"Whatever ..." she mumbled and looked away, her hair falling in front of her eyes—another way to hide. His concern showed, but he didn't push the issue. The way he held her hand or put his arm around her whenever they were together was his way to support his girl.

"Hey, Jeff, will your cousin from Jackson be there? What's his name? Tony?" I asked, trying to be nonchalant.

Tony was so hot, with long dirty-blond shoulder-length straight hair and sky-blue eyes. He was taller than me but not what most people would consider tall. His bad-boy persona had me hooked; his go-to leather jacket with a concert t-shirt underneath and acid-washed jeans was just my style.

"Like you really don't remember his name." Alli rolled her eyes.

Zip it!" I grinned.

Charlie: January 8, 2005

"I LOVE THIS place!" With a smile that spread ear to ear, I found it impossible to hide my pleasure. I paid the two dollar entry fee to the door attendant and entered AllSkate. AC/DC's "Back in Black" assaulted my ears in a good way.

Teenagers packed the roller rink—all kinds of teenagers. No matter how they dressed, they all talked to each other. Boys with long hair or mullets, dressed in leather jackets and acid-washed jeans, talked to good girls. You know, the ones dressed in knee-length cotton skirts and tight light blue cashmere sweaters, with pristine straight hair pulled into a pony or hanging down their back.

Everyone happily mingled with everyone else, which surprised me. Unlike at school where cliques caused constant anxiety, this gathering place was like church; status didn't matter.

Lights flashed from behind the DJ table as Alli, Sara, and I passed it on the way to the dancefloor. The scent of buttery popcorn from the dining area made my stomach grumble.

Even though the venue was almost as packed as a concert, we had no need to push people out of the way. This place was different; taps and nudges with an "Excuse me" here and there worked just fine.

"Hollaback Girl" started to play; it took the entire length of the song just to reach the middle of the rink. Once we got settled at 'our' spot on the floor for the next few hours, I lost myself in the music. In this place, my mom couldn't yell at me, my sister wasn't a dick, and my dad's sad eyes didn't make me want to cry.

With my eyes closed, my feet and hips moved to the beat; this was my happy place. I stretched my arms to the ceiling as my body turned in a circle without thought. I sang along with the songs I knew so well, and my heart swelled. Stress left my body like exhaling smoke from a Marlboro Light.

Before we collapsed from exhaustion, we agreed to take a break. A line of chairs at the back wall offered an area to catch our breath. Tony found me and grabbed my hand; he had just arrived and wanted to dance. He pulled me back onto the dancefloor and wrapped me in his arms. He smelled of my favorite cologne, Polo, and cigarette smoke.

Joey Lane, one of Tony's friends, asked Alli to dance. She thought he was cute but not nearly as hot as her brother's best friend, Tex Sanchez; she danced with him, anyway. Joey was taller than most guys in our class, thin but not skinny, and sported a spiky brown mullet that covered his shoulders.

The kind of guys we typically chased leaned more to the stoner crowd and dressed accordingly. Joey's family had money; he told us that his mom pretty much forced him to wear sweaters and khakis. Jeans weren't allowed at his house. He and Alli looked cute together, so there wasn't any reason to judge based on his clothing choices. He was still a hottie.

The next two hours flew by. We all danced

together, song after song, only sitting out when we needed to catch our breath.

"Shit! It's midnight." Sara pointed to the clock on the wall. "You guys have to go."

Alli gasped and grabbed my arm. "Come on."

Like Cinderella, she must have thought she would lose her glass slipper or my mom's car would turn into a pumpkin. I smiled over my shoulder to Tony, shrugged, and waved to Sara and Jeff before I followed my anxious friend through groups of dancing teenagers.

Alli worried more about the potential of my mom exploding if we made her wait than I did. She had only witnessed a couple examples of my family drama, but she knew how mad my mom could get. I honestly didn't care if we got in trouble. No matter how much my mom screamed about grounding me and refusing to let me leave the house, I always went out when I wanted, anyway.

"Okay, slow down. I'm right behind you. Don't forget our coats." I pushed past Alli and led the way to the locker area so we could snatch our leather jackets.

Alli rushed to the exit door and pushed it open with such force that she tripped and almost fell outside. The cold air shoved us backward, as if we had run into a bowl of Jell-O. We staggered, laughing, into the cold night air just as my mom pulled to the curb in her black Camaro.

"Oh, thank God. We're not late." Relieved, Alli

relaxed. Her shoulders eased, and she exhaled; steam bellowed into the air.

My mom watched us cross in front of her car with squinted eyes. I could tell she wondered why we were laughing. God forbid we enjoyed ourselves. After we piled into the passenger side and back seat, Alli and I traded a look; we agreed to keep our mouths shut as we settled in for the thirty-minute ride home.

We never talked in the car with my mom. When my sister Sam drove, it was a free-for-all, but my mom didn't need to know any of my private life. One time, Alli had said something about a cute guy who had talked to me, and my mom had blown up on me in front of her. For the rest of that weekend, all I'd heard was how irresponsible I was and how I would probably end up pregnant before I graduated and how I would never amount to anything. All because a cute guy had talked to me.

Needless to say, Alli understood and didn't make the mistake again.

Cat Scratch Fever

Sara: August 25, 2005

"MRS. SUMMER, these are the best cookies I've ever tasted. Better than store-bought, for sure. My mom doesn't bake; she's diligent about keeping her girlish figure. She doesn't really cook at all." Another bite of chocolate chip deliciousness quieted my rambling mouth. "She would kill me if she knew I ate two of these instead of an apple or celery."

I could never figure out why Alli's mom made me so comfortable that I almost spilled my emotional beans every time I talked to her. Was it her smile or her sense of calm? Her mothering skills far outweighed my own mothers, and she encouraged me to open up without even speaking to me. She listened intently and acted as if she really cared about what I said. Not just me, either, but all of her kids' friends.

"Well, Sara, if you want an apple, you're welcome to it, but I doubt two cookies will hurt." She winked and smiled. "And thank you for the compliment, but Alli makes all the cookies and cakes in this house. She's not only a talented singer but a fantastic baker. I'm surprised you didn't know that."

Alli shrugged when I gaped at her, grabbed the entire plate of cookies, and led us into the garage where Charlie, Kevin, and his girlfriend Shelly waited. I followed her and peppered her with rhetorical questions. "You cook? You bake? What the hell, Alli, you never told me that. You always let me assume it was your mom."

Mrs. Summer followed us, carrying a tray of glasses filled with iced tea and lemonade. During practice, she always served us something to drink. "I have to keep the big stars hydrated." Her singsong voice made us all roll our eyes. Alli's mom was supportive but a bit of a helicopter. "Are you all ready for the concert tonight? Who are you seeing again? Ted something? Kevin, you're driving, right? And Shelly, you're going too? You know I don't like Alli, Sara, and Charlie to be alone in such a large place. They're just a little too young yet."

"Mom, we got it under control. Don't you worry." Kevin cooed his practiced bullshit and flashed his best good-boy smile.

Once we climbed into Kevin's black-and-yellow-striped car, he let us have it. "When I drop you off in Jackson, you better fucking behave. If you get in trouble, I get in trouble, then none of us can go anywhere. Got it?"

"WELL? SPILL, Charlie. What happened backstage?" Tony ran his hand through his long blond hair and replaced the feather that had fallen from behind his ear. He was kinda cute when he got jealous, not annoying like most guys. Charlie lucked out with this one.

She hadn't told him that Alli had won VIP tickets on Q106 until we entered Pine Knob and were on our way to find an empty spot on the lawn. That may have been a little cruel, but the three of us wanted it to be as special as possible for us, as a band. Who knew? This could be our first 'foot in the door' opportunity. If given the chance, we planned to introduce ourselves as an up-and-coming rock band.

"Oh my *God*! That was the best hour of my life," Charlie answered for all of us.

Joey hung his head a little, not that anyone noticed except me. He had been jealous in an entirely different way than Tony. His insecurity showed through in the form of sad puppy-dog eyes.

My boyfriend wasn't jealous at all; he had been excited about me meeting and talking to famous rock stars and would stand by my side no matter what. "I can totally imagine how our backstage experience will be in the future. Not sure it will be as wild as what we saw tonight, but we'll have fun, for sure."

I snuggled into Jeff, and he kissed the top of my head. The pressure of his fingertips squeezing my hip raised my temperature; I could feel my face blush. I doubted I could stand any closer to him if I tried.

"It smelled like stale beer, weed, and sex. There must have been a hundred people in that room. One of the bandmembers was making out with some girl on one of the couches; his hand was up her skirt, and she was really into it. I tried not to look, I swear, but he was just so bold." Shots of tequila not only made Alli a bit tipsy, but she also tended to ramble on after the hard stuff.

Charlie continued to tell the story of meeting the band. "Ted shook our hands, and a roadie gave us a shot. The rest of the band talked with other fans, but Ted made time for us."

"I'm sure we looked and sounded like bumbling idiots." Alli's tempo sped up as the pitch of her voice rose three octaves. "But I don't care. Oh my *God*, we met Uncle Ted!"

"Alli, you only babbled for the first, like, thirty-eight minutes. After that, you were smooth."

"Whatever."

I loved it when she rolled her eyes at me; it warmed my heart and made me smile. "When I caught Ted's eye …" My hand raised to my heart as I tilted my head backward, taking a deep breath. Releasing it in a slow exhale, I glanced at Jeff and laughed at his expression.

Wide eyes telepathically said, *I'm standing right here*. He couldn't wait to hear what I had to say about the one rocker I wanted to meet, mostly because he was from Michigan. And also, because he was sexy as hell. "What about when you caught Ted's eye?" An air of suspicion resided in his tone.

"Sweetie, don't be silly," I tsked. "You know you're the only one for me." With a smile, I raised on my tiptoes and kissed his cheek. "But *mmm*, those leather pants." I laughed at Jeff's frown.

"Charlie, I don't know how you kept your cool. I thought I was going to puke."

"Classy, Al," I joked.

"After another shot," Charlie continued the story, "the roadie led us to another set of couches where Ted was relaxing with a couple blondes. We introduced ourselves, told him where we were from, and how we are his biggest fans—you know, typical small talk. I could tell we were starting to bore him. Everyone said the exact same things, right? I decided to take my chance and reintroduce myself as the lead guitarist, Sara as bassist, and Alli as lead singer of Heaven Scent."

"He looked genuinely interested and perked up a bit," I added and nodded for effect. "Actually sat forward in the chair and put his forearms on his knees."

"He called out to one of his roadies, who handed me his tiger-striped ESP," Charlie continued. "Ted said, 'Play me something,' so I acted as if I wasn't in total awe, somehow didn't freak out, and played "Cat Scratch Fever," since that is one of my favorite riffs. Alli sang, and Ted backed her up. I've never experienced anything like that in my life."

"Yeah but tell them what he said about how you played." Alli's eyes widened; she found it impossible to contain her excitement.

"Get this. He told me—a nobody from Brooklyn, Michigan—'You play that thing like you're making love to it. You and your friends certainly have that special something, the look, the energy. If you work your ass off, you can make it.' He said that after Heaven Scent played the bar scene for a year or so, to reach out to his manager. He gave me his name and said, 'You'll be able to find him if you're serious.'"

"Are you fucking kidding me?" Tony smiled from ear to ear and threw his arms around Charlie so fast that it looked as if a football player was tackling her. Her feet came off the ground as he spun her in a circle. And I thought Alli and Charlie were the only ones as excited about this prospect as me.

After Tony set Charlie down, he gazed into her eyes as if four thousand people weren't surrounding them. "I can hardly believe you had the balls to play in front of someone so famous."

"It's not brave if you're not scared." Charlie winked.

"Dude"—Tony turned his attention to his friends and announced to everyone within earshot—"my girl is gonna be a rock star. You'll be begging for front-row tickets when Heaven Scent is playing New York City and Vegas."

THE ENERGY of the concert blew me away. The first two bands proved to be incredible, as we had all anticipated. Between bands, our group chatted about nonsense, as usual, until a familiar voice made me turn around.

"Where the fuck have you been?" Tex, Kevin's best friend, spotted us on the lawn and pointed us out to Alli's brother. Kevin, Shelly, Tex, and some other girl had driven to the concert separately from Charlie, Tony, Alli, Joey, Jeff, and me. Once we had split up in Jackson, it didn't matter who rode in which car, because we would eventually meet up at the concert; everyone we knew had tickets. Finding others from our town happened with minimal effort.

Kevin put his arm around Alli's neck in a pretend older brother chokehold and gave her a good ole noogie with his free hand. Shelly poked him in the ribs and made him release her.

"Dammit, Kevin. What's your problem?" Lucky for Alli, it wasn't possible for her pestering brother to muss her hair in front of her friends—or, more importantly, in front of gorgeous guys. Multiple layers of Aqua Net held every strand of hair perfectly in place.

Joey gabbed at Kevin like they were old friends and ignored the fact that Tex stood entirely too close to his girl. Not able to comprehend a word Joey said, Kevin just smiled and repeated, "Yeah, man." He had smoked way too much weed to have an actual conversation; the perma-grin and squinted eyes gave him away.

Tex stood beside Alli; she gaped at me and tried to hide her grin. Everyone except Joey knew she had the biggest crush on Tex. He took advantage of the fact that he made his best friend's little sister uncomfortable and rubbed her arm with his, 'on accident,' every time he moved.

She literally shook from anxiety. If she moved away, it would look like she knew what he was doing. Standing between two guys who she cared for in a way she never expected was nerve-racking.

When her smile faded and her face lost all color, like she had seen a ghost, I decided to relieve her of her misery. "I gotta pee." Reaching for Alli's hand, I glanced at Charlie and led the way toward the bathroom.

Charlie chuckled and stayed right on our heels. She knew how easy it was to get lost in the crowd if she didn't. From experience.

"Shit."

Women stood beside the wall in front of the bathroom in a line that wrapped around the corner and down the stairs.

"There must be fifty people in front of us. Ugh.

Glad I didn't really have to go." I smirked at Alli. "I just knew I had to get you out of there. The look on your face was priceless."

Alli's mouth dropped open as she turned to look at me.

"Yeah, like that," I said, laughing.

"What do I do?" Red fingernails tapped white teeth as Alli's wide eyes darted from left to right. "I can't stand between Joey and Tex. Oh my God, I almost reached out for him." Talking about Tex made her cheeks redden. She had it bad for that guy. "I had to physically hold my own hand and tell myself no. Did you see him grab my ass? Right in front of Joey? I have to tell you it was a little hot, though. Not only the feeling of his hand touching me but the thought of getting caught." Alli fanned her flushed face as she tried to catch her breath.

"DUDE. THAT was the best concert, ever!"

"Joey, you don't have to yell. I can hear you," Tony yelled back at his friend with a scratchy, overused voice. We had screamed so loudly for so long, it was a wonder we could understand what others were saying.

Couples walked in droves, holding hands, arms around each other, smoking, and drinking. Not unlike our group. The night was cool for August in Michigan.

A slight breeze blew my bangs from my forehead, cooling my skin. Joey held Alli's hand, not letting her wander away but keeping a loose rein. Tony, on the other hand, kept Charlie close with his arm around her shoulders. Jeff and I walked as if joined at the hip, our usual position.

"How far away did we park? Holy shit, there are a lot of people here. We'll never get out." My voice was as raspy as the boys'.

Alli opened her mouth but only squeaked, then laughed in little squeak spurts.

The amphitheater had been packed, a sold-out show. I always forgot that so many people would all be leaving at the same time. At every concert, some people leave early, which was unfathomable to me, but it seemed like tonight, everyone had stayed until the very end.

"Do we have to go home?" Alli finally found her voice. "I'm so fucking amped up that I want to party all night." Thumps emerged from under her hand as she drummed on each car she passed, bouncing at the end of Joey's reach, then back to plant small kisses on his lips.

Horns honked between cars as they pulled from parking spots and squeezed into the line that crept at turtle speed. One backfired, causing people in a fifty-foot radius to duck, and several tire squealing sessions took place during the ten-minute walk through the parking lot.

"We'll be stuck here for a while, waiting for traffic. Wanna stand outside and be surrounded by thousands of people or get in and be alone, surrounded by thousands of people?"

"Outside," Alli, Sara, and I agreed in squeaky unison.

Tony opened the passenger door and retrieved a full pint of Southern Comfort from under the seat. He took a long swig and passed the bottle around, followed by a two-liter of Mountain Dew.

The Interview: January 8, 2015

"I'VE NEVER HAD a connection with anyone the way you all do. It's almost serendipity, isn't it? Like y'all were meant to find solace in each other?"

Alli nods. "It really does feel like that. We naturally complement each other. The moon and stars aligned, and just like that, we became best friends. Jenni, why don't you tell us something about you?" Interested if a young lady from their hometown would have the same experiences as the rest of the band, Alli tilts her head and waits.

Not expecting to open up about her own troubled past, Jenni tries to blow it off. "Nah, I'm not that exciting. Besides, I'm just a writer. Who wants to hear about my boring life?"

All four bandmembers simultaneously raise their hands.

Jenni surveys the room, chuckles, and grins. "Okay, but you asked for it. Um, where should I start?"

"How did you spend your free time in Brooklyn? What do you love about the Irish Hills? What made you want to become a writer?"

"It's so weird being on this side of the interview." Jenni pauses and smirks as memories flood back. "Well, I did the same things all y'all did: bonfire parties, Supersport, cruising the ave, MIS, dances at Fun Spot. I had a few close friends who I hung out with religiously through high school, but we went our separate ways to go to college. I got serious about writing, because one of those friends has done some odd things—for fun or money, who knows. When asked why she decided to do these things, her response was, 'Why not?' I love that. So much so that I wrote about our time together, getting in fun, harmless trouble."

"Details, girl." Charlie lifts an eyebrow.

"Okay, okay." Searching for the right words, Jenni pauses before sharing more about her past. "Every weekend, I either cruised the ave in Jackson with my girls, looking for guys; you know, if we didn't already have a boyfriend, of course." She clears her throat.

"Mm-hmm ..." Sara lifts an eyebrow.

"Or we would drive down US-12, taking the curves as fast as we dared, while trying to find the back road where a friend of a friend had a bonfire party. We usually stayed out late, ending up at someone's house at Wamplers or Vineyard or Devils Lake for a euchre game, midnight swims, or dancing or whatever. You know how it is. I loved that there are so many lakes and so many people our age to hang out with."

All the girls nod and smile, remembering their own time in the Irish Hills area.

"One night, though, we congregated at the golf course parking lot and sat on the hoods of cars or tailgates of trucks, just talking. Just getting to know everyone. That was our form of social media; we formed our own little groups and showed up to discuss life, meet new friends or potential mates. The cops broke up our party. No one got in any trouble, but we probably shouldn't have been on the road. Just sayin'.

"My mom usually didn't wait up, but that night, she did, and I got in trouble. Look, my parents didn't do me any favors; I resonate with your mom issues. I protected my little sister Daisy from my 'monster,' which is another book in itself. My escape from my shit life, besides spending time with friends, was writing. I would write stories about dragons and fairies and ask Daisy to draw me pictures as I recited them to her. She's a successful artist in Denver now. Has her own shows at galleries and everything. Anyway, after my mom went to prison—don't ask—we went to live with my aunt Molly and changed our names. The end." Jenni smiles, confirming she's moved past her horrific childhood.

"You changed your name?" Sara tilts her head, intrigued.

"I just wanted to disappear. It's hard to hide when your name is Rose Gardner."

"Jenni," Charlie sits forward. "Your sister Lily and my sister Sam are friends. I knew Daisy sounded familiar. You're the Rose who Lily used to bitch about when she came over. God, she was jealous of you; this makes so much sense. She used to talk about how you never studied and came home with straight A's."

Jenni grins and shrugs. "Another reason why I follow you—you made it. I want to be like you when I grow up. I always wanted to write professionally, but life got in the way. Now I live by the same philosophy as my friend in Brooklyn: Why not? I want to do things that are not what everyone would call 'normal.' I want to travel to unexpected areas of the country and do off-the-wall things. Because, why not?"

"Good for you." Tommy hands Jenni another beer. "Normal's boring."

"Y'all, I have to agree. There's no way I could be happy working in an office, or warehouse, or restaurant. This off-the-wall life is all I ever want to do."

"Alli, I hear a southern twang in your voice." Jenni segways back to the interview and away from her past. "I like it, but it's odd knowing you're from the North. I've read articles where your sound is compared to a mix of Alannah Myles and Stevie Nicks—or Alanis Morrissette and Mylie Cyrus. Which band or artist has been your biggest influence?"

Alli responds with a shrug. "First, I'm a wannabe. I

love the slow, easy rhythm of a southern accent, and I love how it feels rolling off my tongue. You've said y'all a couple times; it's so easy to pick up. Second, I love and respect each of those artists, and it's an honorable and flattering comparison. I'm proud of the unique twang of my voice; I just let my soul flow and whatever it sounds like seems to be working."

"Indeed." A smile forms on Jenni's lips.

"Lifestyle, look, personality, and attitude also play a huge part in who I would consider an idol. I'm attracted to the dramatic, wild, fun, and lively side of being a rock star. But now that we've been some places and seen some things, I tend to focus more on happiness, doing the right thing, and non-political aspects of music."

Growing more comfortable, Jenni sits back in the chair, crosses her legs, and reviews her notepad. "Before I ask these next questions"—she raises her eyes and focuses on Charlie—"I'm intrigued; what was the 'Rob and Bob' incident?"

A snort escapes from Alli, and Charlie shoots her a playful glare. The memory of her first heartbreak used to be difficult to tell. It's been long enough now, and her life has changed so much for the better that the story is much easier to tell than it used to be.

"Picture it, Labor Day weekend, two thousand and four." Charlie explains how Alli serenaded her and convinced her there was more to life than some stupid boy. "One of my darkest days had been made brighter by the love of my best friends. Alli, Sara, and I planned to go to the last party of the summer, but at the last minute, my mom fucked everything up—like she always did. Sara's mom was being a dick, and Alli's brother didn't think she should go. So, at least we couldn't all make it together. We told our boyfriends we couldn't go and sulked on a three-way call. At the last minute, Sara snuck out and picked us up. She just lived a road over from me. We made it to the party and decided it would be so much fun to surprise our boyfriends. Well, imagine our surprise when Alli and I walked in on our boyfriends having sex with my arch nemesis."

Jenni's eyebrows rise, and she leans forward. "Both of them?"

"Yeah. Both of them." Charlie purses her lips and squints. "It almost seems funny now, but that day, I felt the worst pain in my heart than ever before. Honestly, I've never felt that kind of heartbreak since. Any mean words from my mom or punches from my sister paled in comparison. I thought I would die from his betrayal. I decided that day that I needed to do something big with my life. Big. Not just go to college and become a hairdresser or secretary, but something monumental. As I sat in my room, I talked to Squeekers, my cat, and made him promise in purrs that he would never betray me. Alli showed up in my room and asked who I was talking to. Scared the shit out of me. It was after ten o'clock, and even though it was a holiday weekend, Alli's mom never let her go out that late. There was no way she should have been at my house."

"I begged Kevin to take me, since he was already dropping off Shelly, who lived kiddy-corner," Alli adds. "I didn't think I could leave you alone that night, after what had happened." The memory floods back like it happened last week.

The girls recite the 'Rob & Bob incident' like they took turns reading from a book.

"You pushed a half-empty bottle of cinnamon Schnapps into my hand; you started without me." Charlie chuckles at the memory. "Then you told me that you had told your mom about what happened, kinda."

"Yeah, no details for my mom." Alli raises her eyebrows and shakes her head. "It did help to talk about it, even if in generalities. It put me in a good spot to help you realize that stupid boys existed everywhere. My mom knew the right, if not cliché, words to say: All young love comes to an end, there are other fish in the sea, every rose has its thorn, blah, blah, blah."

"Your mom is so smart, but I was so sad, so confused. Even though I knew there was no real future for Rob and me, it would be impossible to introduce him to my mom, because of how she treated me. Still, I didn't want it to end the way it did. When I started to cry, Alli took my noodle-loose arms by my wrists and forced me to look at her. With a serious glint in her eyes, she talked in a weird, lyrical way."

"So, you think that it's over," Alli repeats the words she used that day. "That your love has finally reached the end. Anytime you call, night or day, I'll be right there for you when you need a friend."

"She continued to sing the entire song with perfect pitch in her beautiful, unique voice." Charlie grabs her guitar and strums the chords to "Love Song", and Alli sings the lyrics directly to Charlie, like it was 2004 all over again.

"You're still the biggest fucking weirdo I know," Charlie says, laughing.

"Yeah," Alli sings.

The entire band joins in for the last few syllables of the song.

I know
Do do dondo do
I know
Do do dododo do dooo dooo

"This. This is why I love you so much." A genuine smile reaches not only Charlie's lips but her heart.

Alli brushes away a tear. "You needed some fresh air, so we went to find Sara."

Sara takes over. "They pounded on my window until I answered and crawled out. We walked in silence to the park and found our picnic table. Alli addressed us both. She let us know she would never betray us, never hurt us like those assholes hurt her and Charlie. She would never hurt us like our moms did."

"I told them that they were my sisters and that I loved them." Tears fill Allis eyes again. "Then I picked up a knife."

"What?" Jenni gasps.

Alli lifts her left hand and shows her palm.

Charlie and Sara lift their hands, as well. Charlie admits, "For a minute, I was a little concerned as I watched Alli lift the knife. Crimson red seeped through a slit in the palm of her left hand. But once I understood what she was doing, a calm feeling ran through my veins. When she was done, I reached for the knife and made an identical slit, watching the blood come to the surface. Then I handed the knife to Sara."

"And I did the same thing. We became blood sisters that night. We continue to have a bond so much stronger than anything I've ever witnessed. Nothing can break us."

"Wow." Jenni sniffles and reaches for a tissue. "I don't know what to say. That's beyond beautiful."

A smile dons Alli's face. "Keep rollin', Jen. What other questions do you have?"

Friends, Jenni thinks. *These complete strangers are already treating me like we're friends.* After clearing her throat, Jenni takes a drink. "Where did your love of music come from? Who are your biggest influences? What was the first song you wrote, and how did that happen? How long did it take to polish it to perfection? Where was your first gig, and how did you land it?"

Charlie sits back, takes a long drink, and allows Alli to answer.

"Summer vacation." Alli reaches back in her memory to her childhood home. "Every morning, my brother would wake me up by blaring the stereo with a different record. Our parents were at work, so there was no one to tattle to. One morning, it was the Doors; the next, Metallica; the next, Anthrax or Ted Nugent. I still love Metallica because of their sound, Anthrax because their lyrics are funny, and Ted Nugent for more reasons than just he's a hometown star. Hated the Doors." A shake of her head indicates her opinion stands true to this day. "I tried to be mad at Kevin, but I really fell in love with the music."

Charlie raises one eyebrow. "It was a little different for me. You all know my mom is a dick, but that's a story for a different day. Jenni, for you and your readers, books are or can be an escape; music was and still is my escape. When a song or beat touches me, I'm transported to a different place—a place where I can be myself and totally let go." Raising her arms to her sides and closing her eyes made it look like Charlie could take off and fly at any moment. "Writing lyrics is a way for me to release frustration, almost a form of therapy."

"Our love of music grew naturally, and friends introduced us to different bands," Alli added. "Every penny we had, we spent on gas money to get to Jackson or Adrian to visit friends and to buy CDs. There was this little record store on Michigan Ave where we got ticketed for loitering once—I forgot about that until just this minute." She closes her eyes and revels in the memory.

"We were such rebels; weren't we?" Sara giggles.

"Metallica, among so many other groups, influenced us to the point where we felt like we had to start a band. Just had to," Alli answers another question. "For me, so many bands added a touch of something to my spirit. Girl bands like Vixen, Heart, Jo Dee Messina, Reba, and Whitney proved that strong, confident singers could lead their group to the top. Different ways to write and find the beat, like some seventies and eighties groups—Aerosmith, Bon Jovi, Mr. Big, Tesla, Poison, New Kids on the Block—helped keep writing fresh and interesting. On the other hand, other hometown heroes, like Kid Rock, Eminem, Uncle Kracker, showed me that you can open up and speak your truth without losing your fans' respect."

Alli: October 22, 2005

"ONE DAY, we'll have to write our own songs, you know. If we're going to do this, we can't just do covers," I regretfully informed Charlie and Sara as we walked toward the lake during one unseasonably warm fall day. None of us had ever tried to write more than an English paper.

Picnic tables dotted the small Vineyard Lake Park, and we climbed onto two facing each other—our tables. We threw out words, places, and rhymes that took us back to our favorite season: summertime.

"Sunshine, lotion, lobster burn," Sara started.

"Lakes, long days, longer nights." Charlie smirked.

"Lakies, lovin' under the moonlight, breakin' curfew," I added and giggled.

"Boonesfarm, boats, bikinis, boys, and barbeque."

"Nice, Sara; rockin' out the *B* words." An approving eyeroll came from Charlie.

"School's out, top down, cruisin' the ave, honkin' at hotties."

"Dirt roads, day drinkin', garage bands, bonfires in cornfields."

"NASCAR, Supersport, Irish Hills."

"Tailgate sittin', Southern Comfort sippin'."

"Warmth from the bonfire, and chills from his touch."

"Ooh, yeah. Sneaking out the window, parking on a

deserted back road."

Then we all sang, "Summertime in Brooklyn, Michigan."

"Hey. What are you girls doin' out here?" Tex snuck up on us and literally made me gasp. My brother's best friend was absolutely untouchable. That didn't stop me from daydreaming about how it would feel if he kissed me, though. His perfect smile was seductive and infectious. Looking directly at me, his dimples accentuated his pretty face. "We've been looking for you." Tex reached for me with an outstretched arm.

Without missing a beat, I curled up next to him as he pulled me into a half-hug. My arm slipped around his narrow waist, as if it belonged there. His cheek met the top of my head, and my nose touched his collarbone. I inhaled to revel in the scent of his cologne—Polo, my favorite.

Kevin broke the spell. "You know it's not safe here so late at night."

"Oh, sorry, I forgot about all the mass murders in Brooklyn. I'll be sure to pack my nine next time we roam the streets," Sara joked and blew him off, as usual.

He opened a small cooler filled with beers and handed us each one before he lit a bowl and passed it to Tex. For the next three hours, the band, plus Tex, enjoyed the night. With drinks in hand and our friends beside us, not much else mattered. Once we got back to Charlie's, we grabbed a notebook, wrote down all the words we had brainstormed, and that became our first original: “Summertime”.

Hazy Shade of Winter

Charlie: February 11, 2006

I BEGGED MY sister Sam to let me take her car to Jackson, but she refused, as usual. What's the point of being sixteen if I couldn't drive? It's not like my mom would buy me a car even if we did have the extra money.

Instead, Sam offered to drop us off somewhere, since she was heading to town, anyway. We didn't have a choice, and Sara was waiting for us at the Michaels' house, so Alli and I followed Sam to her car. I could hardly wait to see what kind of fun we would find in Jackson. We always seemed to stumble upon some sort of adventure.

She liked to go through Napoleon and take South Street to I-94; it has the most curves. Camaro. Need I say more? The snow from last week's storm had melted, so Sam took the curves as she should. My hair fell from side to side as I struggled to keep upright in the front seat.

The radio station announced the next song, and Sam

asked me to turn it up. We shared a look, smiling from ear to ear. "Animals" by Nickelback blared inside the small cabin. I played air guitar, and we all sang at the exact same time as Chad.

Sam turned the Camaro to the right, from Cooper St. onto North St., the old prison on the left. We turned onto a couple more side streets before she stopped the car in front of a two-story white house with black shutters.

Alli and I bounced from the car and yelled our thanks to Sam over our shoulders. We walked up the driveway, past the enclosed front porch with an old couch sitting under the window, to the side door.

Never needing to knock, I opened the door and climbed the two steps that led into the kitchen. Smoke hung in the air, thick as fog; we tried not to cough as we said our hellos.

The guys sat at the table playing euchre and barely noticed that the door had opened and closed. Tony, his twin brother, Steve, Joey, and Jeff each had a can of Budweiser in front of them and a lit cigarette in their own ashtray. Sara sat in Jeff's lap and threw out cards for him.

"We've been waiting for you," Tony said without taking his gaze off the cards.

I raised my eyebrows at Alli, and we exchanged a smirk, both wondering why they'd been waiting.

"Euchre! Yeah, baby!"

"Sounds like Tony and Jeff won," I remarked into the open air of the kitchen. The room had barely enough space for the table and four chairs. Alli and I stood against the cabinets, as Sara passed us on her way to the refrigerator. She pushed fresh Budweisers in our hands before serving the guys.

"Quarter bounce?" Jeff asked everyone.

"Yes!" seven voices said in unison. This. This was why they had been waiting for us. Tony never played quarter bounce without me; it was kind of a tradition.

We managed to wedge in another two chairs, and Sara sat on Jeff's lap, again.

Mrs. Michaels burst through the side door; a blast of snow followed her into the house. "Shit, it's freezing out there. Welcome to winter in Michigan, everyone."

"Hey, Mom," Steve greeted the thin blonde woman as he took the beer and paper bag from her hands. Polite son that he was, he gave her a peck on the cheek. "Quarter bounce?"

She rolled her eyes and left the room. As she passed the stereo in the living room, she turned it up. The steps creaked as an indication of her going upstairs to get out of our hair. She had to be the coolest old person ever.

"Hey, girls. Have you heard this, yet?" Steve bopped his head along with the beat. Nickelback's "Animal" blared from the speakers. I didn't want to burst his bubble by telling him that we had, so I shrugged. Discovering music was kind of his thing, and he pouted whenever he wasn't the first to hear a song.

Everyone stopped what they were doing and made it a point to listen. Jeff really got into it; he stood and grabbed Sara by the waist to dance. He was the best dancer of all the guys. If I didn't know any better, I would say he was gay. Sara swore he wasn't, though. She would be the one to know.

She spun like a top around the living room, with Jeff's guidance, before falling to the floor, dizzy.

"Come on, you guys, quarter *boooouuunce*."

"JILLY!" JOEY yelled over the music as Alli, Sara, and I followed him through the front door into his sister's living room—although, stumbled may be a better word for our entrance.

A local band who played in small bars around Jackson and Ann Arbor had set up in Jill's house. The living room was tiny to begin with, and the equipment forced everyone to squish on and around the sparse furniture.

"How cool is this?" Right up our alley, the idea of having the band play inside gave me all kinds of ideas. "We could totally do this during the winter."

"Not at my house," Alli slurred. "My mom would freak."

"Don't even look at me." Sara raised her hands, palms out. "Not an option."

Too loud to discuss now, I promised myself to remember how cool setting up in someone's house would be. The band was really good. The lead singer dressed like Slash and sounded just like Daughtry—his voice literally tickled my ears. His long blond hair and a lean frame made me stop and stare. When he smiled at me, I almost melted. Sara had to push me into the next room to snap me from my trans.

Jill had moved the TV from the living room into the tiny kitchen to make more room for the drums. It was dangerously balanced on the counter, just waiting for a drunk person to bump into it and send it crashing to the floor.

My head spun from the mandatory shots while we played yet another round of quarter bounce. The music that radiated from the living room was so loud there was no reason to even try to talk.

From our position in the kitchen, we could watch the lead singer and guitarist, but the bass player and drummer were out of sight. No big loss; they weren't as hot as the other two, anyway.

After only three songs, the band took a break. Alli took it as a sign from the heavens and maneuvered through the crowd, dragging Sara and me behind her.

Lead Singer Guy's gaze started at my chest and rested on my lips. I nibbled my bottom one, and he smirked as his eyes met mine. A brunette demanded his attention, like a Chihuahua nipping at his heels, but he ignored her and winked at me. “Ladies.”

“The band sounds great. How long have you been together?” Not waiting for an answer, Alli’s drunk self babbled, “Hey, if you’re taking a break, do you mind if we step in for a song? We’re perfecting our first release and would love to play for everyone.”

Without taking his gaze off me, Lead Singer Guy shrugged and handed Alli the mic. “Be my guest.”

I grabbed an electric guitar that was resting in a stand next to the drumkit and nodded toward the bass on the other side of the makeshift stage. Sara lifted the instrument, threw the strap over her shoulder, and smiled. We had played “Summertime” so many times during our daily practice sessions we could do it in our sleep. Or drunk, whatever.

Everywhere we went, we would sing the lyrics of our first song: Bill’s IGA, Swiss Swirl, cruisin’ the ave, Supersport. Everywhere. During each practice, we would play our first original, and all our friends loved it. They would invite other friends to watch us play in Alli’s parents’ garage. Soon after, our following had grown. Friends of friends would see us out and about and ask when we would record and release our first album. They would offer to call local radio stations and request they play “Summertime”.

I forced myself to focus on Alli instead of the hot guy with a voice that gave me chills. Thank God Tony decided to stay home. The 'I don't feel like getting out; it's too cold' excuse worked out well for us both.

I strummed the first chords of "Summertime" and thought about how our first time performing in front of strangers was a trip. I think. Maybe.

The next day, I only remembered that I thought we had knocked it out of the park, so to speak. But honestly, I have no idea if anyone had even enjoyed our performance.

Charlie, February 18, 2006

THE CURLING iron was hot enough to burn my fingers if I let them touch it for too long. My forehead, too. A couple old scars proved how long it had taken me to get it right. As I released the hair from the iron, it formed the perfect curl. This routine had become second nature. Spray, let it dry for five seconds, then expertly brush the curls into place and spray again.

Alli stood beside me and performed the same ritual. Sara's straight hair didn't need much work, so she sat on my bed with my cat Squeekers curled in her lap. The unmistakable scent of burned hair and Aqua Net signified an unforgettable night. The three of us made it a point to find fun in everything we did, even if all we did was hang out in my room.

Goo Goo Dolls played on my little radio at a volume that if we wanted to talk, we would have to raise our voices to the point that others in the house could hear what we said. At 10:00 p.m., we didn't want the entire household to know about our plans. We were just going for a walk, but still.

Growing up in a small town forced us to be creative with our time. During the winter, it had been difficult to find much to do without driving somewhere, so going for walks at least got us out of the house.

The lyrics coming from the radio seemingly developed directly from my mind. I had been thinking a lot lately about how the words of their song, "Sympathy," described my current psyche.

I longed to escape—my house, my family, my town. The only reasons for me to stay were with me in this room. One watched my reflection in the mirror and stuck out her tongue every time I gazed at her. The other sat on my bed and loved on my cat.

Alli and Sara—the people who meant the most to me in this world. We understood one another like we were sisters. We finished each other's sentences, gauged each other's mood, and knew when one of us needed our unique cheering-up services most. Even better than sisters, one of my blood sisters was just as bad as my mom.

Once we were happy with our hair, we sprayed some more, added the scent of our favorite vanilla perfume, and put on our coats and gloves. We weren't planning to see anyone, but we must look our best, just in case. You never know who else would be roaming these streets on a cold February night.

Alli led the way out the window to the second-story roof, followed by Sara. I climbed out last and lowered the window but didn't close it all the way; we would need to climb back inside later. The only way to the first-story roof was to shimmy down a less than sturdy rain gutter.

Once we reached the ground by way of a rogue tree limb and through the gate into the Jones's yard without anyone discovering us, we stopped long enough for a quick shot of Southern. Gloves warmed my hands, which made it harder to screw the lid onto the bottle after a round of shots. There wasn't time to snuggle it into my inside pocket before the light over the kitchen sink in my house turned on; my mom was up.

Sara hissed, "Light."

I grabbed Alli's arm and pulled her into the shadows of my neighbor's house. "I don't think she saw us," I whispered, letting my eyes adjust to the dark. "Be careful but move fast."

We walked sideways, our backs to the house, like thieves hiding from the cops. My mom shouldn't have been upset that we were outside, but knowing her, because we didn't run it past her first, she would have said we were being sneaky. Well, I guess we kind of were.

My heart thudded against my chest so hard it pulsed in my ears. Could Alli and Sara hear it, too? I hardly noticed the brisk night until we reached the road. Turning away from the lake led us toward the main road of the neighborhood.

Sara's teeth chattered so loud that I didn't really need to ask, "You cold?"

She wrapped her arms around herself and shivered. "Fucking. Cold. Why do I let you talk me into this silly shit? It must be twelve fucking degrees, Charlie. Jesus."

"You'll live." I smirked, took another shot, and returned the bottle to my inside pocket. "Would you rather be at your house or here?"

"Here. Definitely."

Alli continued the line of questioning. "Would you rather be … hmm … here or in Hawaii?"

"Are you two in Hawaii with me?" Sara responded with her own question.

"No. Just you."

"Here." With a nod, she took a bottle from her inside pocket, took a sip, and handed it to Alli.

I didn't notice before that she had brought her own. Nice. Never count on anyone to give you what you want. Gotta win on your own.

"Seriously? You would rather be here—twelve fucking degrees, with snow on the ground, slippery roads, and chilled to the bone—than Hawaii? Eighty-five degrees, sun, beach, palm trees, volcanoes, waterfalls?" I shook my head. "Girl, you're weird."

"Okay. Let me ask you the same question. Would you rather be here or in Hawaii? Just you."

"Hawaii. Definitely," I replied without missing a beat. I marched forward, alone, for at least ten steps before I realized Sara and Alli weren't beside me anymore. Confused, I turned around. "Hey. Why did you stop?"

They stood in the middle of the road, arms crossed, and eyeing each other, then glared at me.

"Fuck you, Charlie." Alli's voice was low but stern. She was pissed. "Why the fuck would you say that? You would seriously leave us behind? That's not how this works. We're all supposed to be in this together, period." She turned and started back toward the park.

"Whoa!" I trotted to catch up with her, grabbed her arm, and turned her around. "Hey, I was going to say I was kidding, but you didn't let me. God, you're fast. Of course, I would rather be here in my shitty fucking life, with my shitty fucking mom and sister kicking my ass, than anywhere you two aren't. I would rather suffer in twelve-fucking-degree, ice-filled fucking Michigan than eighty-five-degree, sunny, warm, gorgeous Hawaii if you guys aren't there. I can't do this without you. Don't you know that, yet? I need you." Tears warmed my eyes as I panned back and forth between my two best friends. This time, I didn't care if they saw me cry.

"Charlie …" Alli's smile softened. "I was going to say I was kidding, but you didn't let me." She put her arms around me and pulled me to her.

I felt like such a goober. It did ease my mind to admit that I needed them, because it was true. I think they knew it, but if they didn't before, they sure did, now.

Sara's arms wrapped around the two of us, and we hugged until we shivered, then we laughed and let go.

I pushed them away with exaggerated force before I wiped my eyes. "Hawaii, huh? What about Iceland?"

We turned back toward the main road. Alli hip-checked me and knocked me off balance.

"Why do they call it Iceland when it's green, and Greenland when that place is all ice?" Sara asked. We had pondered this question for the last six months, but none of us had come up with a great answer. We just knew we wanted to see for ourselves. One day.

Each step grew more difficult. It really was cold, and I wasn't sure how much longer I could stand being outside. I looked in Sara's direction to suggest we go somewhere warm, but she had disappeared. It took three whole seconds before I realized what had happened. About five steps back, she was laying in the middle of the road. Flat on her back, arms outstretched. Silent.

Alli had literally fallen to the ground, laughing.

"Snow angels in the middle of the road? Really, Sara?" I teased, knowing she had slipped. If she was seriously hurt, she would have said so.

"I. Hate. Ice. God damn. My ass is frozen to the road. Can't … move." Her eyes closed, and her lips pursed. She shook her head.

I reached for her hand, and after she had a hold of me, she wriggled on the ground like she was stuck. My feet slipped from under me, and I went down on top of her.

Alli laughed even harder from the yard beside the road. "Guys, stop it. I gotta pee."

"Ugh, Charlie. Shit." We managed to right ourselves and crawl to an area beside the road without any ice. Once we had traction, we stood and brushed the snow and dirt off our knees, asses, and elbows. Then we realized just how cold we really were.

A siren let out a single *whoop* behind us. We jumped, screamed like little girls, and giggled.

"Again?" I groaned. My mom would not be happy if the cops took us home. Again.

"Girls?" The familiar voice of Officer Thompson made me smile. We're good.

Fred Thompson was a friend of my sister Sam. They had been in the same class, and he had a forever crush on her. After he graduated from the police academy, he requested Jackson County, specifically Brooklyn, for his patrol area, because that's where our family lived.

"Hey," we sang out to our friend.

"It's a little late for you to be out here, isn't it?" He checked the clock on his dash like he didn't know it was past curfew. "Not to mention a little cold. Seriously, what are you crazy-ass kids doing?"

"Just out for a walk. You know, had to get away."

He knew.

"Yeah, I get it, but you can't be out walking the streets this late. A neighbor called. Look, I have to take you somewhere. It doesn't have to be to your house, but somewhere." He pointed to the passenger door. "Get in."

His smile warmed my heart. At least he was aware of my world and understood how detrimental it could be to leave me with my mom.

"I guess it's too much to ask for a ride to Jackson?"

If only.

Sara: July 22, 2006

"HEY, GIRLS." Kevin sauntered into the garage and picked up his drumsticks. Something seemed different about the way he moved, like he was trying to contain something exciting. His normal bloodshot eyes and perma-grin didn't fade when he sat behind his drums.

Alli and I glanced at each other; we both sensed the change but blew it off as Kevin being his normal weird self. Charlie had been tuning and didn't notice.

After he beat out a couple rhythms, he stopped abruptly. "I got some news."

We all ignored him; his usual so-called news wasn't ever anything we cared about. Either a friend of his broke up with someone we didn't know or the super-cool exhaust he had his eye on dropped in price. Our instruments were first on our agenda, and we stayed focused on them, including Alli singing a scale.

"You want to hear this or not?" His voice raised as if he was pissed, but his smile widened.

We rolled our eyes and faced him, waiting for the next unimpressive thing he had to say.

One hand rested on Alli's hip as she posed in her best 'I'm annoyed' stance. "Yes, Kevin, the protector and King of Heaven Scent, our wise almighty master. What's your news?"

Without missing a beat, literally, he banged his bass drum, then stood. "Well, it seems that the three of you galivanting all over hell and back has finally paid off. Someone saw you performing at a house party in Jackson a couple months ago and …" He leaned over and played a drumroll. "Aaron Loomis just happened to be in that small crowd. He said he heard you two"—one drumstick flittered between Charlie and me—"rocked it, and you"—he pointed the same drumstick at Alli—"sounded like an angelic devil. Whatever that means."

Before we had a chance to respond, he sat back down and beat out the bass to "Summertime". "He wants us to play at his season-opening garage party in two weeks." He ended the news with three hard beats on both cymbals.

"What?"

"Holy shit!"

"No fucking way!"

Our reactions overlapped.

Dying to know more and tossing every question we thought of at Kevin, he raised his hands, palms out. "Girls, girls, relax. Let's behave like adults now."

"Fuck you, we're sixteen. Spill," Charlie joked,

making Alli snort.

"I wanted to tell you before our biggest fans showed up to watch today's practice." Kevin filled us in on the details. "He's charging everyone a five dollar cover, which will pay for the kegs and us. Who knows, maybe we'll make a little bit of money. He's going to leave a tip jar on the stage and ask for donations."

None of us believed what had just happened. Had we heard Kevin right? We actually had a gig? Someone wanted to pay us to play?

Practicing and spreading our name all over Jackson County for the last six months had actually paid off. This was our big chance to prove we had what it takes to make it. The continued support of our friends and their friends had led us to land our first gig.

Charlie played a hard riff, I beat out a loud bass rhythm to accompany her, and Alli jumped up and down, screaming, "Yahoo," into the mic. Her voice was so loud that Mrs. Summer opened the door to the garage to see why we were making such a commotion.

"We got a gig! We got a gig!" Alli bounced toward her mom and wrapped her arms around her neck. "In two weeks, we will officially be a garage band."

"Girls, Kevin, that's fantastic!" An honest smile spread across her face, and she placed her hand over her heart. She and Mr. Summer supported their kids in anything they did as long as they didn't hurt anyone. "You're really going to make this happen, aren't you?

I'm so proud of each and every one of you." Her gaze landed on each of our faces, and she held eye contact long enough for us to sense her love.

I'd never seen anyone's mom smile so big. She hugged all of us tight, then rushed through the door. When she returned a few moments later, she carried a pitcher of fresh lemonade in one hand and a stack of plastic red Solo cups in the other. She presented a lemonade toast—you know, because we were too young to drink—then returned to the house.

We all agreed we'd have plenty of time to continue our own kind of celebration after practice, so we warmed up. As usual, a group of friends stopped by to watch—you know, eight or ten. After an hour-long session, Alli ran into the house to ask her mom for enough lemonade for everyone. She delivered it with a smile to her 'good kids' and our 'good friends,' completely unaware of our far-from-innocent intentions.

Kevin waited until his mom left the garage before he broke out a pint of Southern. Tex grabbed the red Solo cups and distributed mixed drinks to the crowd. His gaze landed on Alli; his smile lingered a little too long. He laughed when her cheeks reddened.

As a band, we announced the date and details of our first garage gig to our following and toasted to our future success. Another round of "Yahoos" followed.

Jeff came over to me and hugged me tight. "I'm so

proud of you." He tapped his cup on mine, and we drank. His eyes expressed how much he believed in me.

The entire group downed the spiked lemonade, then we played another short set. We didn't celebrate like that very often, though. Alli's parents would have banned us from the garage if they had any idea that we mixed liquor in our drinks. Then where would we practice?

By the time the parents called it a night, we were only getting started. We packed up our gear, then piled into Kevin's "flame mobile" and followed four carloads of our friends toward the racetrack.

Bonfire parties popped up in random pastures most weekends. In a small town like Brooklyn, there wasn't much else to do but stand around a fire, bullshit with friends, and drink some beer. Everyone who was anyone would be at this party, the first of the season.

Of course, we shared our good news, and our friends who hadn't been at practice promised to attend Aaron's party. Shared enthusiasm spread like wildfire. A couple strangers approached Kevin at the cooler as he went for another beer. They asked if he was in the hot new band everyone was talking about, the one opening at Loomis's garage in two weeks.

With a giant smile, he said, "Yes. Yes, I am."

Flames from the bonfire lit the night sky as they talked; the strangers wished him good luck and raised their cans of Bud in a cheers. Shelly beamed at him from her place beneath his protective arm.

Kevin had started taking classes at the local community college the previous year and had already mentioned quitting. He admitted later that he never felt like he belonged someplace, like he truly fit in, until that night at the bonfire.

FOR THE NEXT two weeks, we practiced every night. After word got out about Loomis's party, it wasn't unusual for twenty or thirty people to show up at Alli and Kevin's house to watch us play.

Mrs. Summer took it all in stride and would serve snacks and refreshments. As a rule, we didn't allow any alcohol while we practiced. On site, anyway. During breaks, we would go for a short drive to wet our whistle, if you will.

Mr. Summer couldn't believe how much our fanbase had grown; he said he should charge a cover, too. He got into our original songs and looked like he enjoyed watching us but wasn't much for, as he called it, the new-age-style music we covered. Although he supported our band, he showed it in different ways. One of his friend's sons worked the door at the oldest local bar in the area: Callaghan's. He asked for an introduction to the owner.

We met with Bud Wright, the owner of the bar, but he didn't think a group of teenagers could possibly have talent enough to book a paying weekend gig. It just wasn't worth it to book a band who wouldn't bring in a paying clientele. He turned us down without even hearing us play. That was our first rejection. Rejection, you see, is absolute motivation to keep trying.

Sara: May 6, 2006

ON THE NIGHT of our first gig, we prepared mentally and physically for our debut concert. Charlie and I stuffed every piece of clothing we owned into bags and took them to Alli's. We mixed and matched for hours. We had to get our outfits exactly right; after all, this was the most important night of our lives.

Potential wardrobes covered Alli's bed, chairs, dresser, and floor. After discarding multiple options, we settled on our favorite concert t-shirts and jeans with holes in the knees, all artificially made by rubbing scissors over the fabric.

Alli's mom took one look at her brand-new Guess jeans and got pretty upset when she realized what she had done. "Allison Benita Summer, I spent a lot of money on those pants. What were you thinking?"

Charlie faced me and mouthed, *Pants*. We giggled at the old person term. "Sorry, Mom. But don't worry. I'll pay you back when we're famous."

Mrs. Summer frowned, shook her head, and walked

down the hallway. We overheard her talking to Mr. Summer, who chuckled while saying, "It's not the end of the world, dear."

An hour later, Alli's aunt, Kat McIntosh, arrived to do our hair. Everyone adored and respected Kat; she treated all the kids who entered her home as her own. Good and bad. Her kid's friends, her nieces and nephews, and any random kids in the neighborhood all received the same affection.

She promised to make it to the party with her husband, Dan, but admitted that they may just linger in the back. All the younger people wouldn't want to feel like a couple of old chaperones were watching their every move. Besides, her sons Ted and Brandon, otherwise known as the apple brothers—get it? McIntosh. Apple—would surely be in the crowd rooting for us to have the best show ever.

We arrived at Aaron Loomis's early enough to set up and loosen up with a couple beers and a bowl. His garage was technically a pole barn with high ceilings and a permanent stage against the back wall. His older brother had regular monster parties with bands, so for us to have made it this far was really something.

Both Charlie's and Alli's voices shook when they talked, and I couldn't stop smiling. My steps landed a little heavier than usual as I practically trotted back and forth along the stage.

Kevin didn't show any signs of anxiousness. Like, at all. To this day, I have no clue how he had remained so relaxed. He had this calm that I envied. To him, this was like any other day of practice. To me, it was life or death. In my mind, if we rocked this party, we would certainly make it. However, if we bombed, we were over.

During soundcheck, cars rolled into the driveway and excited teens and twentysomethings found their way to the barn. They stood around two pony kegs that sat just inside the roll-up doors, filled their cups, and made themselves comfortable. As more people gathered, they chatted with each other as if they were already friends. Maybe they were.

Once we saw familiar faces, we decided our instruments were ready. Our friends deserved our attention, and we took some time to mingle. Kevin wandered over to where Shelly was talking to friends and Tony and Jeff found their places beside Charlie and me. Joey couldn't make it because he had to babysit his sister's kid. Alli wasn't all that bummed, though; Tex couldn't keep his eyes off her, a new common occurrence.

Forty-five minutes later, people packed the entire property. Aaron gave us the go-ahead with a nod. Kevin moved to his place at the back of the stage and beat his drums to the first song.

We girls had previously discussed and agreed upon

what songs to play in which order. Kevin didn't care to give much input; he just wanted to be in the spotlight. He knew girls would notice him and guys would want to be him if he simply played in a band. He wasn't wrong.

Alli took the folded notebook paper from her back pocket and secured it on the stage under the microphone stand. We decided to open with "Animals", because it surprised people that a band consisting of mostly girls could pull off such a heavy guy-band song.

The lights dimmed, and I knew right then that all I needed was twenty seconds of insane courage. That's it, just twenty seconds and something wonderful would happen. Alli stepped toward the mic, wrapped her hand around it, and positioned herself in her signature lead singer stance.

With my eyes closed, I breathed deep and let Charlie's lead-in pulse through me like a wave. I instantly felt like I was home; we were destined to be rock stars.

The first line flowed from Alli's mouth before I opened my eyes. Everyone in the crowd stopped their conversations and faced us, as if they were at a concert, and stared in awe. Success—we had gotten their attention. It was a high I had never felt before. I instantly became addicted.

It was a totally different feeling to be up in front of thirty people during practice or twenty people all crammed into the living room at your friend's house in Jackson.

By the time we were into our third song, "Live Like You Were Dyin'," there must have been two-hundred people pushed into and around the barn. Lighters held above the crowd illuminated the night sky like a stadium.

From our perch on stage, three feet higher than the crowd, I glanced above the sea of faces to the cornfield next door. When cars had jammed the driveway and back yard, the cornfield held the overflow. Let's just say I didn't see any corn.

When it was time, Alli turned to face Kevin, looked at Sara, then me, and we all smiled. Kevin led us into our original song, "Summertime".

The few people who had heard us play this song already cheered, and it became contagious. The entire crowd erupted in an uproar even before Alli started to sing. That was probably the coolest feeling ever; people were cheering for us. For Heaven Scent.

Sunshine, suntan lotion, lobster burn
Pontoons, long days, longer nights
Lakies, lovin' under the moonlight
Bonfires in cornfields, garage bands
Oooh, yeah
Summertime in Brooklyn, Michigan

As Alli belted out the lyrics of the song we had written about our hometown, I focused on the hundreds of faces I didn't recognize. The roar from our new fans was so loud I almost couldn't hear us play. I guess they liked the lyrics.

Boonesfarm, boats, bikinis, boys
Breakin' curfew, barbeque
School's out, top down, cruisin' the
ave, honkin' at hotties
Dirt roads, day drinkin'

Bonfires in cornfields, garage bands
Oooh, yeah
Summertime in Brooklyn, Michigan

Boonesfarm, boats, bikinis, boys
Breakin' curfew, barbeque
Summertime in Brooklyn, Michigan

NASCAR, Supersport, Irish Hills
Tailgate sittin', Southern Comfort
sippin'
Warmth from the bonfire and chills
from his touch
Sneaking out the window, parking on

a deserted back road

Bonfires in cornfields, garage bands
Oooh, yeah

"Ooh, yeah," our fans sang along.

Boonesfarm, boats, bikinis, boys
Breakin' curfew, barbeque
Summertime in Brooklyn, Michigan

Bics and Zippos sported flames of all sizes. A wave of lights like fireflies spread through the crowd. Reserved for love songs or ballads, the meaning that we took from this show of approval was just that: everyone loved our song and loved us.

We played the rest of the set, and for the first time, we knew we had gained hundreds of fans.

Sara: July 15, 2006

THE FOLLOWING weekend, Mr. Weber invited us to play in the same cornfield by the racetrack where we spent so much time on weekends. Some friends and the owner rigged up electricity so we could plug in and built a stage so our equipment would stay clean and dry.

Kevin and Tex had also made arrangements for us to play bonfire parties throughout the rest of the summer. Shelly's family owned a large chunk of land outside Manchester, and they agreed to let us play there, too.

Jeff and I pulled into a twenty-acre clearing, surrounded by tall trees on three sides and a barbed-wire fence on the other. A deer stand stood in the far corner facing the neighboring cornfield. Flames reached toward the heavens at a stunning height. The contrast of the black night sky was staggering. Embers floated to join a million stars, some brighter than others.

The firepit, if you could call it that, must have been more than twenty feet across. Smoke billowed off red-hot logs stacked high, creating a ten-foot flame. Cars parked facing it in multiple half-circles acting as chairs or couches, something for the guests to sit on or lean against.

"*Sarrraaa*!" My ears perked up at the sound of someone yelling my name. Cocking my head to each side like a dog reacting to a high-pitched sound, I tried to figure out where Alli was standing. I must have looked like a top spinning in a circle.

Jeff chuckled at the odd sight and reached for my arm to stop me.

Alli leaped from behind the first row of cars, almost landing on top of me. "Oh my God. I can't believe we're actually playing here. We're the first band in Brooklyn to have an official bonfire tour. I overheard someone asking if we were selling t-shirts."

"I know it. I can't believe it, either." I looked around, stunned by the number of people who had come to watch us perform. "There must be a hundred cars here," I said barely louder than a whisper. A pint of something clear reached my hand, I wasn't sure from where, and I drank a quick shot before shaking off the horrible taste. "Let's do this."

Over the next half hour, we set up our equipment and did a soundcheck. They had built the stage on the far side of the bonfire, and it worked out perfectly. It was sturdy enough to hold us and all our equipment. However, without a building to reflect the sound, I worried that the crowd wouldn't be able to hear us very well.

I was wrong.

I think the entire town of Brooklyn could hear us; we were so loud my ears grew numb. After we played our first song, I relaxed enough to look out among the guests.

The Jackson crew, as we lovingly referred to them, along with friends from school and friends of friends from neighboring towns stood in front of the stage, danced, and sang along with every song they knew. And every song they didn't know, yet.

At the end of the night, almost five hundred people had paid five dollars each, plus tips. Split four ways, we each walked away eight hundred dollars richer.

I'm Not Alright

The Interview: January 8, 2015

MEMORIES OF the first time they performed in front of a bunch of strangers bring smiles to the faces of the girls in Heaven Scent. Tommy observes from his spot at the bar and enjoys the stories, some he hasn't heard before.

Charlie admits she was nervous as hell at the Loomis place until after they played "Animal". "That song is so fast, and we knew it so well that it was hard to focus on anything except playing. It was almost impossible to let nerves overcome me when I was so focused on letting my fingers do their thing."

Sara adds, "The bass from Kevin's drums matched my rhythm so well that I just closed my eyes for a minute and plucked the strings. Didn't even need to think. By the time I let myself take in the crowd, they were jumping up and down, playing air guitar, and singing along. Just unreal."

"It's really hard to fuck up when everyone is so into you," Alli agrees. "The energy flowed right through me. It's hard to describe the buzz in my ears and the ease of anxiety; it was easier to breathe somehow. Until you've felt it, it's impossible to understand. It's positively magical."

As he hands the girls another round, Tommy admits, "I love hearing these stories. I had almost the exact same experiences at the beginning of my career. Smalltown crowd, we practiced in my friend's barn, and played for the first time at a dive bar. But we just played covers. Nothing original."

Alli nods her thanks to Tommy, takes a long sip of her drink, and changes the subject. "You asked earlier how our families felt about us forming a band. Well, my story is a little different from Charlie's and Sara's. All our mothers couldn't have been more different. You can probably tell by now how my parents loved the idea of their kids having a dream, a vision, and doing whatever it took to make it come true. My mom is very well-rounded but not one to make a scene or be confrontational. Everything must be nice and neat and in its place. My parents listened to country oldies and songs from the seventies but never pushed their tastes on Kevin and me. Charlie's mom, on the other hand, seemed to thrive off drama, and when we first became friends, she wouldn't let her listen to music at all. I brought my little radio to her house one weekend so we had something to listen to in her room, and Natasha took it away. Hid it somewhere until Kevin came to pick me up. Her older sister Sam felt bad for us and shared her radio."

Explaining her own parental struggles, Sara's lips tightened. "My mom is mentally abusive. It took a lot of years and a lot of therapy to be able to say those words out loud. She hasn't ever laid a hand on me, but she's the reason I only wear black and never eat. She didn't approve of most of the choices I made while living under her roof: the band, my boyfriend, my friends. All the most important things in my life, my mom despised."

Charlie, Sara, and Alli exchanged understanding glances. They talked about how to publicly approach this situation many times in the past. Their fans already knew most of their story and heard about how Charlie's mother treated her worse than a dog. Everyone understood Sara's mom was mean, but specifics were never made public.

When Jenni asked for the interview, the band felt compelled to explain why they preach 'anyone can do anything if they put their minds to it'. They were the perfect example of beating the odds.

"Early in our band days, my mom almost convinced me that I wasn't good enough. There was one instance where she took her parental power too far and crossed the line. This isn't an easy story to tell, but I think it's important for your readers and our fans to understand that if you believe in yourself, you can do anything. Including overcoming abusive situations. In late two thousand six, I forced the band into a dangerous slump.

The summer passed too fast, and our days of playing at bonfires were over."

Jenni anticipated the band sharing some hard times during the interview but didn't think it would be so difficult to grasp. Reality can be so much more shocking when the story comes straight from the source. After only spending an hour or so together, Jenni felt as if she was a part of them—a friend.

Charlie: November 3, 2006

"IT WAS JUST a phase, Charlotte. It's over. Done. You're back to being a nothing, a nobody. Did you really think your little girl band would be anything but a summer fling?"

Because we didn't have anything booked for this weekend, my mom thought our success had ended. I frowned and stared at my feet. Negative words cut deeper than any punch ever thrown. In my heart, I knew my mom was just jealous; she lived for attention and overexaggerated every word she spoke. Her level of dramatic storytelling exhausted me.

"Oh, you did. That's so cute." Her teeth gleamed through a fake smile. "Now you need to get off your lazy ass and really consider what you're going to do with your life. You can't just sit around all day like a bump on a log. I don't work my ass off to put food on the table for you to take advantage of my generosity."

It took everything I had to not roll my eyes. I knew damn well that if I did, she would reprimand me. Every time I showed any bit of disrespect, she found a way to inflict pain. One day, I wouldn't have to care anymore.

"God only knows how someone as stupid as you will even graduate. Unless, of course, your so-called friends break into the school again and change your grades." From her spot on the couch, she leaned forward and rested her forearms on her knees. "Hoodlums," she huffed.

For the record, they weren't my friends, and they didn't change my grades. I wasn't the best student, but I didn't need to cheat. If she had only paid attention, she would know I did study, and I did earn decent grades with a little effort. By this time, it wasn't worth trying to explain myself anymore; she didn't listen.

"Ooh, I know." A smirk formed on her thin lips as she stood. "You could offer your teachers some sort of disgusting favor. I hear girls in this town can get away with just about anything if they give it up."

I tried so hard, but I couldn't stop myself. I did it. I rolled my eyes and smiled. Thank God I didn't laugh out loud; that would have certainly earned more of a punishment. In her twisted head, she had turned me into some kind of ingrate, and it was preposterous.

"Charlotte ..." Her fingers wrapped tight around

my arm, and I tried not to squirm as she pulled me closer to her. “Why would you disrespect me like that?” Her eyes turned black, and I knew I was in trouble. Her face stopped within an inch of mine. Stale cigarettes and cinnamon scented the space between us. She’d been drinking. “Wipe that shit-eating grin off your face before I do it for you. You think this is funny? You think this is fun for me? That this is the way I want to spend my Friday night? At home, with you?”

I wasn’t even smiling anymore, but she thought it added to her rant. Her single throaty laugh made me shiver.

She released my arm, walked to the kitchen, and opened the fridge. A beer appeared in her hand, and she opened it, chugged the entire can, and slammed it on the counter when she finished.

A calm vibe spread through my body, like a current of water had cleansed my soul. Courage took over—or was it teenage stupidity? Either way, it was about time I spoke my mind and stood up for myself, even if it backfired. I would at least know I had tried. “No, Mother. I never thought spending time with me was one of your priorities. In fact, I know that every time you look at me, it makes you sick.”

She slowly raised her head until her squinted eyes found mine. I paid attention, for maybe the first time, as the rapid change of emotions spread across her chunky face. Her expressions fascinated me. Squinted dark eyes and tight lips morphed into wide eyes and slightly parted lips.

With a tilt of her head, she understood I had responded to her rhetorical question. A twitch at one corner of her mouth developed into a half-grin, then ended in a full-on smile, showing teeth and everything. She was actually a little pretty if you didn't know her.

"Well, Charlotte. That is quite an observation. It's also a rotten thing to say to your mother. How selfish can you possibly be? I have given you everything you have ever asked for, and this is the thanks I get?" Tears formed in my mother's eyes, and her chin quivered. That was a first. "What would you do without me to do everything for you? You would never make it without me. You'll never be anything without—"

"Without you pushing me to be my best," I interrupted, my hands on my hips. "Yeah, I know. You've told me so many times. How could I ever think any differently? The problem is that you only know how to push me away. You constantly tell me how I'm so self-centered and I will probably end up pregnant and alone unless I do everything you say. You're wrong."

My head jolted to the side; my cheek burned. An imprint of fingers rose on my skin. I turned my head to face her and stood tall—as tall as my five-foot-four-inch frame could stand. I looked straight into her black eyes and said, "No." Only, it came out as a whisper.

She let out a low, throaty laugh, sneered, and bared her teeth. The black, dead soul stared back at me and made me gasp. I shuddered as a single word popped into my head. It described her to a T: Evil.

Then she slapped me again. This time for real.

Anyway, it didn't stop there. I spent the weekend in a broom closet off the kitchen. There was plenty of time to think about my life and how to escape from my shitty family. I mentally channeled Alli to ask for help. Unfortunately, she had gone camping with her family and wouldn't return until Sunday.

Charlie: November 5, 2006

"HOW DO YOU do it?" Alli stood in front of my dresser and tried her best not to meet my eyes in the mirror's reflection.

My eye had purpled, and the bruises on my arm still hurt; I could barely pick up my guitar without wincing. I refused to let my monster rain on my parade. Pissed would not be the right word to describe my mood, but in my teenage mind, it was the first word I could think of when I had called Alli. Furious with a heaping bucket of disappointment mixed in would be more accurate.

The first thing Alli had done after her family had returned home from the weekend getaway was call me.

She had made it to my house in record time. Later, she would tell me how lost I sounded and was worried I might do something stupid.

"Do what?" I asked, plucking the strings.

"Play and sing and move all at the same time. I can hardly walk and talk without getting all tripped up. You are so much better than me."

I couldn't help but smile; this girl cracked me up. I knew she was blowing smoke to make me feel better. It worked, and I secretly thanked her. When I told her about what happened on Friday, she hugged me and cried. Then I cried for the first time since Alli and I had become friends. Somehow it was easier to let my guard down with her and Sara.

"Remember when we used to march in band? I wore mittens to play the sax because, dammit, it's cold on that field in December." I shook my head and closed my eyes.

"During practice, Mr. Stone said something was off, and it was coming from our section. He had us all play our part to see who was fucking up, but I hadn't played a note since we started marching, so I knew it wasn't me. It was impossible for me to play and count my steps on the field at the same time. No way would I be the reason the C-shape was crooked, so I didn't play. I was so nervous, because I had only played the part, like, twice while we practiced inside. Luckily, by the grace of God, I played the right notes in the right order. I never played it again. Somehow you, Sara, and Kevin can actually do more than one thing at a time. Now that's what I call talent. My talent is having a naturally unique voice and naturally big hair."

She wasn't wrong; Alli had always been a little clumsy, but, man, could she sing.

"We can do this. We *are* good enough. *You* are good enough. Fuck Tashi. Let's prove her wrong and make it big. We can't let her kill our dreams. Let's become famous rock stars and rub her jealous face in our success."

My emotions calmed as I plucked the strings in the right order to sound like "Smoke on the Water." I appreciated that Alli was trying to get me pumped up and to remember the night we had decided to form Heaven Scent. "Easier said than done."

Alli interrupted the memory, her attitude changing from excited to pissed. "You know what? This is bullshit. No one should be treated this way. You haven't done anything wrong. You're a good person. You have a great heart, and you love life. She's just a dick. Tell me again why you don't just leave?"

"We have to be twenty before we go to LA. Your mom made us promise, remember?" I sighed.

Alli's face lit up, and she smiled. "I've had an epiphany."

"What is your bright idea, Ms. Summer?" I played

along.

Digging through my closet, Alli found a tote bag and tossed it in my lap. "Pack your shit. You're coming with me."

THE KITCHEN table in the middle of the Summer's dining area was so clean they could serve dinner to the president. As Alli explained our unusual situation, I tried so hard not to cry. It was even hard to look at Alli's parents, but I managed to meet Mr. Summer's eyes once.

Tears rolled down Mrs. Summer's cheeks when her fingers touched the bruise on my face. Then she stood to give me a hug, and I lost it. I'd never had a mother who hugged me when I cried. My mom always called me weak and stupid as she walked away.

Despite myself, I hugged her back. Mrs. Summer let me hold on tight for as long as I needed. It seemed like an hour, but it felt so good to be in the embrace that I didn't want to let go. The love in one simple hug was like nothing I had ever experienced.

Once I reluctantly relaxed my grip, we returned to our seats at the table. Alli grabbed my hand. My sister from another mister, as we always said, literally stood by my side during the worst part of my shitty childhood.

Mr. Summer explained that there would need to be some house rules if he were to allow me to live there. I had to pay for my own long-distance calls and help clean up after dinner. I agreed. "I've never had a rule that made sense. More than happy to follow yours."

He had no idea how life changing this moment would prove to be. Mr. Summer may have understood that he had saved me from my monster, but I doubt that he knew he saved my life. He suggested he call my mom and tell her what was happening. I tried to persuade him not to bother, but he said he wouldn't harbor a fugitive.

We all chuckled; he had a way of lighting a dark situation.

I shrugged. "Fine, have it your way, but don't say I didn't warn ya." I leaned back in my chair, arms crossed.

Mr. Summer dialed my home phone number and introduced himself when my mom answered. At first, we only heard his side of the conversation. "Your daughter, Charlie, is going to stay with us for a while."

A split second later, Mr. Summer pulled the receiver from his ear, and everyone in the room witnessed my mother's loss of control.

After Natasha threatened to call the police, she said, "Charlie is my daughter; she belongs to me. No one is going to take her away. You have no right to steal what is mine."

During the commotion on the other end of the phone, Mr. Summer stared at me with raised eyebrows, then smiled and nodded. He closed his eyes, took a deep breath, and shook his head. Interrupting the screams as they came through the phone, he said, "Look, Mrs. Stanley, I just wanted you to know your daughter is safe. We'll take good care of her."

He disconnected the phone and rested his hands on the counter. With pursed lips, he fought the anger that heated his face. After a deep sigh, he took three short steps toward me and wrapped me in his arms. "Honey, I'm so sorry," he whispered. "Stay here as long as you want." He held me at arm's length while I wiped my cheeks with the sleeve of my sweatshirt.

My voice failed me; all I could do was mouth, *Thank you*.

He reiterated one of the rules: we could not leave for LA until after we turned twenty. Mr. Summer fully wanted his children to go to college for at least a couple years to get an education. He wanted them to have a career to fall back on. Just in case.

On the flipside, he also understood how much talent us 'youngsters' possessed; our passion would most likely propel us through plenty of other tough situations.

He and Mrs. Summer agreed, behind the scenes, to support their kids in their dream. That night, I became one of their kids.

A BLOWUP mattress covered most of Alli's floor, our floor—after all, this was my room, too. I sat on my new bed, and we discussed our dreams, even though we had absolutely no idea what it meant to go to LA, what it looked like, where we would stay, or how we would make money to pay for food. We had, however, heard about the places where A&R reps, people who had been assigned to find and sign new talent by record labels, had discovered young bands. Most of those places only allowed people twenty-one and over through the doors. Possibly problematic but not impossible.

The phone rang a little while later, and Alli's mom brought the receiver to our bedroom. On the other end of the line was the mom of one of Kevin's friends. I sat beside Alli on the bed, and she tilted the phone away from her ear so I could listen.

"My son Scott saw Heaven Scent play at a couple different parties, and he told me that he heard, through the grapevine, how you approached the owner of Callaghan's. From what Scott said, you asked for permission to play, but Bud Wright turned you down."

Still confused why Scott's mom had called, Alli hesitated. "Um … that's true."

"I know this call must seem awfully odd to you," the woman said, chuckling. "I'll get to the point. Bud Wright is my husband's best friend. Scott asked me to talk with him to see if he would reconsider."

"Okay."

"I talked him into letting you play a gig at Callaghan's."

"Seriously?" Alli's eyes widened, and she gaped at me. "That's so awesome. Thank you. When?"

"Just before Christmas. You're playing on December sixteenth."

Alli thanked Scott's mom a hundred more times before she hung up. A loud "Yahoo!" came from nowhere. We stood and danced in the middle of the bedroom. Alli jumped on her bed. "Oh my God. Oh my God. Oh my God!"

Mrs. Summer knocked twice on the door before she opened it. "What's all this about?"

"We"—Alli bounced off the bed, put her arm around me, and paused for affect—"are playing at Callaghan's on December sixteenth."

"Girls, that's just fantastic. Good for you." She hugged us, then turned to the door. "I need to tell your dad."

"See! We are good enough. We're going to do this. You, me, Sara, Kevin—we're really going to make this happen. We are rock stars."

Alli hugged me so hard I couldn't breathe. It was the first time I'd smiled in days. She was right, and we both knew it. That night, we wrote "All Right" in about an hour. As we digested how quickly our future was changing, we promised to always be all right.

I need to get away from it all
Just get away

Heaven Scent

Forget everything I was taught when
I was young
And be a strong confident human
I'm gonna board an airplane and fly
around the world
Or maybe I'll just write a song

Just get away
It may be scary, and I might just fail
But dammit, I can say I tried
What am I without some pride?

Somehow, I'll always be all right
I need to get away from it all
Just get away
Forget everything I was taught when
I was young

Why do some people try to hold you
back?
What do they want from me?
How do they expect me to love them
if they don't love me?
Somehow, I'll always be all right

I know I'll find true love
But first, I need to find myself

I might be sick and a little twisted
But with my friends by my side, I'll
always be all right
All right, I'll be all right
Somehow, I'll always be all right

Livin' on a Prayer

The Interview: January 8, 2015

"CHARLIE, I don't know what to say." Tears filled Jenni's eyes, and she reached for a tissue.

"I didn't tell you that story for you to feel bad. It's a part of my past. It's one gigantic reason that I pushed myself to success. It's okay, Jenni. But thank you."

"So, a friend's mom took it upon herself to book a show for you? That's pretty incredible." Jenni sets her beer on the table and picks up her pen.

"You can say that again," Sara agrees. "She's still one of our biggest fans. Sends Facebook PMs and emails about what's happening in Brooklyn. She's great."

After scribbling a few words on her notepad, Jenni lifts her eyes to find the band waiting for the next barrage of questions. "So, that's how you got connected to the music world, but how did you sustain and grow the connection? What was your average crowd through all this? How did the increase in crowd size impact your performance? Did you ever have stage fright, and how did you overcome it? And of course, how did that change how much money you made?"

"Jenni, let me tell you that our performance has drastically changed over the short time we've been together." Alli twirled her hair. "Our first performance inside a real establishment, although memorable and fun, was quite different from the level of performance at one of our current shows."

Alli: December 16, 2006

WE LANDED OUR first gig at the hole-in-the-wall dive bar in Brooklyn called Callaghan's. It smelled like ass, cigarettes, and stale beer. Big dance floor, sketchy crowd. You need to remember; we only had a little over a month to get the word out.

We enlisted my aunt Kat to help make flyers and connect with her Jackson community. My cousins, Ted and Brandon, had tons of friends around Napoleon and Adrian. They all supported our summer bonfire tour, so we felt confident they would help with promotions and attend for support.

We promoted and marketed the show all over the Irish Hills area. All our friends talked about our first concert and shared the date everywhere they went: the grocery store, other friends' houses, parties, and we were the talk of the high school.

The principal wouldn't let us hang flyers, though, because he said it wasn't appropriate. Whatever, we didn't need his permission. We put our homemade advertisement under the windshield wiper of every single car in the parking lot. Every day.

We posted every day on our individual Facebook feeds and created a Heaven Scent Facebook page and shared posts there. Bud Wright let us post on his Facebook page and he updated his website. He even sent emails to his subscribers.

WE ARRIVED AT Callaghan's the night of, what we considered, our first real gig. Sure, we'd played at parties and in garages all summer, but the season had ended, and it was getting colder; this seemed like the most natural progression.

Unfortunately, we couldn't do much about the venue because of its old bones. It must have been built in the Middle Ages, because the bathrooms were orange and yellow and the carpet a dirty deep blue. This was only my second time in the bar. You have to remember we were only sixteen at this point and usually not allowed in any drinking establishment. Usually.

We arrived early and got our setup and practice duties accomplished before anyone showed up. Doors opened at eight o'clock, and the bouncer collected a five dollar cover from everyone as they entered. We were scheduled to take the stage at nine, so we sat in the back room for a half hour. We waited, paced, got all kinds of worked up.

I had been so much more nervous than I had been at any other show. When Charlie noticed my shaking from anxiousness, she told me I needed to release some energy.

So, I did jumping jacks, of all things. Then I ran in place, then punched the air. This was the start of my pre-stage ritual—my way of prepping for a crowd. If I wanted to perform at a level that impressed and entertained, I needed to relax and regain confidence before we took the stage.

Believe it or not, I used to be shy. I don't need to continue the ritual now, but it's kind of a superstition, so I do it anyway. After I worked out some of my energy, I settled my stomach with five crackers and goat cheese. No one else ate before the show.

Another ritual is our pep talk, a practice we still do. We recited our favorite phrases for confidence, success, love, and adoration and agreed this would be the best show ever.

"My choices are mine and mine alone."

"I am worthy of happiness and success."

"Not everyone has to like me. I'm okay with that."

"This is my new comfort zone."

"I love you to the tallest mountain and the deepest sea."

Kevin ordered each of us a shot of Goldschlager

and a beer. We toasted to our first gig, threw the shot back, and slammed the glasses on a table. In true football team fashion, we chanted, "Heaven Scent, Heaven Scent, Heaven Scent." We still do this before every show, too.

At precisely nine o'clock, Bud turned on the mic and tapped it. Piercing feedback got the attention of the entire bar. "Now, the moment you've all been waiting for. We are happy to present the very first indoor arena performance of Heaven Scent." The crowd cheered, and Bud pushed down their sound with his hands. "Thank you all for coming tonight to make their debut performance memorable."

As we took the stage, my heart raced, and my palms sweated. Plywood rumbled like an earthquake under my feet. It was as if the venue was too small to contain so much excitement. If I had to describe it in a word, surreal couldn't even come close—out of body, maybe. It was almost like someone else took steps with my feet.

All the nervous energy had upset my stomach, and I worried I would puke. Whose bright idea was it to eat goat cheese before a performance?

Callaghan's had just gone through some lighting renovations, and from my vantage point on stage, it was hard to physically see the faces in the crowd. Blinded, I raised my hand above my eyes to deflect the spotlight, and the inexperienced lighting guy got the hint. I searched for familiar faces, and it hit me how many people were crammed into the bar.

Before I allowed myself to freak out, I spotted Aunt Kat sitting beside Uncle Dan and my parents at the bar. When I caught Aunt Kat's eye, she raised her signature 7&7 in a toast. I nodded my appreciation and breathed a little easier. Ted, Brandon, and their friends took up four tables along the wall. Joey and his sister sat at a table with Tony, Jeff, and Steve. I knew our Jackson crew wouldn't miss this. Kevin's buddies took up another three tables, Tex included. Shelly entered later with another group of girls.

I told myself I needed to pretend we were just at one of our bonfires or in Loomis's garage. This was nothing different from anything we had done before; it just happened to be in a different venue. And making twice as much money.

After we all settled into our designated places on stage, Kevin played a warm-up beat. Charlie plucked at the strings of her guitar while she pushed a couple pedals at the edge of the stage. Sara threw the strap to her bass over her shoulder, and I stood in front of the mic. From experience, I knew if I thought through it too much, I would fuck up. I talked myself into just losing myself in the music. After a couple deep breaths, I turned to look at our band, nodded, and smiled. That was their queue. I was ready to rock.

Charlie played the entry chords of "Manic Monday". Even though the Bangles had originally played it on a keyboard, she had perfected her own version of it on guitar.

My hands were still sweaty, so I didn't trust myself to hold my microphone. I leaned in close and belted out the first lines of the tune. You see, we had chosen this song to lead for a reason. The Bangles were obviously a girl band, and we wanted to judge our audience before we surprised everyone with our next song, like we had at Loomis's.

Most of the crowd turned their attention to us, but a few people chatted at the bar and others huddled around a couple tables in the far corner. They glanced in our direction a few times but did their best to ignore us. Four guys surrounded one of the pool tables, smoke rising from the ashtray and beers lodged in their hands. They laughed at their own jokes instead of watching us play. Challenge accepted.

As expected, most of the patrons applauded after the first song, but when I howled my best "*Hellllloooo*, Brooklyn," everyone cheered.

Each of our bonfire and garage gigs had prepared us for this moment. In the beginning, we felt like impostors and ensured to let our following know we appreciated their support. Now, as we had before, I said a little thank you for coming out. One of our Jackson buddies screamed, "Heaven Scent!" and everyone cheered again. From the voice, I was sure it had been Steve, but I lost him in the crowd.

We chose the second song on purpose, to get the attention of those few patrons who struggled to pay attention. “This one’s for you, Tony.” I pointed to him as I hammered out the lead-in riff to “Seek and Destroy”. Tony had introduced us to the badass Metallica album, and this was my way to thank him.

For a moment, the crowd turned silent. Or maybe I got into my own head. But as soon as I looked up, I saw everyone standing in front of the stage with their jaws dropped in awe. The guys at the pool table turned and stared. That was probably one of the best moments of our early days. Mission accomplished; we had surprised the shit out of everybody.

Halfway through the set, I gave Charlie ‘the nod,’ and she played the intro to “Summertime”. Some of the crowd recognized the tune and applauded.

“This next one is our first original. It’s become quite popular around town. Some of you know it already, and for those of you who don’t, we hope you love it.” My raspy low voice sang the intro:

Sunshine, suntan lotion, lobster burn
Pontoons, long days, longer nights

Those who hadn’t heard the song listened intently until I sang:

The group in front of the stage erupted. They went crazy. It was so cool to see how much our hometown enjoyed what we considered our personal art.

We went through the rest of the setlist as if we were practicing in the garage, confident and comfortable. The only difference was that we didn't make any mistakes. We played perfectly, I sang the lyrics without error, and the crowd loved every minute of it.

Everyone in the bar sang along to our eclectic groupings of songs, danced, and cheered us on. It was simply the best experience. The best connection with the crowd and with each other. The best time I could ever imagine being on a real stage in a real bar. The best time in front of people who had paid real money, not just our friends and family.

At the end of the night, we sat around a group of tables with Bud and revisited our first conversation. He admitted he hadn't been sure if we would have been the right band to play at his bar, only because of our age.

"You sure as hell proved me wrong," he admitted. "Anytime you want to play here, you just let me know the date, and I'll make a space for you. In fact, I own another bar with a better setup and higher-paying crowds. When y'all think you're ready to step up your game, in the next year or so, I'll help you book events around Royal Oak."

Kevin drummed his sticks in the air, and us girls gaped in disbelief.

"Might seriously think about hiring a manager, because your band won't be playing dives like this for very long." Along with the cash we made, twelve hundred and fifty dollars, he handed me a CD when he stood.

I passed the money to Kevin to split four ways and asked Bud, "What's this?"

"My gift to you. I took the liberty of recording you tonight. Make copies of this and send it to everyone you can."

Famous in a Small Town

Charlie: December 24, 2006

BETWEEN practices the next week, we gathered in Kevin's basement bedroom to discuss who we should ask to be our manager. We agreed we could probably hire a booking agent to schedule our gigs but thought we needed more. It made sense to hire someone who would also look out for our best interests, not just take a cut of our proceeds.

"Oh my God. It just came to me. Like, duh, your aunt Kat." Once I blurted out my epiphany, it didn't take us long to agree on the one person who would be our best choice. The room grew silent as the rest of the band processed the thought.

"Of course!" From an overstuffed chair in the corner, Alli slapped her knee. "Seriously, we have obviously been thinking about this too hard."

"That's the best idea you have ever had," Kevin joked. "Like, ever." He and Shelly sat on his bed with their backs against the brick wall.

"No need to be a dick," Shelly sneered and stuck up for me; her tone was out of character, and it took me by surprise. I wondered what he had done to deserve a snide remark from the only person who thought he was a king.

Hair wrapped around Sara's finger as she nodded her head. "Aunt Kat is the perfect person to ask. Think she'll do it?"

Alli leaned back in her chair and searched the sky—actually, the drop ceiling covered with flags from multiple concerts—for affirmation. "Yes. I do. And listen …" She leaned forward. "Between her, Dan, and the boys, they know almost everyone in this area, Jackson, Adrian, and Ann Arbor."

Their uncle Dan worked at a restaurant supply company in nearby Chelsea and had built meaningful relationships with many business owners.

The boys, Ted and Brandon, went to high school in the neighboring town and spent a lot of time in and around Jackson and Ann Arbor. I was sure they would be supportive in helping us gain more followers and find places to play.

Plus, the entire family had attended every one of our performances. Sometimes I really did have great ideas.

Not wasting any time, everyone except Shelly jumped in Kevin's car. She gave some lame excuse about how she had to be home for dinner. We all thought it was a little fishy; Shelly never hung out with her family.

It only took ten minutes to get to Napoleon, where Kat lived with her family. Drive-by hugs were her favorite, and we intended to make this one extra special. In our own little world of smalltown living of 'everyone knows everyone,' it simply meant you didn't have to call before you stopped over. Kat loved surprise visits.

Christmas lights lined the roof of the two-story house, and the heavily decorated tree stood on the other side of the picture window. Dan and the boys cleared snow off the driveway, leaving piles along one side. They had just finished shoveling paths from the house to the garage. When we pulled into the driveway and spilled from the car, we waved, and they followed us into the house.

Kat greeted us at the door, thrilled we had come over. Dressed in an apron with a festive sweater underneath, she obviously had been making her signature caramel popcorn. The entire house smelled of the sweet drizzle, and my stomach growled. She dished up some of the treat for each of us and pointed to the living room. There wasn't much room to sit in the cozy area, so we squished together on the couch and love seat, excited to share our idea.

When the small talk subsided, I smiled at one of the sweetest people I had ever known. "Kat, I would first like to thank you for always being there for us, not only as kids who need direction"—it was impossible to hide a grin—"but as a band. You're one of our biggest fans and one of our biggest supporters. You are the reason we all look incredible during our shows, and your entire family have been to every gig we've ever played. Things are really starting to get more intense and more serious." I paused to smile and take a deep breath. "You guys were at the show on Saturday; I think you can see we're getting quite a large following. From on stage, it looked like everyone had a blast."

Kat chimed in, agreeing, "Everyone had the best time. I lost count of how many people came up to me and said how great you were. I am so proud of each and every one of you, and I'm so excited to see where this takes you."

Alli's shoulders relaxed a little. "I'm so glad you said that because that's kind of why we're here. We have a proposition for you."

Kat tilted her head and gave a little smirk. "Go on."

Before we had arrived, we'd agreed Alli should be the one to say: "What would you think about being our manager?" She paused to let the question sink in before she added more details.

Kat glanced at Dan, Ted, and Brandon with a straight face.

Brandon stood, twirled in a circle, and whooped as he punched the air.

From his position on the couch, Ted smiled from

ear to ear and nodded.

Dan reclined in his chair and smiled. Not a man of many words, he showed his approval in his expression.

Kat, however, frowned. She leaned forward and put her elbows on her knees, clasped her hands, and stared at her pink-painted fingernails. A few tense moments passed while we waited for her response. When she lifted her eyes to meet Alli's, they shimmered with happy tears. Touched, her voice trembled. "I don't know if I can do a good enough job for you, but I will damn well try my hardest."

"Yes!" Kevin drummed his fingers on the coffee table.

Sara and I stood and hugged each other.

Kat and Alli rose at the same time, and Kat pulled her niece into one of her signature tight, warm hugs. She pulled back and smiled. "This is the best Christmas gift ever. Thank you."

"Who wants a beer?" Dan asked. "This calls for a celebration."

Charlie: February 1, 2007

DAILY PRACTICES, writing sessions, dreams of studio time, and playing at Callaghan's most weekends kept us busy over the next few weeks. Kat called when she was ready to discuss our first local bar tour, so to speak, and we were anxious to review her plans. Excited for us, Kat took the liberty of naming the tour, A Step Up, which signified our minute traction toward success. Certainly, we would climb more steps in the near future.

Making the right contacts, Kat found unique ways to promote the band. She spent most of her time weeding out offers to play in exchange for an audience versus paying gigs that would maximize our exposure. Not only did she put one hundred percent of her effort toward finding gigs, but she also used her exceptional sales techniques to convince the most unlikely venues to book us on Saturday nights.

Between Valentine's Day and the beginning of summer, we had a gig booked every Friday and Saturday night. Kat even booked a couple special events: a birthday party and a college graduation. It baffled me how she worked so hard to please us. She believed in our talent just as much as we did—almost more.

The recording that Bud Wright had made during our first indoor gig at Callaghan's helped other bar owners determine whether they wanted to book us or not. Only one place said no; Kevin's now ex-girlfriend Shelly tended bar at Stingers, and she had a say in who played.

Ever since they had broken up right after Christmas, Kevin drank more, and his normal happy-go-lucky attitude had turned to 'I'm-a-jerk' in an instant. He would make most decisions either in haste or with one of us getting our feelings hurt by some off-the-wall comment—usually Alli. Kevin called her stupid all the time, and it was wearing on her.

One of the first locations we played on the tour was a local smalltown sports bar called Aggie's. In our own way, we all had a connection to this place. Kat and Dan lived down the road and knew the owners, and Kevin knew the owner's sons. Before she had met Jeff, Sara had dated another of the owner's sons. Alli and I were friends with the bartender's little sister. It made sense that Aggie's would be on our tour.

Back in those days, the stage was tucked in a corner on the opposite side of the kitchen. It was barely big enough for Kevin's drum set, let alone two guitar stands, pedals, three mic stands, and four teenagers.

As we set up, a few customers entered for a late dinner and pretty much ignored our activity. We combined three tables closest to the stage with other tables to clear some space. A win-win—bigger seating areas and more room for us to spread out.

Alli's entire family attended that night. Her parents had invited their extended family to support their kid's first official 'tour.' Most of them made it. Of course, Kat and her family were there, along with the entire Jackson crew, except Joey. Tex and most of Kevin's friends took up another three tables.

It took less effort to pack Aggie's, a smaller venue

than Callaghan's. Once our regulars found their seats, it only took fifteen or twenty more people to be considered sold out. Before we even got on stage, people lined the walls.

I didn't expect my family to show up because they just didn't. Ever. Halfway through our first set, though, Alli stumbled over the lyrics to her favorite song, "I Hate Myself for Loving You". Something had gone wrong, and I picked up on it right away. When I glanced in her direction, I saw her eyes were wide, and she nodded toward the door.

My dad stood there with the warmest smile, and stared at me as if he hadn't seen me in forty years. Tears filled my eyes, but I didn't cry. Through all the bullshit with my mom, my dad had been on the road most of the time and hadn't experienced the terror she inflicted on me. He wouldn't doubt me when I'd told him about the things she'd done, but he hadn't been home enough to protect me. For me, his attendance was monumental.

If I tried, it would have been impossible to stop the smile that spread across my face. The one person who mattered showed up to support me. I pursed my lips and jammed even harder. My dad leaned against the far wall throughout the rest of the show. It was clear he enjoyed watching his youngest daughter do what she loved most in the world.

It's My Life

Sara: May 1, 2007

AS MUCH AS Kat loved drive-by hugs, we loved surprise band meetings. Our manager planned fun and exciting adventures, as far as gigs went, and she loved to keep us guessing. When she summoned the band, we gathered and made a beeline to Kat's house.

After we settled in our respective chairs at the modest kitchen table and finished our small talk, the matriarch of our group stood. "Girls, Kevin. I have some news." She paused, then turned away to hide her smile. "Nah, you're probably not interested."

Each of us sighed and grumbled in protest.

"You're killin' me, Smalls," Kevin quoted from one of his favorite movies.

"Well …" She turned back to face us, her smile gleaming. "I guess I can let you decide if you're interested in this event or not."

Silent, we waited for her to continue. I leaned forward and put my elbows on the table. I found myself holding my breath in anticipation.

"Okay, I'll just say it. Here goes … Heaven Scent is

one of twenty contestants in Jackson County Fair's Next Top Band contest. As your manager, I took the liberty of entering you today. This could be the perfect step for you. It's a great opportunity."

Not understanding quite what this news meant, we eyed each other and shrugged. Were we supposed to treat it as just another gig, or was there more to it?

Kat tapped her foot. "The winner of the contest is not only awarded one thousand, five hundred dollars, but also four hours of studio time. At any location you choose. In a real studio. With real equipment. To record a real CD."

By the time we had understood all the details and had agreed to Kat's terms, the sun had disappeared behind the trees, and we were ready to party. It was a day to celebrate, for sure.

The first bonfire party of the year was an impromptu get-together. Wouldn't you know it, Kevin and Tex had called friends who had called more friends, and two hours later, cars filled the field on Taylor Road.

Although a chill hung in the night air, warmth spread by way of excitement of the unknown. None of us had any idea what the future looked like, but we couldn't wait to follow Kat's path. During any normal bonfire party, Heaven Scent would play a set, but that night, we celebrated our next step up the rock-band career ladder.

Until my mom showed up.

I had to do a double take to recognize her, thinking how someone who resembled my mom was approaching me. Then I recognized the Givenchy dress and Prada bag. No one in their right mind would come to this field wearing that getup.

Except my mom.

She stopped in front of me and sneered. “Couldn’t you find something more flattering than that to wear? That shirt makes you look even fatter than you are.”

Mortified, I backed away. “Why are you here?” Blinking away the tears, I refused to let her see me cry. From years of practice, she would purposefully choose specific words to hurt me. It was just like her to push every button in front of my friends.

“Now, Sara. Is that any way to greet your mother? There’s no need to be rude. I came here to save you from the local riffraff. I can’t, for the life of me, understand why you’d want to spend time in the middle of a dirty, disgusting cow pasture.” Once clean, Gucci heels poked holes in the mud. She wrinkled her nose. “These people are not our kind. This place smells worse than that kid you claim as your boyfriend. We’re leaving.” She turned, took three steps, expecting me to follow, and lost her balance. To keep from falling, she outstretched her arms like an airplane and teetered.

Don’t laugh, don’t laugh, don’t laugh ...

She turned back toward me and clenched my arm

with her clawed fingers. "Now, young lady."

"No." I wriggled away, a scratch streaking my arm in the process. I glared at her as I stood beside my friends. "These people are *my* kind. They're the only ones who care about what I want to do with my life. They don't push me to be their vision of perfection."

Jeff put his arm around my shoulders to prove my point.

When I refused to go with her, she raised her voice and made a scene. "How dare you associate with such filth."

"I don't expect you to get it, *Mother*." I spat the last word and crossed my arms.

A group of concerned people surrounded us, ready to help if I needed them.

"Sara Jean."

I stood my ground and smiled. "I'm not going anywhere with—" My cheek stung as welts raised on my skin. She thought she could wipe the smile right off my face. She was right. She had successfully humiliated me in front of everyone I knew. Slumped on the ground, sitting cross-legged, I cried tears of embarrassment as she walked away.

"What the fuck was that?" Jeff squatted beside me and brushed loose strands of hair from my face. His gaze followed my mother as she drove away in her BMW. "Come on, let me take you home." He helped me to my feet, but I refused to leave.

"Not a chance. No way in hell am I going back there."

Jealousy can be worse than any drug. It can make almost anyone do things that, to most others, seem unimaginable. Leave it to my mother to ruin the best day of my life in three minutes flat.

Sara: July 12, 2007

BACKSTAGE at the Jackson County Fair was laid out differently than any other stage we'd played. For one, you didn't just jump off the front of the platform to the dance floor. Or push past tables to go to the restroom. Or feel the heat from a giant fire twenty feet away.

Throughout the entire week of the fair, we prepared for the contest by practicing at least three hours a day, every day except the day prior. Our experience had taught us that one day of rest helped form an osmosis of sorts. When we practiced the day before an event, it never failed; we would make a mistake.

On Wednesday, the day before the contest, we went to the fair as guests. Our Jackson friends met up with us, and for hours on end, we rode rides, played games, and ate fair food. We spent precious time as regular teenaged kids. Without a care in the world, we just focused on having fun.

The next day, we packed the only gear the contest judges allowed us to bring and headed back to the fairgrounds. It surprised me how weird it felt to congregate in the same crowded area with twenty other bands; we all had numbers on our clothes, like cattle.

In addition to being 'tagged,' the whole thing seemed so hurried. But with that many bands playing two songs a piece, I guess they sort of needed to rush it. Everyone took the time to showcase their talent in the three-hour slot the fair had allotted.

They called it 'plug and play.' No time to tune our guitars or test the pedals or microphones. The fair had put some volunteers, who we couldn't communicate with, in charge of the sound. If, musically, something was off, there was nothing we could do. Our control remained in our ability to gel as a team.

They had told Kat that the contest would run from two o'clock to five o'clock when she had booked us. Of course, the bands needed to arrive at ten in the morning to go through the entire process of checking in, preparing, and whatever other bullshit the directors deemed necessary.

At the last minute, whoever organized the details of the stage timeslot portion of the day had forgotten they had booked a talent show for two o'clock. Because all the bands had arrived early, they forced us to take the stage three hours prior to what they had communicated.

For two months, we had marketed, advertised, and

spread the word that we needed the support of our fanbase to win this thing. Not only had we posted to all our social media, but at every show we had played, we'd ensured to announce the date and time of the contest.

Tons of our followers had planned to be at the fair by two o'clock to hear us play and cast their vote. Unfortunately, there had been just enough time after the change of events for us to post updates on social media and call our immediate family.

The contest began with absolutely no audience. Zero. Lucky for us, they didn't schedule us first. It would have sucked to perform to chairs and dirt. We had a chance to watch seven bands perform before us. The first five were pretty good, not spectacular. Not to toot our own horn, but we were way better.

The band two slots before us didn't have it together. During their first song, the lead guitarist missed his entire solo, and the singer forgot the words to the end of the song. Flustered, she turned her back to the small audience who were trickling in and walked off stage.

The band directly before us watched in horror and admitted they were more nervous than expected. The singer threw up just after getting on stage, and they couldn't continue.

Before our scheduled time to take the stage, Alli did her ritual prep, but the fairgrounds had a no-alcohol policy, so we could not include our ritual shot. We had prepared the two most appropriate songs for people who were not our regular fanbase. We understood regular fairgoers would be listening, too.

Country music was growing in popularity among our followers, and each time we played "Fancy", the crowd went wild. We chose that for our first song and played it without a hitch. Twenty people in the crowd cheered. I counted. The other seven weren't paying attention.

Jeff and Tony made it to the fairgrounds early, along with Alli's family and Tex. Joey didn't show up again, though. Alli had been more than understanding each time he missed a show, but this time it was almost literally in his own back yard.

She was already pissed, because of how the day had gone, but this was the icing on the cake. Later, she admitted it had already been over way before that. Besides, her heart had always been with Tex.

For our second song, we played something a little more our style. "Animals" grabbed everyone's attention, because the jackass controlling the sound had turned up the guitar volume so loud. Having no way to communicate with him, we had to deal. Charlie played spot on, but it overpowered the vocals. Alli sang her heart out, but it didn't matter, and we all knew it.

Disappointed doesn't even come close to how I felt: outraged and annoyed because of the last-minute change, and out of control, because someone who knew nothing about our band had managed the soundboard. We were all heartbroken because we were good enough to win this.

We had worked so hard to not only perfect our sound, but our performance, our crew, and supporters were top notch. Sure, a lot of the other bands were pretty good, but I wasn't the only one who knew we deserved to come in first place. In fact, some of the other bands' entourages voted for us.

Most of our followers had arrived right on time, just as they announced the winner. Figures.

In the end, we came in second place. I guess we could consider it a win, but at the time, it sure didn't feel like it. The fairground personnel had severely diminished our chances because of miscommunication. It was a shame, but we lived with it, learned from it, and moved on.

Sara: July 21, 2007

GRADUATION came and went; it wasn't as big a deal as everyone made it out to be. Sure, we walked across a stage in front of hundreds of people, but that wasn't anything new. We got a piece of paper telling us that our high school career had ended successfully. Big whoop.

All our friends had selected their college of choice

months ago, or a college had selected them, depending on who you asked. They were all excited about starting this new phase in their lives, but we had already been living our new phase for a couple years.

My parents hadn't planned a graduation party for me because I had told them not to bother. At the beginning of the school year, my mom had acted like it would take an act of Congress just to free up enough time to send invitations.

After the stunt she had pulled at the bonfire, I refused to speak to her in more than one syllable replies. Unfortunately, I still needed a roof over my head, so I came and went when she wasn't around. My dad had tried to ask what was wrong, but he wouldn't understand. To get him to stop asking, I had told him, "Girl stuff."

I didn't care about not having a graduation party. Besides, Charlie's parents had flaked on her, too, so at least we weren't alone.

Mr. and Mrs. Summer felt the need to celebrate, though. They treated the entire band as their own and promised graduation would be special. As a surprise, and an attempt to make things different from what our friends were doing, they planned a joint party for the entire band.

They correctly assumed that, wherever we were, we would want to play. Mr. Weber, the man who owned the land on Taylor Road, where we'd spent so many nights around a bonfire, had agreed to let us have our party there.

Relaxed and happy, we took some time to just jam with our friends while we hung out. It wasn't like a real practice session; we weren't 'on,' so to speak. Plus, all Alli and Kevin's family came, and there was cake. Cake changed the dynamics of any party. I felt like a little kid celebrating her birthday—giddy and dancy.

However, after the aunts and uncles left and we'd consumed the cake, things changed.

"I love nothing more than the smell of a Taylor Road bonfire. This has got to be my favorite place," Charlie said, beaming.

Smoke billowed off red-hot logs stacked three feet high and created a ten-foot flame. Heatwaves radiated and reached us as we strolled to the stage.

"Rotisserie chicken." Alli turned in a slow circle two feet from the bonfire. She held a red Solo cup filled with keg beer, likely warm by now, in one hand and a bottle of Mountain Dew in the other.

Tex kept a close watch on Alli. He had stood beside her all day and would bring her food and beer. Whispers between the two of them made it obvious that their feelings for each other had moved to a new category. It had taken them forever to connect, but when they did, it was clear to everyone that Tex wanted to be with Alli. Although they hadn't made it official yet, she was playing hard to get.

Insert eyeroll here.

Charlie grabbed her guitar and ripped a sweet chorus right away. Kevin and I held the beat, while Alli stumbled up the steps to sing. Words she had yet written on paper flowed from her soul like a waterfall. It was completely possible that alcohol influenced our actions that night.

Can't find my socks,
I just put them down
Why did I walk into the kitchen
again?
Where are my keys?
Oh, they're in my hand

Walkin' around here like a clown
Thoughts of you cloud my brain

Alli pointed at Tex.

Stupid love, Stupid love, Stupid love
My love for you makes me stupid

I yelled, "That's fucking awesome! Don't forget this one. Dammit … write it down!"

Charlie and Alli had a bad habit of forgetting incredible riffs after jamming. This song ended up being one of our favorites, though: “Stupid Love”.

Part 2

Drunken Armadillo Feb 14, 2009

♡ ♡ ♡ ♡ ♡

Raise your Glass	Pink
Kiss	Prince
NASCAR	Heaven Scent
Party in the USA	Miley
Summertime	Heaven Scent
Come to My Window	Melissa
Let Me Be Me	Heaven Scent

BREAK

Call Me When You're Sober	Evanescence
Love Song	Tesla
Yourself	Heaven Scent
Watch Me	Heaven Scent
Miss Independent	Kelly
No Sleep 'til Brooklyn	Beastie Boys

The Interview: January 8, 2015

"TELL ME MORE about your influences. The way you dress, the way you dance, your stage presence, is it all one hundred percent the natural you coming through? Or do you pull from what you admire about other celebrities and mix it into Heaven Scent?"

Charlie shrugs. "Most of it is just our goofy, silly, stupid ideas. Somehow, whatever we did turned out to work. There were some influences, obviously. Because specific bands inspired us, we strove to rise to fame as they did. It's easy to emulate what is attractive to you." She shakes her head and laughs. "When Alli started dancing like Steven Tyler, though, I had to put my foot down."

"Hey! I resemble that remark." Alli stands and struts to the bar to grab another mixed drink.

"Our look changes with the times, but our sound, Alli's voice, is like nothing else out there. We are able to be unique and genuine based on one small aspect of who we are."

"We didn't want to be poppy, like Britney,

Madonna, and Miley," Sara adds.

"Although we love Miley," Alli interjects, while Tommy dumps a shot over ice. "I can dance to her music all day." A raspy version of "Party in the USA" fills the room. Like Miley, she raises her hands above her head and shakes her hips.

The girls sing their parts, and Tommy taps his fingers on the bar, keeping the beat.

"Actually, "Party in the USA" inspired one of our songs," Sara says. "We wanted to be more hardcore, though, so it's pretty guitar heavy."

"Do you mean "Yourself"?" Jenni guesses.

"Impressive, Ms. Brooklyn." Charlie offers a sly smile. "Sounds like you may know more about our story than you're letting on."

A shrug accompanies Jenni's wink.

Sara names more rockers who have influenced Heaven Scent. "We love Heart and Vixen and have a little more of an edge, like Joan Jett, Avril Lavigne, Sheryl Crow."

"I love Lady Gaga's voice, but she puts on too much of an act—not that there's anything wrong with that. We're just all about being ourselves and speaking our truth." Alli and Charlie share a nod.

"Jewel." Sara's smile is infectious. "Above and beyond her amazing voice, she has a phenomenal success story. Then there are country stars, like Miranda

Lambert, who flat out kicks ass, to the legendary Reba. Greats like Whitney, Aretha, and raps own Queen Latifah, and heavier artists, like Evanescence."

"Speaking of Reba." Alli lifts her hand. When she has Jenni's attention, she continues. "She was a huge influence because of her shows on stage—in fact, one of our favorite songs to perform is "Fancy". When Reba plays, it's almost like you're going to a movie. Our stage presence is focused more on playing, though."

"Not many acts can pull off Reba's style of performance," Jenni adds her own opinion. "Pink, too, has an incredible stage presence."

"To be honest, if we never got any further than playing the bar scene, I think we would have been fine. As long as we gave it our all and knew we tried our hardest, that's all that matters. On the other hand, I thank God every day for the grace He gives us."

"That's beautiful, Alli." Progressing with the interview, Jenni asks more questions. "You worked so hard to begin your proverbial climb. When did you start getting recognized? Has there ever been a time when you thought about breaking up? When did you make your first recording in a studio?"

"Wow, so many questions. Let's see if we can answer them all in a few stories." Alli giggles. "We finally got enough of a following to land small bars north of Detroit, which scared the shit out of my mom. Mention the word Detroit, and she freaks out."

Squinting, Jenni tilts her head. "But most of the bars where your type of music is popular is in a pretty safe area. Besides, your aunt Kat wouldn't dream of putting you in jeopardy. Why was she so scared?"

"Smalltown momma. Jackson and Ann Arbor have their sketchy areas, just like any other city, but my mom always felt better when we played closer to home. Even came to watch us play a few times at Frasier's Pub." A smile forms at the memory.

"Yeah, one of the funniest things I've ever seen is your mom sitting at a table in the middle of rowdy college kids playing quarter bounce. She was so confused." Charlie pursed her lips. "My mom probably would have joined them and drank them under the table. I digress. The more we played, the more the crowds grew, and it seemed like a natural progression to be in front of more people. It didn't affect us as much as I thought it might."

Charlie: March 1, 2008

IN ADDITION to our usual Irish Hills area bars—Callaghan's, City Saloon, Aggie's, and Jerry's Pub—Kat booked several other bars in southeast Michigan. The intent had been to expand our reach and to grow our following. Pay ranged from one hundred fifty to two hundred fifty dollars depending on the day of the week and location. Total, not each.

In larger, more upscale towns, like Dexter, Chelsea, and Ann Arbor, we gained another level of fan. College kids always spread the word about their latest and greatest discoveries. The promise of more money was alluring, as well.

Right around this time, personal agendas changed. Kevin dropped his college classes to be a fulltime drummer. After all, it was way more fun and, as he said, chicks dig guys in bands. They didn't really dig drummers, except for Tommy Lee, Dave Grohl, and Lars, but that didn't keep him from bragging.

Michigan State University had accepted Sara, but she struggled with mixing classes with gigs. For a semester, she scheduled classes only Monday through Thursday and drove home, from Lansing, on weekends. Even though we hadn't been playing as long as some bands, she wondered if our dream would ever come true.

Alli and I played with the idea of getting a waitressing job at Jerry's Pub on Wampler's Lake, because we played there some weekends and knew the owners, but the only way to make any real money was to wait those weekends. That wouldn't work for our tour schedule. We each applied for positions in stores in Brooklyn and worked for minimum wage. Seven-forty an hour didn't amount to much at the end of the week, but it helped with gas money.

Aunt Kat developed a great plan to promote us and worked feverishly to ensure everyone she met learned about Heaven Scent. It was apparent we would need more than word-of-mouth marketing if we wanted to increase our presence across the tri-state area.

Behind the scenes, we all agreed we needed to have individual social media pages. We would post something on them at least every other day, even if it wasn't band related. At least it would help keep us in front of our friends' and followers' faces. Everywhere we went, someone we knew greeted us and wanted to know where we would be playing next. We invited fans to follow our social media to keep them up to date.

Kat controlled the band page by updating our schedule and posting during gigs. We all added to it here and there, too. When she felt it was time to spread out, Kat booked bars in Novi, Royal Oak, Birmingham, Rochester Hills, and Detroit.

These areas had been on her radar for quite some time, but she waited until her Spidey senses confirmed we were ready before she contacted Bud Wright. As promised, he helped with bookings at higher-scale venues.

With performances every Friday and Saturday night, we were profitable the first half of the year in many ways. We made more money by raising our booking fee to a six-hundred-dollar minimum. Our friend zone and Facebook following exploded almost overnight.

One afternoon, after practice, we drove to Dexter to see if Aubree's on Main Street had an area for us to play. After we met with the owner and shared an amazing pizza, we headed back to the car.

A young couple passed us on the sidewalk, walking the other direction; the girl did a double take and nudged her boyfriend. It was then when we saw the fruits of our labor.

I was the only one who overheard her whisper loudly, "Oh my God. Is that *them*?"

"Who?" the boyfriend asked.

The girl turned to get a good look, squealed, then jogged down the sidewalk to catch up with us. She touched me on the shoulder, a cloud of CK One surrounding her. "Excuse me. Are you Heaven Scent?"

I smiled and nodded. "We sure are."

Alli laughed, exclaiming, "Wow, we have fans!"

The girl dug through her purse and retrieved a pen and an envelope from an old piece of opened mail. She shoved them at us and talked so fast I could barely understand her. "Oh my God, I can't believe it's you. It's really you. I love your music. I've seen you a few times in Ann Arbor and Royal Oak. When are you coming back? I can't wait to see you again. Are you going to play in Dexter sometime soon? Can I have your autograph?"

Charlie: March 15, 2008

GIGS IN THE upscale areas on the outskirts of Detroit played a big role in the number of additional unique followers we gained. From where we started—smalltown USA—I would have thought it would be more difficult for us to make a name for ourselves among the young, professional crowd. Somehow, we fit in.

Our original lyrics hit a much-needed chord in the psyche of kids who, mostly, were just like us. Everyone has a need to be accepted and loved. Everyone has a reason to be pissed off at someone for something; our songs brought us all together.

We were all the same in the end. Everyone excels at something, and we all make mistakes. Whether we're rich or poor, white or black, or somewhere in between, young or old(er), we all still bleed red.

"The cars these kids drive are just insane. Seriously, a twenty-two-year-old in a Porsche or Jaguar?" Outside Mr. B's, Kevin leaned against the brick wall during a break in our set. He passed a bottle of cinnamon Schnapps around our little circle.

"Did you see that chick climb out of the Beamer? She couldn't have been much older than us. And she's in a fucking BMW." I took a shot and continued in my best Arnold Schwarzenegger voice, "Who are her parents and what do they do?"

"Think they'll adopt us?" Sara laughed and pointed at a passing Cadillac.

Once we took our places on the stage, Kevin tripped on a cord and made a ruckus as he caught himself with his cymbals. I turned to see if he was okay and followed his stare into the crowd. The girl we had just watched exit the BMW sat alone at a table directly in front of the stage. Dressed in a short, tight, black dress, and black stilettos, she looked ready to rock. When she stared at Kevin and licked her bright red lips, I thought he might trip, again.

Charlie: March 16,2008

BLUNDERS seemed to follow us around the entire weekend. The next night in Rochester Hills, my guitar ended up unplugged somehow, forcing me to play acoustic.

Alli, quick as a whip, started singing "Love Song" to make me relax. I changed my perspective and accepted that we were acoustic for one song. Fortunately, we had started covering it during every show after Callaghan's, so it came to me like riding a bike. The crowd had gone crazy for it the first time we played it in Brooklyn, so we had kept it in the lineup. Because of the mistake in Rochester Hills, and how well we had adjusted, we continued to cover the great Tesla song.

In the end, I recovered, and the crowd was happy—didn't even know it had happened—but I saw it as a loss. Fans lined up to tell us how awesome we sounded. These rich city kids loved the way us country kids played. They cheered for us because they connected with us.

However, my mom still lived in my head, and I heard her tell me how I would never amount to anything. Shit like that stays with you, whether you want it to or not. No matter how much praise we got every night we performed, I seriously thought about throwing in the towel after one small mistake.

Alli and I worked through my gloom in a way that became normal for us: we wrote a song. "Yourself" reminded us how we were just normal people, and so was everyone else. It helped uplift people who may have endured a tough time and felt like they'd lost their purpose.

We'd had fans write to us to thank us for creating this song. Listening to it on repeat had helped one fan get through the loss of her father, inspiring her to refocus and get back on track.

As a band, we learned a valuable lesson about who

we were and who we wanted to be. Those types of stories would really get to me and remind me of why we do what we do. We loved entertaining, but when we touched someone, it confirmed we were where we were supposed to be.

Charlie: March 29, 2008

"WE REALLY need to push marketing before we play the Pig." I typed an update on our Facebook page, added an image of us playing at the Roadhouse in Jackson, and hit Post.

"*What*? We're playing the Blind Pig? You're fucking joking, right? Oh my God! How did that happen?"

"Seriously, Alli? Do you even listen to anything Kat tells us?" I shook my head and raised my hands, palm up. "She's been over the schedule a thousand times. The Pig is this Saturday."

Over the last hour, Alli had wrapped cords and reorganized her equipment a hundred times. She stopped mid-wrap and stared past me. An orange chair caught her as she sank. "I …" With a shake of her head, she frowned. "It's just …" Stuttering wasn't usually Alli's MO, but lately, she had been spacing out at the most inopportune times.

"Hey."

With her eyes, she traced an imaginary map on the wall behind me.

"Al."

When she didn't respond, I crossed the room and put my hand on her head and mussed her hair. "Earth to Alli. Come in, Alli."

Tears formed and she covered her face with both hands before they streamed down her cheeks. Through faint sobs, she admitted, "I haven't been listening, really paying attention, for a while. I know you've seen it; my mind is all over the place. I'm sorry." She sniffled. "With Tex going off to school and the band getting bigger, I just don't know where I am. I'm so afraid of losing the person I love most on this earth."

Kevin walked through the open garage door and punched Alli in the shoulder. "Quit crying, you baby. What could you possibly be sad about?" He didn't wait for a response. "You're the lead singer of a rock-and-roll band, you work with your best friends, and your brother is the coolest guy in the world."

Somehow, the comment made Alli laugh. I didn't understand their sibling bond, but if something so simple could bring her back to reality, I was good with it.

"What happens when we start landing gigs outside of Michigan? What about our friends? What about—" She didn't need to finish the question about Tex.

Once she voiced her concern out loud, I had to

admit, the future had been weighing on my mind, too. Only my version of the future looked pretty damned good. "In my perfect scenario, fans demand we headline a concert, we all get rich, and my family finally fucks off."

Kevin tilted his head and panned from Sara to Alli, then back to me.

I shrugged.

Alli pretty much ignored me. "Okay. But what about when that actually happens? Aunt Kat has been making contacts all over the place. What happens when she connects with an agent in California, and we end up getting a record deal?"

"Um, we fucking celebrate?" Confused, Kevin ran his hand through his hair. "Alli, if you don't remember, that's kind of our dream. That's the plan, right? To make a name for ourselves and live the life of rock stars. Make a shit ton of money, buy a mansion and four Lamborghinis. The end."

Anxiety spread across Alli's face, and she leaned back in the chair. "Yeah."

"Shit's getting real, guys. I'm so excited that I could pee," Sara spoke up from her spot in the garage. "This is happening, and I think we need to be smart about everything. For real."

"We need to make sure nothing comes between us." Alli followed Sara's lead and took it one step further. "We all smoke every once in a while, but Kevin, that's as far as it goes. No drugs. Okay?"

"Why you comin' at me? That's kinda been a gimmie from day one, so, yeah."

"We don't date each other's crushes or exes." Alli glanced from Sara to me.

We shared an eyeroll and spoke our minds in unison. "Duh."

"We always do things together. At least two of us at all times." I picked up my guitar.

"Yeah, so creepers don't hijack us." Sara threw her strap over her shoulder.

"Exactly," I agreed. "Kevin, since you're the honorary big brother, I think it goes without saying that you're our protector."

Satisfied with our little pep talk, Alli stood, grabbed her mic, and turned on the amp. It was the first time I noticed her smile all day.

Kevin lifted his eyebrows, beat the bass drum, and nodded. "Of course."

Don't You (Forget About Me)

Sara: June 1, 2008

KAT LIVED UP to the band's expectations and beyond. She booked us at venues all over the tri-state area: Michigan, Indiana, and Ohio. She worked extra hard to ensure our future success while we focused on songwriting and practice.

A map lay spread across her kitchen table, with cities highlighted in green, yellow, and blue. As she talked, she pointed to cities from Lansing and Battle Creek to Grand Rapids, Traverse City, and Saginaw.

Even though we had only spent the spring in the Detroit area, Kat convinced us that it was time for us to move on. Numerous bar owners had the pleasure of experiencing Kat's art of persistence; she talked us into places we would never have heard of if not for her.

The four of us sat around the table as Kat explained her latest plan. "This summer, you will be playing in over thirty cities. I have a schedule set up for you, starting in Lansing next weekend."

Surprised by Kat's ability to book our band so

effortlessly, or so it seemed, we all stared at her with our mouths agape. She had an uncanny ability to act like it was no big deal.

"Now, keep in mind that the venues are kind of all over the place. Literally." She giggled. "One night, you're in a dive bar that pays your minimum, the next, you're at the Allegan County Fair, opening for Daughtry. As you can imagine, that pays much better."

"You got us opening for Daughtry? How the hell did you manage that?" I asked, dumbfounded.

With a wave of her hand, she dismissed my reaction. "Eh, I got a guy." She winked.

Where the fuck was Allegan County, we all wondered, but Kevin was the only one to ask.

"Holland." Our eyes moved to the green area highlighted on the map along the Lake Michigan coast. Each of us bobbed our heads in understanding.

Our southeast Michigan comfort zone had been excluded from this tour, and, I have to admit, I was excited about going somewhere new and also terrified about going somewhere new. Ann Arbor, Novi, Dexter, and Jackson weren't incorporated into the new tour area. Neither was Brooklyn, our safe place.

I still had more questions. "So, where will we stay through all this? Hotels will eat up all our cash; won't they?"

"You're right, sweetie. That certainly would happen

if you were to stay in hotels. I've thought about that and already solved the problem." A nod confirmed the statement. "Green tacks represent June, yellow are July, and blue—"

"Wait, what about the hotel solution?" I interrupted, unsatisfied with her dismissive answer.

"Oh, that. Well"—Kat pointed to Alli and Kevin—"your dad agreed to let us borrow the motorhome."

Silence.

"Isn't that great?"

More silence.

Kevin squinted, Charlie pursed her lips, and Alli and I exchanged a questioning glance before Kat elaborated. "Free of charge. Actually, better than free. He pre-paid the fees for each of the overnight locations, as well. It's all set up. All you need to do is drive, play, sleep, repeat."

"Makes sense to me." I elbowed Alli and twitched my head to the side.

"Yeah, okay."

Picking up where she had left off, Kat explained the details of each venue in each of the highlighted cities. Michigan was mostly green, Ohio turned into yellow, and Indiana was blue.

She had highlighted Shipshewana, the greatest flea market in the Midwest, as far as most locals are concerned, in blue—August.

"We're spending the entire summer away from

Brooklyn." Alli's forehead wrinkled.

"Yup." I smiled. Was there any better way to break out of this small town?

"That's the plan," Charlie confirmed and gave me a wink. I knew she was thinking the same thing: our moms had held us back enough in our lives; it's our time now.

"What will I do without Tex? I already feel like he's slipping away." Alli sighed and sunk into herself. "Do you think he'll forget about me?" The last question came out barely louder than a whisper.

"Tony and I decided to back off our relationship because of the band, and I'm okay with it. We're not breaking up, just slowing down. I want to pursue this opportunity and not have any regrets. I don't want anything to stop my Zen when I'm on stage. Worrying about what my boyfriend is doing all the time would drive me insane."

"What are you saying, Charlie?"

"It might not be a bad idea to slow things down a little with Tex."

Tears formed in Alli's eyes simply at the thought.

I put my arm around her shoulders. "Maybe just for now. Just for a little while. It doesn't have to be forever. He can do his own thing, too, like finally going to school."

Alli nodded. "He put that off for me, didn't he?"

KRISTI COPELAND

Sara: June 22, 2008

DURING SEVERAL mid-Michigan performances, an older, nice-looking man made it a point to talk with me. At first, I chalked it up to a fan wanting to get close. I remained my polite self, and when he asked me to dinner, I declined. Jeff and I were still together, so I wasn't about to let some guy on the road distract me.

"Why did you tell him no?" Alli asked.

"Um … he's, like, thirty. Gross." A wrinkle in my nose validated my statement. "Besides, we're not supposed to be alone with anyone."

"Oh my God. You don't know who he is; do you?"

"Of course, I do. His name's John Bertolli."

"Sara—*the* John Bertolli."

I didn't recognize the name, so I raised my eyebrows and shook my head. "Honestly, Al, I think he might be a stalker. He's nice and all, but isn't that where it starts?"

Alli sighed and rolled her eyes. "John Bertolli is a record producer from Ann Arbor. He scouts up-and-coming bands, and he's been to at least four of our shows. I'll go with you; let me tell the others."

"Oh, shit."

"Yeah. Wanna see if you can catch him before he gets away?"

I turned and trotted to the edge of the parking lot, looking for his car. I spotted him standing beside a red Taurus with a flat. At least Alli won't have to rush to catch up with us.

By the time I reached his car, he had pulled the spare from the trunk and was loosening the lug nuts. "Hey, John."

Startled, he pushed the wrench too hard, and it slipped off the nut. He swore under his breath and lowered his head long enough to regain his composure. A smirk complimented his blue eyes. For a clean-shaven, well-dressed old guy, he was actually really cute.

I gave my best smile and flirted. "That offer for dinner still stand?"

Sara: August 9, 2008

AS THE SUMMER tour ended, so did our first year of travel. It was a little like going to a community college. We were on our own—out of the nest, so to speak—but not far enough from Brooklyn to feel like we weren't home—or, at least, that we didn't seem like we couldn't resume our previous lives if the tour bombed, like Kevin had been convinced it would.

It didn't, thank God. It was more of a success than,

I think, any of us expected. We learned so much and improved not only our craft but our presentation, preparation, and ability to have fun.

We all got along well enough in small quarters and made enough money to say this was our job; we were legitimately making a living as rock stars. The more shows we played, the more comfortable we became in our songwriting ability. Each night, we threw in at least five or six originals.

Confident in our song choice and skills, we researched studio time as our next step in the process. John Bertolli's dinner date wasn't really a date, by the way. He just wanted to get to know the band a little more before deciding whether he wanted to professionally produce our debut record.

Over those thirty-some gigs, we each pocketed about a hundred each, you know, after expenses. Except Kevin. Somehow, he never had any money. Personally, I think he smoked it all, but whatever.

Three grand over three months wasn't a lot of money, but it was enough to pay for the time needed in a recording studio to make a record. If John Bertolli decided to invite us to record in his studio, we could afford it.

Part of our marketing strategy included mentioning our upcoming tour dates at least three times every night. Therefore, most of our friends would attend as many shows as they could. The support they showed astonished me, but Kevin remained confident that our fans would follow us to the end of the earth.

Only when we were playing too far north to drive home after a show did we see a drop in our following. That's not to say our newfound fans didn't follow us from show to show. They did, and it was the best feeling to know how much people loved our music.

"Summertime," our first so-called release, had been in the setlist from day one. We added "Let Me Be Me", which I pretty much wrote about proving haters wrong. Then Charlie wrote one about breaking away from someone's strong hold; she named it, "Watch Me".

Kevin wasn't much of a writer and pretty much got on board with whatever we suggested. That being said, he wrote a hometown favorite: "NASCAR". About what subject, you ask? Yeah, NASCAR. I thought it would bomb, but our fans loved it. Something about turning left got the guys in the crowd interested in more than gaping at Alli and Charlie.

For our last show, Kat had scheduled us as the headliner in Shipshewana, Indiana, a two-hour drive from Brooklyn—one way. None of us expected to see many of our peeps attend. Despite that, everyone in our entourage considered the summer tour a success. This last gig was more of a celebration than anything.

An outdoor arena on the westside of town housed a stage and plenty of chairs for concertgoers. Positioned beside the cinnamon roll restaurant, my stomach growled the entire afternoon. Two bands played before us, and between the performances was an intermission of sorts. This gave each band enough time to prep at their own pace.

As we took the stage, we went through the normal routine of getting things set up. By then, it was like riding a bike; we could probably do prep with our eyes closed. The sun hung low in the sky as it set, the temperature settling at a comfortable seventy degrees.

Alli and I faced Kevin for the first part of the tune-up. Most of the crowd from the previous group had left the seats to stand in line for refreshments. Or cinnamon rolls.

From behind Alli, a group of people approached, and a voice we all recognized called out, "Heaven Scent rocks!"

Charlie smiled at me, then spun on the ball of her foot and planted the other one spaced three feet away; her best rockstar-lead-guitarist stance. She threw back her head and played the beginning of "Seek and Destroy". We weren't scheduled to play for another fifteen minutes, but what the hell?

The group of friends from Jackson, Kevin's friends from Brooklyn, and the cousins from Napoleon joined to form a strong fanbase for this last concert. Even friends of friends of friends showed up to support us.

Over twenty people cheered, threw their hands in

the air, and chanted, “Heaven Scent,” as they rushed the stage. The remaining fifty or so casually entered the arena and found seats close enough for me to recognize their faces.

Even though it wasn’t time to perform yet, the entire band took our cue from our friends and jammed for fun. It was like we were back at the Taylor Road field, playing for our friends beside the bonfire.

Alli laughed, and Kevin shrugged. After she sang the chorus, she yelled to the crowd, “Hello, Shipshee!”

Tex stood in front of the crowd and as close to the stage as he could possibly get. Our biggest fan, or at least Alli’s, sang along and played air guitar with Charlie.

After the impromptu first song, a crowd assembled; the emcee arrived on stage and seemed confused. “Well, that was a little unconventional, but you all seem to be happy.” He pointed to the crowd, and they responded with applause. “Sounds to me like you already know this band, so I guess there’s no need to formally introduce you to this fantastic musical group from Brooklyn, Michigan, Heaven Scent.”

The mob of our fans roared.

We didn’t plan to play “Seek and Destroy” as the first song, but it obviously went well; the crowd loved it. It just goes to show that when you love what you do and you’re having fun, people respond. A group of random individuals converged on the scene, quickly filling the remaining seats.

One song consistently made Alli crack up. "Kiss" by Prince—you know, the lyrics at the end of the song that Julia Roberts sang in *Pretty Woman*—got Alli every time she performed it. Whenever Charlie felt froggy, like that day at Shipshewana, she would dare Alli to sing it.

Of course, Kevin and I had to play along; come on, it was funny to watch the perfect Alli mess up occasionally. It reminded everyone that we're only human.

As she had every other time, when we came to that part of the song, Alli sang the lyrics and cracked up immediately after the words left her mouth. We had so much fun on stage during our last performance of the summer that it was hard to imagine anything topping this tour.

The next song we played was out of order, too. After all, everyone's emotions were at an all-time high. It only seemed natural to play "Don't You (Forget About Me)."

Alli grabbed the mic, pointed to Tex, and said the first thing that came to her mind. "This one's for the love of my life."

Start of Something Good

Alli: August 10, 2008

STUDIO TIME had eluded us for the past two years. We talked about what it would be like and when we should look into it seriously, especially after our first gig at Callaghan's, but Kat hadn't scheduled it, so the thought remained just a thought.

John Bertolli became a regular fixture whenever we played in or around Ann Arbor, and he brought friends to each show. Soon after our summer tour ended, John invited one of those friends, or I guess more of a colleague, to a gig at The Blind Pig.

Boots, a nickname designated because he didn't wear any other footwear, owned a basement studio in a neighboring town, Clinton. John regularly produced records there and talked us up as a band he may want to work with. Interested, Boots wanted to watch us live before deciding to let us in his personal studio or not.

During one of the breaks, Boots approached us and leaned his weight on one foot. One hand rested in his front pocket, and the other held a cigarette. “Well, John wasn’t wrong. He usually isn’t.” Charlie caught his eye, and he made it clear that he was attracted to her.

“You”—a smirk spread across his face, accentuating a dimple—“are exceptional.” He literally looked her up and down; she didn’t seem to mind his brown eyes roaming over her body.

“You ain’t seen nothin’, yet.” Charlie tilted her head and lifted one eyebrow for effect. Flirting had always been one of Charlie’s strong suits. Just because she was going with Tony didn’t mean she couldn’t look at other guys.

Long brown hair fell past his shoulders and covered the logo on a concert t-shirt. “Why don’t all of you check out my studio to see if it’s the right place for you to lay down a couple tracks?”

“Sounds great.” Kevin stepped forward. “What do you charge?” My brother asked the one question that had plagued all our brains for months.

“Fifty an hour.”

Alli: August 13, 2008

DIRT ROADS twisted beyond the village of Clinton, eventually leading to a driveway that, at first glance, had led to an abandoned property. Only a barn stood beside a line of trees. Confused, I stepped from Kevin’s flame mobile and pulled my sunglasses over my eyes. "Are we recording in a barn?"

Tex stood beside me and rested his arm over my shoulders.

Sara giggled. "Yeah, that would totally explain where we come from. Can you imagine telling this story someday during an interview?"

While Charlie's attention roamed the open pasture, she pointed to a door in the side of a hill. "Oh my God, you guys."

Boots opened the door and greeted us. "Right on time. Come on in." Shirtless, he ushered us through the door; the scent of Irish Spring tickled my nose as I passed. He stepped in front of Charlie to offer a hushed, private, "Hello, darlin'." A purr-like soft laugh escaped her throat.

Some girls would find him too forward but not Charlie. She totally fell for his antics. He paid attention to her the way she wanted him to—completely.

Surrounded by speakers, microphone stands, and guitars, the three-room space made me claustrophobic. "Where's the studio?" Anxious to check it out and leave, I tried not to rush the process too much.

Boots pulled cold beers from the fridge and passed them around, then nodded to a door with a sign that read, *Quiet*.

Kevin told us to stay put as he and Tex followed

Boots into the room and closed the door. Known for his salesy approach, I assumed he would discuss the possibility of renting the space. I didn't think he would hold the discussion in private, though. Obviously, he felt the need to make these kinds of decisions without the rest of us.

Irked, us girls made ourselves comfortable in lawn chairs that passed as indoor furniture, while the boys chatted. A cardboard box covered in joint-rolling paraphernalia sat in the middle of the chairs.

I picked up a joint from the makeshift table and lit it. Pinching it between my thumb and index finger, I brought it to my lips and inhaled. My brother had taught me well. I had observed Kevin smoking so much in the past few years that it might seem like I knew what I was doing.

I held the hit in my lungs, until they burned, then I coughed an exhale, and enjoyed the dizzy wave as it rushed over me. After I passed it to Sara, I watched Charlie stare at Boots as the guys strolled into the room. They stood far enough away so we couldn't hear their conversation but close enough for Boots and Charlie to play googly eyes.

"Charlie, you want this?" Sara spoke while she held the hit and nudged Charlie's shoulder. When she didn't respond, Sara exhaled the smoke in Charlie's face. "Earth to Charlie."

"Sure. Why not?" Without taking her gaze off

Boots, Charlie reached for the skunky-smelling cigarette.

By the time the joint had made it around three times, we were relaxed and reclining in our lawn chairs. With half-closed eyes, we allowed Kevin and Tex to decide our next professional move.

"What do you think they're talking about?"

"Boots keeps looking at you, so probably girls," I determined.

Pleased with the observation, a smile spread across Charlie's lips. "He already told us the hourly rate, so it's not money."

"Probably who has the best weed," Sara added. "Is that why this place smells like a Michigan basement?"

"Probably," Charlie and I chirped an answer to both questions in unison.

I laughed at us, saying the same word at the same time in the same tone. Once I started, I couldn't stop. I didn't know why, but everything seemed hilarious.

Sara's giggle grew into a laugh. When Charlie rolled her eyes, the laugh expanded to a full-out crackup. The contagious game lasted what seemed like hours. The instant I stopped, I spied Sara from the corner of my eye, and she failed to contain her chuckles.

"No laughing in this house. If you continue to laugh, you will be asked to leave the premises," Boots said in a raised voice from the other side of the room. That stopped us for about three seconds.

Sara eyed Charlie, smiled, then looked at me and lost it. We all had tears running down our cheeks and found it hard to catch our breath.

"Oh my God, Charlie. I can't breathe." I leaned into Sara and grabbed her arm with a jerk and a yelp. My feet flew into the air; my chair almost tipped over, and I laughed even harder.

Three beers and a joint later, we signed a deal for six hours of recording time in Boot's Basement. It's not like there was much of a choice; this was the only place we knew to record in the area, and we needed to put something on tape.

Satisfied with our decision, we packed into Kevin's car and waited for Charlie to finish talking with Boots. He grabbed her hand, pulled her to him, and tried to kiss her. She turned her cheek and hugged him instead.

When she reached the car, she nodded. "Yeah, I just got us a free hour." I held the seat forward for her and climbed into the back seat beside her. After falling into the passenger seat, Tex closed the door.

"What? How?" Kevin asked.

"We have a date after our show Friday night."

I rolled my eyes and sighed. "Of course, you do."

Sara gasped, "What about Tony?"

"What about him?"

Alli: August 20, 2008

MIXING equipment lined one wall, and a window above the soundboard stretched the entire length of the room. Boots, already high, explained through slits for eyes how all the buttons worked. At least he tried to. None of us had any idea what the terms meant, so if he used the wrong words, none of us would ever know. John Bertolli had pushed his producing responsibilities onto Boots and didn't make it to assist or support.

Two-inch reels apparently increased the quality of the sound, and pushing specific buttons and turning certain knobs made the sound better or worse—whatever. Just because he could explain the difference between analog and hybrid mixers, in agonizing detail, I was not impressed.

Honestly, I really didn't care. I just wanted to get moving and stop wasting time. My goal was to simply lay down some tracks, so we had something to sell at our gigs. Aunt Kat mentioned she needed something to use for promo material, too, so we asked for a two-track CD for a freebie.

For me, this process contributed to the anxiety-filled feeling in the pit of my stomach. Each time I walked on stage, I had the same thought: if I don't perform perfectly, our set or record or whatever we were doing would be ruined. If I messed this up, like Kevin assured me I would, we would run out of money before we finished the record.

Heading into the studio shouldn't be any different from stepping on stage; my stomach tied in knots. To ease some of the pressure, I did five jumping jacks, ran in place five times, and threw five punches into the air, all while singing a scale. Don't ask what the fives mean because I have no idea. It just ended up that way; it works, so I'm leaving it.

"What the fuck are you doing?" Kevin sneered and shook his head. "You look like a freak. That shit doesn't work. You're making a fool out of yourself, when we're all trying to take the next step in our career. Quit being stupid. You're embarrassing me."

In my mind, there was no exception; if I lost my shit and lost my unique sound, which I had worked so hard to perfect, what would I have? What would *we* have? I couldn't fuck it up.

My brother's negativity was really hindering not only me but the rest of the band. Nothing I did could ever please him. I even had Charlie voice my opinion on other decisions so he wouldn't ridicule me. He continued to be a real dick as he became frustrated with the process, and his energy threw me off.

Wouldn't you know it, my biggest fear came true. The first hour in the studio was completely fucked up. We just didn't understand the complexity of the process and of performing our piece of the pie on our own.

Without any backing instruments beside me, I couldn't find the right sound.

After two hours, we decided to reschedule so we wouldn't waste any more money.

Alli: September 17, 2008

OBVIOUSLY, we successfully recorded, but it didn't happen for another month. Boots asked John to join the session this time. Having him there for support built our confidence and allowed us to trust ourselves and get our bearings. The whole ordeal was surprisingly intimidating.

Recording vocals without any instruments present felt weird. Charlie even struggled to play her guitar without the drums physically keeping the beat behind her. It was almost unnatural. Even though the total song flowed through her headphones, she kept looking back to find Kevin.

Luckily, Boots had a bigger room in the barn, which he didn't use as often. He reserved it for bands to set up as a whole and offered to record there to see if we could find our flow.

Sara giggled as we carried our equipment to the building beside the trees. "We are such rednecks."

Inside, Boots led us to a large room with padded walls and another full set of recording equipment. We plugged in and played. That did it. Once we figured out the process, we nailed it and rarely needed more than a couple takes.

John put his finishing touches on the production of all our songs, and the end product blew us away. Listening to the playback reminded me of the nights we had spent in Jackson listening to some new cool rock group that Steve had discovered. It was truly unreal.

Not long after we had finished recording, we sold the CDs at our shows. Like, by the hundreds. I, for one, couldn't believe how fast they went; good thing Aunt Kat had decided to stock more than she thought we would need.

One afternoon, I stopped at a light in Jackson and heard "Summertime" in the distance. I glanced around and realized the car beside me had our song turned up loud enough for the world to hear. I couldn't believe it; it was the first time I had heard our sound come from someone else's radio besides mine.

I lowered my window and motioned for the car beside me to do the same. "Hey, who is that band? I love their sound."

The driver raised his eyebrows, "It's this new group called Heaven Scent. Dude, they're so awesome. They're local, from some small town around here. And they're fucking hot."

I smiled, laughed, and waved as I drove away.

God Blessed Texas

The Interview: January 8, 2015

"WHEN DID you venture farther from home? If none of your fans followed you, how did you build your name again?" A thought pops into Jenni's head, and she sits upright. "Hey, are there guy groupies? I've never even thought about that until just now. Are there guys, men, who will follow you from city to city and try to meet you or want to follow you wherever you go? All of you are gorgeous, so I can't imagine there aren't some guys out there who act like girl groupies. Have you had any scary moments or close calls?"

Charlie chuckles and eyes her bandmates. "Yeah, one situation in Texas stands out."

Jenni leans forward to adjust the recorder on the table. She needs to ensure she captures everything in case she gets caught up in the story. "Would you feel comfortable telling me about it?"

Charlie: December 23, 2008

After our tri-state summer tour, we became antsy. The band agreed that there wasn't any reason for us to stick to only playing in and around Michigan. We expressed an interest in traveling and were anxious to spread our wings. The timing fit, so Kat got creative and made a few calls.

North Texas, the Dallas area specifically, had a huge bar-band boom in late 2008. John Bertolli had a connection to Patti Littleton, who owned a string of bars in Texas. In exchange for a percentage of our proceeds, he offered Kat a warm introduction. The two of them hit it off and, from what I understand, are still friends.

We were so excited to play somewhere far from our everyday lives, somewhere warm. We even had a gig in Shreveport, Louisiana. This was not quite on the level of the world traveling we daydreamed about, not yet. It had always been our dream to play in Vegas, but we would just have to wait a little longer for that.

Uncle Dan also had family in north Texas—complete coincidence—so the location seemed like a win-win. If we toured in an area where we had support, Kat and the rest of Alli's family would be more comfortable about us traveling. The fact that it would be January by the time we began the tour somewhere warm was just icing on the cake.

"Look, everyone." Kat clasped her hands and began a speech that sounded practiced. "It breaks my heart that I can't spend the winter with you in Texas. Truly." Tears filled her eyes, and she pulled Alli into a tight hug.

"Ah, come on, Aunt Kat." Kevin had always been uncomfortable watching any girl cry. He broke out the cooler that he carried with him everywhere. "Wipe those beer tears. This calls for a celebration." He handed us all a Lite and sang:

Beer tears
Beer tears
Wipe away those beer tears
Push away those beer fears

Sara added to his words with her own lyrics.

Drink another beer, dear
This calls for a beer cheers

I grabbed Kat and twirled her in a circle, while I added my own lines.

Ah, baby, come here
Let me wipe away your
Beer tears

Even though his simple attempt at making us all laugh worked, Kevin didn't know that he had started to write another song. Alli broke out her notepad and jotted down the lyrics and her thoughts.

"I have spoken with Patti multiple times," Kat said, returning to her seat at the table, "and she seems like a very nice person. She owns a string of upscale honky-tonk bars called Seven Springs Saloon and agreed to let you play a rotation at each of them. Oh, and you can be sure that I have every intention of staying in close contact with her. Once you gain a little bit of a southern following, we'll revisit expanding." While Kat made the rounds and hugged each of us, we tried to keep our emotions in check.

"This will be such a wonderful experience for all of you—or, as they say in Texas, *y'all*. I have nothing but positive vibes about this next step up."

Three days later, we headed south. Alli's dad continued to let us use the family motorhome. *Winnie* became a staple in our life, and we ensured to respect it and be thankful for having it available. We pretty much treated it like part of the band—reliable, trustworthy, and always on time.

The stretch on the road, in forced proximity, allowed us to calm each other's fears and reflect on our past and how we got to this point in our lives. Getting along with everyone in such tight conditions proved the perfect way to learn how to communicate, have compassion, and compromise.

Alli cried through the first day; she missed Tex something awful—that's how you would say it in Texas.

Deciding to put their young relationship on hold made her sad but hopeful for the future.

Sara and Jeff had a huge fight and ended up saying some mean things to each other. She said it wasn't worth trying to salvage; they had been having issues with trust anyway. Jeff used Sara's touring against her, saying he was lonely and that they should just call it quits.

Surprised at the revelation, we questioned if Sara was okay. She always shared most of the details about her relationship with Alli and me.

"Yeah, it's for the best."

I ended my relationship with Tony, too; it only made sense that distractions would happen. It had already started with Boots and a couple other prospects at shows. If we weren't attached, neither of us could be unfaithful. It was sad to think about leaving someone I cared so much about behind, but it, too, was for the best.

Kevin pretty much kept to himself. As the designated driver, he listened but didn't participate much in our conversations. He did nod a lot, and scoffed, or snickered, so we were all aware that he listened.

I, for one, had been thrilled at the idea of leaving Michigan. The image of my mom followed me everywhere. "I swear I see her in every store I go into and at every stop light. She's fucked with my brain for so long, how can I make her just go away?"

Alli tried to comfort me. "It all takes time, Charlie."

Without being in my shoes, she didn't understand; I didn't blame her for that. "Yeah, I guess. Look. I don't want you to feel sorry for me, but we have time, and maybe it will help to get it off my chest."

"It will. I'm sure."

"Spill, dude."

I hadn't told my friends the worst of what I had been through. To be honest, I thought they would pity me if they heard about my experience of her locking me in a closet for the entire weekend. But here we were, with hours and hours on the road and no way to escape. I felt the need to add a detailed story. "Remember that weekend that neither of you could reach me?" I nodded to Alli. "Just before your dad let me stay with you? She made me drink until I puked, then locked me in the closet." She knew how to get to me, and every time I would build a wall, she crumbled it.

With these two beside me, it went without saying that silence equaled empathy, not pity. Thank God.

"Each time I thought my monster would let me out, she just 'punished' me with another one of her sick ideas. You wondered what happened to Squeekie?" I couldn't say the words to explain what she had done to my cat. "She made me watch, then threw his body in the closet with me and locked the door."

I kept my eyes closed so I didn't see their reaction; their gasp was enough to make me cry. Sara and Alli sat on either side of me on the couch and put their arms around me. Compassion flowed through their soul directly into mine. This was what I needed to heal: the love of my true family. My sisters.

Once our tears had dried and Kevin had made a stupid joke that made us laugh, we stopped for gas and snacks.

Sara opened a granola bar. "Every time I even smell a donut, I can hear my mom: 'Five pounds, Sara,' or 'I can't afford to keep buying new clothes every time you eat a candy bar.' Do you know she would literally hand me a stick of celery for dinner? How do I not have an eating disorder?"

"You know you're gorgeous, right?"

Sara scoffed at my comment.

"The photo of you is on our CD cover. That must mean something?" Alli smiled. "Not only are you the one and only super-talented, beautiful, perfectly proportioned Sara DeVille, but you are also officially a model."

"Yeah, I know what you see, and that picture turned out fine, but when I look in the mirror, I see my mom standing behind me. A size zero with a perfect C-cup, straight blond hair, a straight, perfectly shaped nose, and plump lips. Did you know she has her makeup applied by the highest-acclaimed makeup artist in Ann Arbor? Refusing to dress in anything less than, as she says, 'the most expensive clothes,' she orders direct from Paris."

"And every bit of it is fake. Every. Single. Bit," I reminded her. "You, my dear, are a one hundred percent natural beauty. Your mom's just jealous that you don't have to work at it." I squeezed her hand for emphasis.

At least she smiled. We all had our issues. Bouncing them off our best friends helped cure our need for acceptance. At least we had each other.

Charlie: December 29, 2008

KEVIN PULLED into an RV park in a town that was an hour outside Dallas, called Terrell. "Honey, we're home," he joked and parked *Winnie* in front of the office.

Aunt Kat had chosen the perfect place for us to stay while in the area. Not only was there a pool, but a stage and seating area spread across a beautifully green manicured acre. When we weren't playing at one of the local bars, the RV park owners had invited us to play there.

It wouldn't always be warm, but if people wanted to watch us perform, he offered it as an option. Besides, we needed to practice, so if there weren't paying customers in our off time, we still needed to play, anyway.

We took a couple days to set up our winter home and get comfortable with the area before meeting up with Patti. One of her bars was right down the road—or highway, I guess—from where we set up camp.

We walked through the doors of Seven Springs Saloon, Terrell, and it felt like we had entered a cabin up north; all the wood trim made me wonder if trees had been cut and designed specifically for this venue. The bars and tables, along with the dance floor, all shined like they were brand new.

They had decorated the bar for Christmas, and the décor reflected that New Year's Eve was just around the corner. Patti had offered to meet us before this venue's celebration to discuss our tour.

Kat was right about Patti; she was a very nice person. I could tell right away how she put others first. Caring about her community and what would work best for the areas around each of her saloons came before her own agenda. She found a way to work her unique ideas into the needs of others.

While Patti explained a little about herself, she told us how she had decided to open her first venues around her hometown of Athens, Texas. "There wasn't one single good place to see live music. My family and I teamed up with other local businesses to brainstorm what would work best for our area, and we made it happen. I designed and created an opportunity for bands to play and make decisions to give back to their community. I brought music to Athens, and the venue thrived. It was the best thing I ever did. A year later, I quit my day job and began the process of opening bars in other local areas—you know, Canton, Tyler, then here, in Terrell."

We passed glances around the table and shrugged.

"No, I'm sorry." Patti shook her head and chuckled. "I guess y'all wouldn't know what I mean by local. Well, not to worry. You'll get your bearings soon enough." She paused to signal to a waitress to bring us another round. "This is my fourth venue and, honestly, the most successful. We added locations in The Colony and Rockwall over the past eighteen months, and I'm sure both will surpass Terrell's revenue in no time. My husband and I love Shreveport, so we decided to open another venue there. Along with the casino, we're the top-grossing concert venue in western Louisiana. Well, that's enough about me. Tell me a little about you. I've heard some interesting details about y'all, but I would love to get to know you on a more personal level. Not simply as a band that's playing at Seven Springs."

I began with how we had met in high school and how we had dreamed about living the life of rock stars. "Brooklyn is such a small town that nothing exciting ever happens. Well, besides NASCAR races twice a year. We wanted to break out of our families' *everyone who's born here, dies here* cycle. No one we know has even traveled out of the tri-state area, let alone across the country. We wanted to see it all, do it all, have experiences that no one else had."

"What better way to do that than combine it with what we love," Alli added. "I love to sing. My mom put me in voice lessons just after my ninth birthday, and I've never wanted to do anything else."

Sara explained her love of music. "The beat of each song I hear travels through me like electricity. The minute I picked up a bass guitar, when I was twelve, I never wanted to put it down. It was a gift from my grandmother. My mom despised it, which only made me want to play it more."

"Kevin? What about you?"

"Yeah, I don't have a great story like the rest of them. I played drums for one season in band, hated the discipline that the teacher pushed on us, not to mention the stupid songs he made us play. I just wanted to rock out with my—"

Alli kicked him under the table and made a face.

"Hey," he snapped at his sister, then cleared his throat. "I'm just along for the ride. Ma'am." Kevin had almost forgotten how to use his manners.

Wide-eyed, Patti smirked and sat back in her chair. When the waitress served the second round of drinks, Patti changed subjects. "I've seen your tour schedule and helped tweak it a bit. You'll love the areas that you'll play. I know you're from a small town, so most of these locations will fit your personality just fine. Besides all my venues, I've got you booked in fifteen smaller cities all around the DFW area. However, you're playing in Dallas, Arlington, and Fort Worth, which are all considered the 'big city,' but you'll be fine. I hired a man for those locations to be your bodyguard. His name is Eddie Francis, and he'll keep you safe. He grew up on the eastside of Fort Worth and is a former bouncer in one of the roughest neighborhoods in that area. His reputation for keeping the peace is the reason why I chose him for this job; he's a natural protector. If you cross him, though, you'll be sorry."

Alli and Sara laughed, but Patti wasn't kidding. They met her straight face with silence.

"I'm serious." A smirk tugged at the corner of her lips. "Your first gig is right here on Friday. Y'all ready?"

"Can't think of a better way to start the new year than with a new adventure," I answered for the entire band. "Bring it on."

Charlie: February 14, 2009

ONE OF THE less-than-spectacular places we played was in Fort Worth. Sure, The Drunken Armadillo had a reputation for being a dive bar, but based on feedback from John Bertolli and Dan's cousin, it was also known for being safe.

Besides, Eddie had been with us during all the big city gigs, and we developed an easygoing rapport with him. His no-nonsense, tough-guy, asshole persona had been a cover. In reality, he could be very charismatic, yet protective. We trusted him.

At the time Kat had arranged the booking, almost a year earlier, this venue hadn't ever had a problem with bar fights or sketchy customers. That changed one balmy Valentine's Day.

Outside after we finished setting up, Kevin passed a joint between our tiny entourage. Mixed with the beers we had already downed on the drive, I tried my best not to fall asleep. A few minutes before we took the stage, the bartender made us all Jagerbombs, and I hoped the Red Bull would combat the effects of the weed.

Bartenders make extra strong drinks for the band, as a rule. This one kept them coming and would continue to unless we asked him to stop. I didn't resist multiple rounds of my go-to sex on the beach cocktail. After the second song, my face grew warm.

Throughout our performance, I watched three clean-cut, fit guys maneuver closer to the stage. I always have an internal safety monitor turned on inside my brain, and I usually made it a point to acknowledge it.

These guys had been to our three previous shows—two in Dallas the previous weekend and in Arlington the previous night. We had become accustomed to regulars following us from gig to gig, so I didn't think anything of it.

At this venue, it wasn't unusual for bands to break away from the crowd between sets. A room at the back of the bar was a designated area for us to relax without interruption. We didn't know anyone at this venue, so we thanked the guests and announced our estimated time to return.

After we finished the last set, we mingled until closing, as usual. The three guys walked out the door during our last song, so I didn't expect to see them again. Well, as I talked with another patron, one of the guys appeared beside me.

He caught my eye and introduced himself as Roy Frankel. At that moment, I thought he must be one of the prettiest men I had ever seen. His blue eyes reflected the neon lights, and I found it difficult to break the stare. His dark hair fell over his left eye, and his smile must have been perfected with braces in his youth.

He asked the typical questions: *Where are you from? How long will you be in Dallas? Where's your next show?* I responded as I had the previous hundred shows. I'd never had a reason to hide any details; we plastered our schedule all over social media, and our story wasn't a secret.

As you can imagine, I had been a little tipsy and enjoyed the flirty conversation. He knew all the right things to say and asked if we could go somewhere a little more private.

Now, remember, the band had made a rule to never

go anywhere without another bandmember. No one sat in the far corner booth, so I waved at Alli and followed Roy to the back of the bar.

After about half an hour and two more drinks, I excused myself to use the restroom. The minute I exited the bathroom, Roy grabbed my arms and pushed me out the back door. It happened so fast that I didn't have time to react.

He must have planned this in advance because he forced me into a parked car right outside the door. He opened the driver's door, pushed me onto the bench seat, and slid in after me. My first thought was, *Who drives a car with bench seats anymore?*

The keys were in the ignition, and he was ready to speed away. In fact, the car had been running for some time; the warm air relaxed me. It took me a minute to figure out what had happened, and when my drunk ass fought back, he elbowed me in the face.

Through the pain in my cheek, thoughts of Alli and Sara flooded my mind. Right away, I knew I had made the biggest mistake; vodka and lust had clouded my judgment.

I had chosen to ignore the red flags about Roy. I should never have agreed to be alone with him, even if we were in plain sight. My internal safety alarm could have saved me if I had only paid attention to it. Instead, a severe lack of judgment may have caused the end of my life. That was the price I would have to pay for being stupid.

I wondered if Alli had seen me when I waved to her, or had I imagined her wink? I hadn't seen Sara since we stepped off the stage, so I doubted she realized I had disappeared. Literally.

I thought this was it, that I would be held prisoner and/or raped and murdered. How many of those TV shows have Alli and I watched together and said, *"Wow, that chick was so stupid. Why would she put herself in that situation?"* I can honestly tell you that you truly never know.

Roy floored the gas pedal and pointed the car toward the road. Trying to stay calm and react through the alcohol daze, I did the first thing I could think of and pulled the steering wheel hard to the right. We crashed into the side of the building, and Roy cursed before he put the car in Reverse and hit the gas pedal again.

I don't know how it happened. Maybe one of the girls or Eddie had noticed me missing. Maybe someone had heard or felt the car hit the side of the bar. But when I looked up, I saw people had filled the entire parking lot.

Thank God.

With the car still in gear, Eddie opened the driver's door and pulled Roy from his seat. My hair was twisted in Roy's hand, and I didn't have a choice but to follow him out the door.

Somehow, I had the forethought to put the car in Park before Roy could punch the gas pedal again. This may be the smartest thing I'd ever done.

Eddie manhandled Roy and slammed him on the car's hood. When he unclenched my hair, I backed into the crowd. Roy's face bounced off the hood, and blood dripped from his nose. Then Eddie tried to secure Roy's hands behind him so he could let the police take over, but Roy's surprise turned to fury. He twisted out of Eddie's grip fast enough to catch him off guard. A knife slid between Eddie's ribs like butter.

A scream alerted the rest of the crowd, and at least twenty people rushed to the car. From the sidelines, I watched the no-nonsense side of Eddie turn vengeful.

He grabbed Roy's arm so hard that it snapped. The knife fell to the pavement and bounced out of reach. I could tell Eddie forced himself to not beat Roy to a pulp—a broken arm would keep him from hurting anyone else.

Once the police arrived, we relayed the entire stupid story, and they took Roy away in the back seat of their cruiser. A year later, a judge sentenced him to eight years in prison for attempted kidnapping and an additional twelve for attempted murder. Turns out, Roy had a rap sheet a mile long. Figures I would be attracted to a lifelong criminal.

The rest of the tour was easy-peasy. No fan attacks,

not nearly as much drinking—for the next few shows, anyway—and no Eddie for the next ten. He needed to heal from the stab wound and caught up with us in Texarkana.

We made, what we considered, good money and learned how to budget. It worked for us; we all pitched in for food and gas, and Alli's dad had pre-paid our lot fees at the RV Park. The balance went in our pockets. Six weeks later, we played our last Texas show in Athens.

Alli: January 28, 2010

THRILLED AT our return to Michigan, the usual bars where we would play accepted us with open arms. To welcome us back from our successful out-of-state tour, they made it a point to fit us into their already-packed schedules.

Callaghan's allowed us to open for another band, and the patrons packed the bar. The unknown group had been excited to have such a large crowd and thanked us for not pushing them out of the limelight.

On one normal afternoon, I went to Country Market, the local grocery store, for supplies. A fan recognized me and said she had attended our show the night before at The Blind Pig. After she introduced herself as Brenda, she told me how she thought my voice was so unique and incredible. "I think you'll be a big star someday. I can't wait to tell everyone that we grew up in the same town."

I listened and graciously thanked her but always wondered what people thought when they said that. I hadn't ever found the courage to ask anyone before. "Thank you so much, but how can you know that?"

"Oh, my uncle works as a scouting agent for *American Idol.*"

I raised my eyebrows, surprised. "Interesting."

"He's always looking for people around the tri-state area who have incredible voices. I've told him about you. I think you should go to an audition."

"But I have a band, and they don't allow bands to audition."

She shrugged. "Well, if you're discovered, you can bring them along with you eventually, right?"

That got my mind turning, and I fantasized for a few moments about being on the *American Idol* stage. I could picture myself in front of Simon, Paula, Kara, and Randy, belting out my best Alannah Myles or Stevie Nicks cover.

"They only audition once a year, right?"

Brenda emphatically nodded. "Yeah, and next month they'll be starting the search for artists to compete on the 2011 season. The Novi Hilton is hosting them between February fifth and thirteenth. You should go. I just know you'll go all the way to the finals, probably even win."

After I got home, I thought more about the strange encounter. I seriously envisioned what it would be like without the rest of the band. One at a time, I mentally removed members of Heaven Scent. At first, I couldn't imagine looking over my shoulder and not being amazed at the way Charlie ripped on her guitar and made faces that one could only describe as her being satisfied, content. Her happy place was in this band. After only glazing over the thought, I moved on.

Sara was more excited to be a part of something big than anyone I have ever witnessed. I took a few minutes to picture Sara not standing on the other side of me. If I alienated her, I wouldn't only lose an incredible bass player who kept us all on track, along with Kevin, but also an exceptional friend. She had always been willing to do whatever the rest of us wanted. She always loved the songs we wrote and happily backed us up with her own unique voice.

But would it really be all that bad to not have her in the band? Yes and no.

Kevin. Now, Kevin is the glue. As much as he loved to throw it in our faces how he held the band together, I hated to admit he was right. If I didn't have Kevin, I wouldn't have the beat or the humor or inventive ways to deceive our parents.

Trying to weigh the good and the bad, the positives and the negatives, wasn't very helpful using my brother as an example. Although he did show me, not to mention the rest of the group and all our followers, different ways to have fun, he had never been the best influence.

I allowed my imagination to revisit a career without

Charlie by my side. I mean, we were going to be the next Heart. Right? Without her, Heaven Scent wouldn't even be. This whole band, our livelihood, wouldn't have started if not for Charlie. I had never even considered the possibility of being on stage alone. Until that day. Not only was Charlie my best friend, but she was also the one person who loved me no matter what, even when it felt like no one else did. She had always been my biggest supporter. And vice versa. I would do anything for her—in fact, I have.

In my mind, I remembered the negative parts of our relationship. We had some hiccups, like any best friends did, but we persevered and rose above all our issues to get where we were. Sure, I had sacrificed a little for Charlie by bringing her into my family; I had to share my room and my parents. If I had the choice to do it all again, I would. In a heartbeat.

Charlie had always been the more confident one and always found a way to make me better—on and off stage. And when she dealt with her family issues, she played her beloved guitar and allowed her soul, her true self, to show through. Her raw talent had been above and beyond any sort of natural talent people told me I had.

Fans wanted to talk to Charlie; they gravitated toward her, not me. At first, I had been a little jealous, because, after all, I'm the lead singer; why would they want to talk with Charlie and not me? We were both pretty and talented, but I wanted to be the one the fans were excited to see.

Maybe it was time for me to get some of the attention and affection. Would it really be that bad to try out on *American Idol*? If I won, all the decisions would be mine; I wouldn't have to give in to anyone.

I daydreamed about the *American Idol* judges passing me on to the next step of the competition. I could see myself standing on the stage at the end, with confetti falling all around me. I thought it might not be a bad idea to take a chance and consider what it would look like to leave the band behind.

Alli: February 1, 2010

GROWING OUR fanbase on social media and through interviews, YouTube videos, and promotions was our focus throughout the winter. Traveling around the icy tundra of Michigan during that time of the year was a huge hassle and not worth the effort, so we stayed close to home for gigs.

We found an internet designer and sold CDs on our website. Kat promoted us to local record stores and persuaded the owners to sell our CDs; we did a couple signing events and gained more followers. Hell, in Jackson and Adrian, our faces graced the front shelf of all the stores that sold any form of music.

We spent some of our income from our Texas tour on a professional videographer and built a YouTube channel. We hired a photographer to redo our band's picture, and we posted it all over our social media. Our original CD cover was a totally unimpressive compilation of photos taken at a concert venue, with our name at the top.

The new cover featured a picture of Sara dressed in a simple black tank top. Her backlit dark hair blew away from her face as she strummed a white bass. Everyone agreed that the contrast between her outfit and the guitar made the perfect CD cover.

We also took some time to reflect on our success and how the tours had taught us to be smart, have fun, and to grow, while keeping an open mind. Discussions about future tours took up hours upon hours of our time in early 2010. During one of those discussions, I decided to blurt out what had been on my mind.

"So, guys. I have something I need to get off my chest." I busied myself with organizing my equipment and cleaning my area of the garage. When I sensed everyone had stopped what they had been doing and trained their eyes on me, I took a deep breath and turned around.

"*American Idol* is in Novi next week. Someone approached me about trying out, and it sounds interesting." There, I had said it. Palms sweaty, the words were out there, and I couldn't take them back.

Although I had rehearsed this big speech in my head, only about half of the words escaped.

"But they don't take bands." Sara tilted her head and squinted, repeating my initial thought.

When I didn't respond, her gaze dropped to the floor. "Oh."

With her guitar still in one hand, Charlie stopped in her tracks. She hesitated before placing it on the stand and pursed her lips. I could tell my comment was making sense. "So, you're quitting us."

"No, that's not—" I tried to explain, but Charlie caught on and created her own version of what I had said. Her interpretation had probably been exactly what went through my mind—only, to her, it meant something totally different from what it meant to me.

"That's just great, Alli." She raised her eyes and stared a hole into my soul. A frown overtook Charlie's face, and a dark cloud seemed to form over her head. "Just. Fucking. Great."

Pissed off didn't come close to expressing Charlie's frame of mind; she was downright furious. Understandably. A red hue rose from her neck to her cheeks, then to her ears. Once her hands shook, I knew I needed to explain. If she only knew how much I had fantasized about this during the past few days, she'd be even more upset.

"Charlie, that's not what I said." My heart did a

slow roll before my pulse increased. "Seriously, someone just mentioned that it would be a good idea. I didn't say I agreed or that I would do it. But I've never gotten such a wonderful compliment. What if—" I stopped myself before the thought slipped into actual words. Three steps across the garage took me within two feet of Charlie and Sara. "Look. Forget I said anything, okay? It's a stupid idea. A stupid thought. Besides, I wasn't seriously thinking about it—"

"The fuck you weren't." Charlie glared at me, and time slowed. It must have been an eternity before she looked away. She packed her guitar in the hard-sided case and stormed out the bay door. In a flash, she was gone.

"Fuck. That was way worse than I imagined in my head," I said out loud but to myself.

"And how did you expect us to handle such news, exactly?" Sara asked as she held her own hard-sided guitar case.

"I … Sara. Wait."

She, like Charlie, walked out the bay door and, I prayed, not out of my life.

"Nice job, asshat." Kevin's words hit the nail on the head. "Fucking idiot …" His continued mumbles followed him into the house.

Oh, shit. What had I done?

Alli: February 14, 2010

TWO WEEKS later, Aunt Kat called us together. Once again, she had some news. We hadn't practiced, or even talked, after my mention of *American Idol*. I did discuss what had happened with Aunt Kat. Okay, I had cried to her and begged for advice.

She suggested we needed a break anyway. Hopefully, spending a couple weeks away from each other would give us time to calm down and rethink our future. It hadn't been easy to convince Charlie that being in the same room with me would be a good idea. Aunt Kat, the talented convincer she was, talked her into it.

When we finally met at the garage, Aunt Kat sat us down and forced us to apologize. Me. She forced me to find the nerve to apologize. Once I started, I couldn't stop. I begged for forgiveness and reiterated how stupid it was to even think about breaking up something so special. I said how sorry I was and how it tore me up inside just thinking about how I had created such a difficult situation.

Then Aunt Kat made us hug and cry. Well, she didn't make us cry, but we did anyway. Thinking back, I can't begin to imagine how I had genuine thoughts of breaking away.

"Now it's my turn to apologize," Aunt Kat started a speech of her own.

Everyone exchanged confused glances. She had never done anything to hurt us, so we didn't understand the need for an apology.

"I have been doing something behind your back. I wasn't sure what the result would be, so I didn't feel it necessary to inform you about what I was working on. I didn't want to get your hopes up. Everyone here has been kicking ass during all these shows and tours that I arranged for you. You've been traveling, finding yourself, relating to each other, growing, gaining experience, and even making some money in the meantime. I thought it was worth a shot to reach out to some managers of bigger bands. So, I did."

"What?" Tears dried on Charlie's cheeks.

"What's going on? Did you know about this?" Sara sniffled and gaped at me.

I shook my head, wiped my nose, and asked Kevin the same question.

Kevin shrugged.

"Okay, guys," Aunt Kat said to regain our attention. "None of you knew. So, do you want to know who you're going on the road with?"

Charlie spoke up first. "On the road? Wait, you can't be serious." She stood and asked again, "Are you serious? Like, on a real tour?"

Aunt Kat nodded, and Charlie jumped up and down. She bounced in circles, appalled that we hadn't joined her. "Don't you know what this means? Oh my God!

We're going on tour. We're going to be a fucking rock band!"

In disbelief, I stood in front of Aunt Kat with my mouth agape.

Kevin repeated Charlie's question. "Are you serious? Like, seriously serious? You wouldn't just fuck with us about this, would you? This can't be some sick joke because that would be the worst kind of torture ever."

"Yes, this is really happening. Yes, this is true. No, Kevin, it's not a joke." Aunt Kat smiled at him, closed the distance between them, and looked up. "It's real. You are now officially a fucking rock band."

"Yes!" He took a moment to hug his favorite aunt before he threw punches skyward.

Sara and I exchanged smiles and giggled. I reached for Charlie's hand. She nodded and grasped it tighter than I thought she could. We all hugged and jumped up and down, then hugged some more.

Stoic, Kevin stood with his hands on his hips and watched us get all girlie. He didn't want to admit how much he wanted in on the celebration, until Sara approached him and wrapped her arms around his waist. "Come on, big brother. You're a part of this bad-ass gang."

Once the dust settled, Aunt Kat mentioned, "Little different from where we were last year at this time, huh?"

"Well," Kevin interjected, "are you going to tell us who?"

"Oh, I haven't said?" After an excruciating pause, Aunt Kat, unable to hide her smile, announced, "Nickelback."

Girl on Fire

The Interview: January 8, 2015

"I CAN'T EVEN imagine the emotions that you experienced when you first heard the name Nickelback. Just, wow."

"Every emotion buzzed through me at the same time," Alli admits. "Literally buzzed. I was happy, scared, overjoyed, content, calm, excited, anxious, all together. The same feeling continues to come to me every time we overcome the next big hurdle."

"At the end of the tour, Nickelback's label gave us a five-thousand-dollar bonus. We decided we would reinvest those funds toward hotel rooms on the next tour. *Winnie* had been a lifesaver, but with the money we made, we could retire her and let her spend the rest of her days in Michigan."

"So, obviously y'all overcame the *American Idol* situation. How long did it take before you were really back to normal, like, one hundred percent?"

"You know"—Sara glances at Alli—"it didn't take much more than a couple practices. The thought of breaking up kinda made us stronger, like with any relationship. We all tried harder to be a meaningful contributing team member."

Charlie teases, "Alli apologized so many times that it became a little annoying."

Alli sticks out her tongue in response, then wrinkles her nose.

"In our hearts, we knew she would never leave us. This kind of temptation to stray away forced us to take a good look at what we had and realize how lucky we were. Not many bands, let alone people, find the connection, love, and respect for each other that we had. Still have."

Jenni scratches some words on her notepad and moves to the next subject. "Was there ever excessive drinking or drug use in the band? Enough to kick out a member?"

"Even though you already know the answer, I'm glad you asked. That situation was not only a very important time in our growth, but so many people fall into the drug-use trap. I'm hopeful our story will help someone who reads your book someday." A frown dims the light in Sara's eyes.

Sara: April 3, 2010

OPENING for a popular band, a steppingstone to landing a headline tour, provided a sense of in-between that I didn't expect. We were well on our way, but not quite on our way. If that makes any sense. The bar scene had been successful, but we hadn't gained enough of a following to be on our own.

CD and t-shirt sales helped bring in some extra money, but I often wondered how much people would recognize us if we didn't get our ass out there. We needed to be on the radio more than just in Ann Arbor, but without being known, Kat had a hard time convincing the right people to take a chance on us.

During our first night on the tour, we took the stage and warmed up for a few minutes. Floor-ticket concertgoers within the stadium talked among themselves. When we played, it was as if we were only background noise. Expecting Nickelback to take the stage in the next hour or so, the crowd basically ignored us.

Until we played "Animal". As it usually did, that piqued the interest of those who thought Heaven Scent had been just a generic opening act.

Once we made our point, we started to play "Summertime". Most people in attendance faced the stage and gave their full attention. The first time we played in a stadium setting was surreal, to say the least.

On a dare, Alli performed "Kiss" by Prince and, for

the first time ever, didn't crack up. None of us believed it at first. The fans loved our rendition of it and sang along with Alli. After the success of pleasing the crowd, we decided to add it to our setlist.

It fit to play one of our originals called, "Watch Me". Since we had written it with passion, aimed at all those people in our past who didn't believe in us, the lyrics flowed with ease.

Don't believe I'll be happy?
Watch me
Don't believe I can do it on my own?
Watch me

You think I need you to take care of
me?
Boy, watch me prove you wrong
Watch me walk away
Watch me break out of your grip

You think you're the only one who
can love me?
If this is love, I don't want to be in it
Watch me walk away

It was a shame we didn't have a chance to interact with the band more. I would have liked to have picked their brains and ask questions about their past and how they had gotten where they were. Their manager kept them busy with meet and greets and focused on playing for their fans, not playing around with a little-known act.

From the little time their management had allowed us to spend with Nickelback, they treated us with kindness. All their roadies helped us with anything we needed. Everyone was friendly, accommodating, helpful, and down-to-earth.

We followed the tour bus all over Georgia and Florida in the spring. The high from playing to such a huge crowd made all of us, Alli and Charlie especially, crave our own headlining show. In our future, we promised to be more involved with the bands we chose to open for us.

Hard choices followed you wherever you went, but for me, the large venues called for more choices. Drugs showed up no matter how many times you said *no*—not from the other bands but guests who came backstage.

It was weird, honestly, how many people think it's okay to bring illegal substances when they visited, like a present or something special they could offer.

This was the one thing Heaven Scent didn't accept, so we made it a point to announce during our shows how passionate we were about not using drugs. Yes, we understood this probably alienated some of our crowd, but it was not an area we, as a band, felt the need to negotiate.

And who called all these gorgeous guys to meet us backstage? Good lord, people falling into the life of being a rock star needed to set some hard-ass boundaries. We didn't need to fulfill the classic 'sex, drugs, and rock & roll' to consider ourselves successful.

Sara: May 21, 2010

AT ONE CONCERT where we played on the outskirts of Fort Myers, Kevin celebrated extra hard. One of his friends, who had moved from Michigan to Florida after high school, had reached out, and they hooked up after the gig.

Casey and Kevin had a relationship where they egged each other on to see who could do something bad and get away with it. All throughout high school, they had both come close to getting into a lot of trouble. I was still surprised neither of them had spent any serious time in jail.

Tex never liked Casey and told Alli how he had always been a bad influence. He just wanted attention and talked Kevin into doing a line of coke with him that night. Apparently, he liked it more than whiskey or weed. It was very unfortunate. Not just for us, but his entire life changed by one single stupid choice.

Anyway, I saw them leave the motorhome, wiping their noses and laughing. The telltale sign. At first, I tried to deny it had happened. The more I thought about it, the surer I was of what I had seen. I tried to talk myself into 'maybe it had only happened one time.' Surely Kevin had suffered a momentary lapse of judgment, and it wouldn't happen again.

I spent the entire day wondering if I should tell Alli about what I had seen. Even though we had strictly written the no-drug policy into the band's code of conduct, we'd always let smoking weed slide. To be honest, it was not a horrific drug, and we all enjoyed a little toke here and there.

If I confided in Alli, which I knew in my heart was the right thing to do, I couldn't help but wonder what would happen to Heaven Scent. In my mind, the drummer was the hardest to replace—that and the fact he was Alli's brother, I didn't think Heaven Scent would survive without him.

Besides, Alli was my best friend and the lead singer. What kind of person would I be to ruin a time in our lives, which had been so absolutely incredible?

If I spoke up, our time as Heaven Scent would surely end. We would have no choice but to stop doing the thing we all love more than anything else. All I ever wanted was to be in this band and to live the life that we lived. As a team, we had worked so hard to make our dreams come true, and, in one little second, I could ruin it all.

I found myself in an impossible situation. At the time, I understood how Alli must have felt when she had to tell the rest of us about *American Idol*. The last thing I wanted to do was disappoint everyone.

All night, I went back and forth in my mind. *Do I say something, or do I keep my trap shut?* I tried to rationalize how it must have been a celebration of sorts, that what Kevin had done was okay, if it was just this once. However, I knew in my heart that wasn't the case.

In the end, I decided to sleep on it. We had a couple days between Fort Myers and Tampa before we headed home. I put it on the back burner and tried to stop my emotions but ended up crying myself to sleep. I never told anyone that.

The next morning, we ate breakfast at a small diner in town. Everyone had a hangover because we had partied the night before. Some of us more than others.

I still tried to talk myself into how maybe what Kevin had done was okay. He hadn't ever done this in the past, that we knew about, and we were all drinking and getting a little crazy. But it still didn't sit right that it was coke. It just wasn't okay.

I watched him eat breakfast, and his demeanor hadn't been any different from any other morning after a gig. We typically found a smalltown diner first thing in the morning, and we all usually felt the effects of alcohol consumption from the previous night. I watched him dip his toast in his egg yolk and couldn't help but wonder how many times he had done this before. Had this been a normal thing for him? Had he been doing coke this entire time?

The thought of confronting him before saying anything to Alli crossed my mind. I was so torn and sad and confused. Alli noticed my mood and asked if I was okay; she always had a way to read my emotions. I blew it off as just being hungover.

I can't count the number of times I tried to mention it to Alli, but I didn't witness it again; I had been watching.

After we finished the tour and arrived in Michigan, I was compelled to come clean. We retired *Winnie* to her spot beside the garage, and Kevin headed straight to the trailer to unload his drums. Charlie and Alli walked their equipment to the garage, and I followed.

Before Charlie had a chance to get in her car, I pulled them both to the side and asked them to meet me at the park. Surprised that I wanted to spend even more time with them, Alli asked, again, if everything was okay.

"Yeah," Charlie agreed. "We've been stuck in the same small area for months, and you don't need a break? I mean, I love y'all, but I have my limits."

I couldn't stop tears forming in my eyes. I never cried in front of Alli and Charlie—or anyone, really. It didn't take long for them to catch on that something was wrong. Really wrong.

"We need to talk." I looked over my shoulder. "But not here."

WE INSTINCTIVELY walked to our picnic table in the park on Vineyard Lake. When I paced from table to table and refused to look at them, random questions flew from their mouths.

"Are you sure you're okay?"

"Are you sick?"

"Did someone hurt you?" Alli checked my face and arms for bruises.

I couldn't look either of them in the eye. The thought of breaking up this band tormented me.

Alli gasped, and Charlie's eyes widened. They'd had the same thought.

"Oh my God, Sara. Were you raped?" Alli whispered.

I almost laughed. "What? No."

"Then what, dammit? You're killing us. What the hell is going on?" Charlie demanded.

I studied my feet, then my hands, and finally decided it was time to spit it out. As much as it tortured me to keep the secret, I also refused to put them through this any longer.

"Kevin's doing coke!" I closed my eyes, held my breath, and waited for the end of the world.

"Shit." Stunned, Charlie gaped at me.

I opened my eyes to my best friends standing so close that I smelled their perfume.

"Yeah, shit is right." Alli hugged me. "You must have been going through hell holding that in." She backed away. "For how long? How do you know? Did you see him do it?" The sincerity in her voice confirmed that her questions were not accusing me of being wrong.

Charlie paced. "Shit, shit, shit." She tapped her teeth with one fingernail, trying to process what I had just said and contemplating what to do next.

"Look, y'all," I started as they took their place on the picnic table. "The two of you are my best friends. The only people in the world who love me despite all my fucked-up flaws. The only people in the world who I would do anything for. Anything. We can't let this break up Heaven Scent. We need to decide what to do about Kevin. Together. To answer your questions: I don't know how long. I didn't see him actually do it, but I saw him walk out of *Winnie* with Casey after the Fort Myers show. They both wiped white powder off their noses—that, I did see—then they sniffed and laughed. I didn't sleep at all that night—or much since then. I tried to tell you so many times, but I didn't see him do it again. I thought about letting it go, but we made a pact. It's the right thing to do. Please tell me I'm not overreacting."

Tears rolled down my face as I sat atop a picnic

table. I found it hard to stop thoughts of our time being a rock band ending. "I'm so sorry. I don't want this to end. I've never wanted to do anything else with my life. I want to tour and perfect our performance on stage and create music forever. I love this more than anything in the world. I love you, and I love what we have accomplished. I love Heaven Scent."

"Don't you dare apologize for something Kevin did," Alli said. "He's the asshole here. He's the one who broke our pact. He's the one who should be sorry. Fucker." Emotions ranging from sadness, to disappointment, to anger, to fury crossed her face.

After a lengthy discussion, we decided to sit on it for a little while and make it a point to observe every detail. We had some time before the shows in Detroit, so we had an opportunity to determine whether Kevin acted differently during practices.

Master of Puppets

Charlie: September 15, 2010

"WANT SOME?" Kevin wiped his nose and raised an eyebrow. "I have plenty." I had walked in on him doing a line of cocaine in the basement bathroom before practice. To be fair, the door had been half open, so there wasn't really a need to knock.

"The fuck?" Confused and surprised, I jumped into little-sister's-best-friend mode. "What are you thinking? You know you're not supposed to be doing this. It's totally against the rules."

Laughter filled the space between us, and Kevin reached for me. He wrapped his arm around my waist, pulled me against him, and whispered in my ear, "Rules are made to be broken, babe. Come on. Release your inhibitions." He placed a kiss on my neck and squeezed tighter.

Warmth from his embrace made me shiver, but I wasn't sure if it had been due to disgust or excitement. Everyone knew I had a crush on Kevin, dating back to junior high. He knew it, too, and always made it a point to flirt a little. A little. It never went beyond a look or a laugh.

Pushing away, I frowned. “Get away from me.” The truth hit me hard. I was disappointed that what Sara had thought she saw had turned out to be real. We all had hoped it wasn’t true, especially me.

It was fun to flirt with Kevin, and I hoped that a stupid mistake or a misunderstanding wouldn’t interrupt our playfulness. I wanted to keep crushing on my best friend’s older brother, but he ruined it.

For a couple days, I kept the incident to myself. Things returned to normal after coming off the road with Nickelback. Surely, we would have seen the signs of abuse before now, right? At the very least, I should have; I made it a point to watch him like a hawk.

We had a show that Friday night at Callaghan’s, and I wanted to see if maybe Kevin hadn’t really been using for the past four months. It was kind of a test. If everything went off as usual, I wouldn’t say anything. But, if even the slightest thing felt off, I promised myself I would have another discussion with Alli and Sara.

Charlie: September 17, 2010

DURING THE intro to “Summertime”, which we have played at every gig from the beginning of time, literally, Kevin fucked up. That was when it became clear how much his drug use affected his ability to play. He never missed a beat. Ever. Even when he had too much to drink, he never messed up our first original.

I caught Alli's eye, and we looked at Sara, silently arranging a Kevin-less talk.

It was impossible for me to contain my anger, though. This couldn't wait until the next day. After the set, I confronted him myself. "What's going on, Kev? You never fuck up. Messing up "Summertime" threw us off the rest of the night."

During practices and after shows, Kevin was usually laid back and apologetic for his mistakes. That night, he came at me. "Oh, because you've never made a mistake? Little miss perfect? Oh, right—how about the time in Rochester Hills when you fucking unplugged? What's your fucking problem? You guys are all drinking underage. Want me to bring that little tidbit up to management? No? Jesus, Charlie. What the fuck?"

Before I could scream at him, like I wanted to more than anything—and honestly, I should have—Alli put her hand on my arm.

"Kevin, when we started this band, all we needed was a laugh. Years have gone by, and I'd say we've kicked some ass. But drugs were never part of our deal. Never will be. If any of us catch you using again, if we even hear a rumor that you may have been doing anything besides smoking weed, we're done."

Finished with us and the conversation, Kevin

scoffed, stood, and dismissed us with the wave of his hand. "Whatever. Fucking little girls. I'm so sick of your shit. I'm going to get another shot."

The next day at practice, Kevin pulled a small baggie containing a cream-colored powder, a bowl, and a straw from his pocket. He acted as if it was the most natural thing to do, as if part of his preparation for band practice ritual included smoking meth.

I can't tell you how proud I was of Alli. She finally stood up to her brother. "Kevin? What the fuck is that?" Except for the one time in the bathroom, none of us had ever seen him with anything other than weed.

He rolled his eyes. "Ugh. You guys are such pussies. I can't even believe how fucking stupid you are." He loaded the pipe and grabbed his lighter off the windowsill behind his drum set. "You can't tell me what to do or how to live my life."

Before he had a chance to light up, Alli got in his shit. "We have a signed contract that says different. Do I need to remind you where it lists the rules and regulations for being a member of Heaven Scent? Do I need to go get your copy? The one you signed when we all agreed that doing drugs is a dealbreaker?" Hands on her hips, she held her ground.

Without a pause in his action, Kevin called her bluff. "What are you going to do? Kick me out? You don't have the balls." When she didn't back down, he raised his eyebrows, lit the pipe, took a hit, and closed his eyes.

Five seconds later, he opened his eyes wide and smiled ear to ear. "Don't you know the drummer is the glue to every band? Without me, you're nothing." Ignoring his sister's tears, he flicked the lighter again.

This time, Alli didn't let him finish. "You're out," she announced, louder than anticipated. I would consider it a shout. She stood tall and pointed out the garage door. "Leave."

Without missing a beat, Kevin stood and walked away. A "Fuck you" followed him into the cool fall night.

Shaking, Alli lowered herself into a lawn chair and buried her face in her hands. Silent sobs turned into a sort of moan.

Not knowing what else to do, Sara and I kneeled beside her and cooed our support. After a few minutes of "Oh, honey" and "It's okay" and "I'm so, so sorry," she regained her composure.

"Well, I guess that's it. He's out." Alli took a deep, cleansing breath. "But what the fuck now? What are we going to do?"

After some pondering, my face lit up. "I've had an epiphany." I stood and paced, excited to tell my best friends my idea for our next move. "I don't think we should wait. I think we need to go to California. Like, tomorrow."

Sara squinted and rolled the idea over in her mind. As if the sun and stars aligned at that exact moment, a slow smile spread across her face. She nodded. "Yup. You're right, Charlie. That's exactly what we need to do."

Stunned, Alli's gaze volleyed between Sara and me as we spitballed ideas, as if writing a song.

"We need to go to LA and make this work. The three of us are dedicated enough. We can make it."

"Let's prove to all those haters that we can do this. Especially our moms. They said we couldn't do it and that we were in over our heads. Let's show them how wrong they are."

"We don't need people in our lives who will just bring us down. Let's find another way around."

"Ooh, this is good. I'm writing this down." Alli turned to grab a pen.

"For once, we need to be us. We need to be happy and free without anyone holding us back. To the world, I say, let me be me."

"Alli, last year you talked me out of my funk about not being good enough, and you know what? You were right. I believed you then; now you need to believe me. Believe us. We can do this."

"We need to call Kat."

Charlie: September 23, 2010

"I REACHED OUT to someone on your behalf." Kat had never lost sight of our best interest and put our success first. "I know you remember the concert where Ted gave you the name of his manager and said you could find him if you were serious."

"Yeah?" the three of us responded in unison and exchanged glances. From the table in the small kitchen, we didn't have much of a choice but to focus on what Kat suggested. We pushed thoughts of Kevin aside for the moment and gave Kat our total attention.

"Well, I found him right after you gave me his name and listened to his advice. He said to call back when you were ready for the bigtime. I've been saving his number for a couple years now. Just waiting for this very moment. You're ready. I can feel it in my bones."

"Oh, boy. Shit's gettin' real." Alli smiled.

"He told me that if you're serious, you need to move to LA, which works out, because that's your current plan. He gave me the name of a man who owns a couple bars and helps aspiring bands get noticed. I thought, *what the hell?* and reached out.

"His name is Mike Allen, and from everything I've heard, he's the one you want to know. But there's a six-month wait to play at his venue—Lisa's."

It didn't take long for us to decide what to do. We packed our gear and said our goodbyes. Even though we had spent the spring in Michigan, we had each been reluctant to rekindle our relationships, because we knew this day would come sooner rather than later.

Tex and Jeff both went to Michigan State, so they spent most of their time in Lansing. They had become pretty close friends while supporting us and rented a house just off campus. Tony had gotten a job and moved closer to Detroit. All three of us thanked the relationship gods for giving us time to pursue our rock star dreams.

Alli had a difficult conversation with her parents about why Kevin wasn't going to LA with us. She said her mom cried, while her dad tried his best to offer comfort through his anger.

They promised to look into rehab and work with their church minister to find him the right kind of help.

Part 3

Callaghan's June 29, 2012

Set Me Free

Choices

Remember Me?

Kiss

Summertime

Watch Me

All Right

Home

BREAK

Love Song

Stupid Love

Yourself

Beer Tears

Clean Me Up

NASCAR

No Sleep 'til Brooklyn

Paradise City

The Interview: January 8, 2015

"YOUR ENTIRE life changed in 2010. What was it like, moving from smalltown USA, to one of the largest cities in the world?" Comfortable with her new friends, Jenni asks questions not on her list. She's genuinely interested in how each member of the band answers.

"You're from Brooklyn. You know what it's like to have everyone in your business all the time. If you don't know them, they know you. Somehow." Charlie reminds Jenni.

"Moving to LA, we quickly realized it would not be a walk in the park. It certainly was, however, worth it," Sara says. "Everything we learned along the way designed a different aspect of our persona. I, for one, was super excited about starting a new life in California. I couldn't wait to prove my mom wrong. When I told her I was leaving, she reiterated that I was too fat to be famous."

"I tried not to be freaked out all the time," Alli admits. "Sometimes it was acceptable, but not all the time. I had never had issues with anxiety, hadn't ever been overwhelmed like our first few weeks in Cali. With so much competition, I had no idea what to expect. Trust me, if we could have done it differently, though, we would have."

Alli signals to Tommy for another round. "Kevin was our rock, our protector, our confidant. Hell, he's my brother. It wasn't an easy decision for any of us. We shed our share of tears and spent hours discussing how to handle the situation. In the end, we had only one choice. For a variety of reasons, the unanimous decision made sense. First, because it was the right thing to do, and B, because he had demons he needed to fight without us interfering. We tried to help him after Shelly broke his heart, but he wouldn't accept the fact that he needed help at all. As it turned out, he chose to self-medicate with whatever substance he could find as a way to forget or to get through the day or to relieve the pain."

"Not to mention," Charlie adds, "it was another thing we, as a band, did not want to be known for. Heaven Scent would not be recognized as drug addicts."

"We made yet another pact when we got to California. We wouldn't write any negative songs." Alli raises her hand to interject. "At times, we all felt like we had, at one point, been standing on the edge of angry. It was as sharp as a knife and seemed like it would cut us in half. We followed a road to what we called *a good place* and refused to look back.

"Kevin was writing a song he titled, 'The Edge of Angry.' I came across it in one of my notebooks and ripped out the page. Remember the movie, *The Wedding Singer*? When Adam Sandler's character wrote a song out of anger and screamed the lyrics? Yeah, that was Kevin. Right after Shelly dumped him, he went on an internal hatred tour, and everything he wrote was negative. So mean and hateful, like he wanted revenge or something. I still think some strong emotions linger with him, even though he's doing better now. The entire situation, the breakup, the other guy, the things she said to him, it took a long time for him to figure out how to handle it or make sense of it. Young love is stupid sometimes."

Intrigued, Jenny tilts her head. "Would you mind throwing out some of the lyrics? I've never heard this story, and I think it would be a really great opposing viewpoint in the book."

Charlie strums her guitar, slowly at first, then almost in a thrash-metal style. Alli recites the lyrics through gritted teeth and closed eyes.

I'm standing on the edge of angry
It's as sharp as a knife
Like straddling a razorblade
One wrong move will end my life

How could you, how could you, how

could you
You lied straight to my face

You said you loved me
You said I was the only one
I hate you, I hate you, I hate you
I love you so much I fucking hate you

I'm standing on the edge of angry
It's as sharp as the teeth of a
carnivore
I can feel myself slipping
But it doesn't hurt anymore

"It's just a ridiculous song, honestly." Alli rolls her eyes and chuckles at the memory. "Tommy suggested we sell his old songs to other bands who thrive on negativity. Maybe we can make some extra cash with words that once kept my brother jailed. Who knows? Someday, maybe."

"I love you, Tommy." Sara smiles. "But I can't help but wonder what would have been different if Kevin came to LA with us. I'm sure Alli's right; he would still be calling her names and would want to run the entire band by his rules and not consider our opinion."

"Of course, being his sister, I was the stupidest person in the world. When I wanted him to consider one of my ideas, Charlie or Sara presented it as a suggestion. The ideas they shared, even when they had been mine, weren't ever stupid in Kevin's eyes. It took us a long, painful year to learn to play the game, and it took a toll on our relationships. Early on, Kevin's ridicule held back the expressive parts of my personality. Once we figured out how to manipulate him, I truly thrived. If Brooke Mason, our manager, had to deal with him, we would still have ended up with Tommy in our lives anyway. Just a little later and enduring a little more heartache."

"Besides, if not for that dark cloud, we wouldn't have left Michigan when we did." Charlie sets her guitar down. "I sometimes think about how things would be different if we waited longer to move to LA."

A beat passes as the girls recall losing Kevin as a band mate.

"Tell me more about you, Tommy." Jenni turns to the elusive drummer. He stayed out of the limelight, quiet, while the girls gave the interview. Now it was his turn to be recognized.

"Well, before I met these jokers"—his smile lights up the room, apparent that he's an integral part of this group—"I used to do all kinds of crazy things. Imagine the Mötley Crüe "Kickstart Your Heart" video. I went skydiving one day. The weather had been perfect, and I was pretty much an expert by then; it was like my twenty-fourth jump or something. Well, the main shoot didn't open. I freaked out, and my life flashed before my eyes. Luckily, I got a grip and pulled the cord on the reserve shoot. I landed hard, broke a leg, and decided then and there that I would get serious about what I wanted in life. The time hit me hard, literally, and I knew I needed to make things happen for myself." Tommy raises his glass in a toast.

"Two months later, he answered an ad in the paper for a drummer. The rest is history." Alli smiles.

Alli: September 27, 2010

TEX AND I said our goodbyes the previous day, in private, so I could focus on my family the day we shoved off for LA. If he had been there, I wouldn't have climbed into the RV.

Kevin didn't show up. I'm sure he stayed away on purpose. I think he was too embarrassed and pissed to be positive about us leaving without him.

To cover for my brother, my mom shrugged. "Kevin wanted to say goodbye, but he had something else to do, I guess." She switched gears and turned to hug me one last time. "Heaven Scent will make it. You girls will find your way, and great things will happen for you. With your aunt Kat rooting for you, it's as good as done."

"Promise you'll get Kevin the help he needs?" I asked, and she nodded.

My dad gave us *Winnie*. He looked so proud and was on the verge of tears. When he hugged me one last time, I thought he would crush my ribs.

Sara had hooked her car to a dolly so we could tow it behind *Winnie*. The ten-year-old Camry was just the right size to zip around the Los Angeles streets. She offered to drive first, hopped into the driver's seat, and we were gone. We left our simple, easy life in Michigan for a chance at success.

The Sunset Strip was the birthplace of generations of rock bands, and we were next on the list. Determined to win, to be somebody, to make our dream come true, we putted carefully through the streets of Brooklyn toward the West Coast.

On the road, the vibe was totally different with just us girls. When one of us had the slightest moment of doubt, the others reminded her that this trip was worth a shot. Without Kevin around, listening to every detail, we didn't need to watch what we said or how we acted.

For the first few hours, we shared fond memories about how Kevin had been silly or fun or accepting. All too soon, those memories turned to disappointment and sadness. At the time, we felt as if he had let us down. It wasn't until years later that we completely understood how addiction takes over even the best, most caring people.

The rules we had implemented for Heaven Scent was for a reason: to keep those of us who decided to make this a life-long commitment safe, happy, and honest. Little did we know, one of us would make choices that would affect the rest of the band forever.

"What do you think happened?" Focused on the road, Sara started the conversation.

"Tex said it started with Casey in Florida."

"I thought maybe breaking up with Shelly triggered something. You know they hooked up after we got back from the Michigan tour," Charlie said.

"They did? Where the hell was I?"

"Hooking up with Tex."

I blushed as I realized Charlie was right. I had been all encompassed by the one who made me swoon. I missed him already.

"Do you think he'll be okay?" Sara asked what we all wondered.

"I hope so." I frowned. "Aunt Kat said she would push as hard as she could to get him the help he needs."

"You can't help someone if they don't think they're doing anything wrong." Charlie sighed. "I just hope he understands what he's done."

After driving six hours, we pulled into an RV park outside Springfield—Illinois not Missouri. Of course, we all commented on the Simpsons: *Where do you think they live? Think Homer and Marge will be at our show?*

Maybe Bart will bring his girlfriend. Think Duff beer is a real thing?

Aunt Kat had fast-tracked bookings for a few acoustic gigs along our route to California. Without a drummer, we couldn't play a full set, but at least the gigs we booked would help put gas in *Winnie*.

We had an hour to set up our equipment and grab a burger before going on stage. The bar owner told us we had made it just in time for the last weekend of outdoor music. He explained how Aunt Kat had been one of the most, if not *the* most, convincing booking agents he had ever worked with over the phone. She always found a way to work her magic at the exact time in our career when we needed it most.

We had to shorten and adjust the setlist. Obviously, songs like "Animals" and "Master of Puppets" couldn't have the same effect without a drummer. Instead, we decided to play some Eagles and REO Speedwagon, with a side of Alabama.

The classics were always a hit and allowed our fans to reminisce. This trip, we shared in reminiscing. We had a great run with Kevin. Sometimes, though, shit just happened. We all kept the faith that better days were ahead.

At eight o'clock, we took the stage and did what we did best, and the crowd enjoyed our set. During the intermission, a group of girls approached.

"You put on a really great show. We've been

coming here every Friday night this summer. Why haven't we seen you here before?"

"Oh," Charlie answered. "Thanks so much, but we're just passing through."

We chatted for a bit, and the girls told us that when we made it big and had a show in Springfield or St. Louis, they would be there. They bought CDs, said goodbye, and walked away.

I couldn't help but fantasize about headlining a tour. Our love of performing had always been obvious, but without Kevin, it became more evident that we had been held back. Only after this specific gig did I feel like fate had stepped in to relieve us of a literal weight.

Alli: October 1, 2010

FOUR DAYS later, we arrived in LA—well, an RV park on Malibu Beach, but close enough. Aunt Kat had done the research, and the park she chose ended up being absolutely perfect.

My dad surprised us again, when he and my mom paid for the first six months of the campground in advance. When I called to thank him and ask how he had swung such an expense, he said, "Consider this your college tuition." Yeah, I cried.

We owe a lot of our success to my parents'

generosity and support. Because we had a roof over our heads, we could wait for the right opportunity in LA.

Venice Beach, known as the playground by the sea and notorious for its eclectic oceanfront boardwalk, was one of the first places we explored. Sand squished between my toes, and the sun warmed my cheeks, while we strolled aimlessly. Sunglasses perched on my nose, and shoes dangled from my fingers.

As we passed the funky shops and beheld the colorful murals, our stomachs growled. Lack of money lured us to a little taco stand on Pacific Avenue called Beach Boys Tacos. To this day, they are still my favorite tacos. I don't know if it is because of the memory of our first week in Cali or because they really are the best.

California had a different atmosphere than Florida, at least this beach did. All kinds of people walked or rollerbladed or rode bikes down the boardwalk or on the beach.

After lunch, we got turned around and ended up walking down an alley. It seemed like any normal alley, but the number of homeless people surrounded by cardboard boxes and grocery carts full of their belongings surprised us. Sara frowned, "Like bodies in an open grave."

Saddened and humbled, we waited until after we were out of earshot before commenting on what could have happened to each of the people in the alley. By the time we found our car, we had created another Heaven

Scent original song detailing how we felt about the current situation of so many individuals in the US. This one we named, “Choices.”

Where did they go wrong?
What happened in their life that brought them here?
Which single choice went sideways?
Choices, it's all about the choices you make

Is it, though? Isn't some of their heartache because of choices made for them?
His wife died and he couldn't hold it together
She lost her job and couldn't pay rent
They didn't have insurance on their home that went up in flames

They lost it all, but it wasn't their choice
I just want to hug them all and let them cry

Being from a small town, we had never had any

experience with the homeless population. It tugged on our heartstrings and stayed with us. While we spent months looking for our real opportunity, we kept these people, who had been down on their luck, in the backs of our minds. After all, that could have been any of us. Maybe even Kevin.

We reflected on how lucky we had been and how much support we had. It only felt right to give back, no matter the amount of energy or cash it took. From that day, we agreed to donate something from each show to the homeless community. In addition, we donate to rehabilitation centers, specifically those which grassroots organizations have started.

Finished with exploring the beach and beyond, we hopped into the Camry and headed toward the Sunset Strip. So many items filled our list of things to do that I wondered how we would possibly have time to see everything. Then I remembered we lived here now. We had fucking moved to LA. How long would it take for the realization to sink in?

No matter how often I had looked at a map on the drive across the United States, it couldn't compare to reality. For four days, I had studied the Los Angeles layout, but I felt lost as we drove down the actual roads.

At this point, we had basically just been sightseeing, trying to get a feel of the city. My senses took in every scene and scent while walking along Sunset Blvd., from the smell of seasoned meat that wafted out a restaurant door as we passed to skyscrapers that towered over the street.

Unusual sounds and energy of crowded sidewalks added to my angst. I tried to memorize the enhanced feeling of each next step. Mostly, though, anxiety crept into the cracks, and I doubted the purpose of this move.

"We're really here, aren't we?" Craning my neck to see the top of hotels and office buildings, I turned in a circle and spread my arms like a bird. "What if we fail? What if we don't make it or everyone hates us?"

"We are really here," Sara confirmed, then teased, "Stop with your silly shit, girl. We won't fail. Believe it or not, we're doing this thing one hundred. I can hardly believe it myself. If this is a dream, I don't ever want to wake up."

Alli: October 11, 2010

BY THE TIME we settled into a routine, Aunt Kat had a nice list of drummers lined up, ready and waiting for interviews. She even rented a space for us to practice—an old dive bar turned restaurant that had no following to speak of. A friend of John Bertolli's owned the place. It was located just off the beach in north Santa Monica. It turned out to be the perfect place to play and meet people.

Now named *Our Place*—yeah, not all that original, but that was what first came to mind, so we kept it—we would invite anyone wandering around outside to come in and listen to us play. The door remained propped open as we played. Before we had a chance to find a neon "Open" sign, we made a "Welcome" and an "Our Place" sign from posterboard and hung them on the windows.

We learned from our early days that it paid to play freebie sessions, aka practice. Those friends who came back again and again learned our music, learned about us, and turned into fans. The best kind of marketing is word of mouth, so we welcomed all our new followers with open arms.

Each drummer we interviewed brought their own unique sound and played really well with us. A couple guys also played in other bands and wanted to use our sets to supplement them. Their end goals didn't match ours, so we thanked them for their time and experience and agreed to keep in touch.

Three more guys and one girl refused to agree to our rules, so we passed on them too. Most of our early relationships stuck and morphed into friendships. It paid to keep a wide array of friends; anyone could be connected to someone who could help you.

In the end, we had to choose from two people: Tommy Tomac or Damon "Iron" Travis. When he introduced himself as Iron and we hesitated, he elaborated. A little. "I got the nickname from having the hardest head."

Charlie's eyebrows lifted, and Sara let out an *Oh*. Not sure if I should be concerned, I sat back and crossed my arms.

"Damon doesn't sound very intimidating, now, does it?" His tattoo-covered arms and long greasy hair gave me pause. "You're waiting for a story?" After meeting each of our questioning gazes, he chuckled and raised both hands, palms out. "Okay, it's stupid really. One night, during a high school football game, a group of us got drunk under the bleachers, and a support broke when some fat lady jumped up and down to celebrate her kid's touchdown. I didn't move out of the way fast enough, and it hit me on the head. When I came to, six guys stood around me and laughed when I asked what happened. My best friend, Ronnie, pulled me up and handed me another beer. I didn't let the guys know how much it fucking hurt. I probably had a concussion and should have gotten stitches. But I'll be damned if I let my dad find out I had been drinking. He would have kicked my ass. Anyway, Ronnie joked it off and said my noggin must be made of iron. Hence the nickname."

Beneath the grunge look, he had a nice smile and pretty green-blue eyes. He was a very talented drummer though—better than Kevin. His connections around town highlighted another good reason why it would behoove us to choose him, but something about his aura just didn't click. Didn't feel right. We couldn't put our finger on it. He hesitated to sign any band rules, but we played with him a little longer anyway. It took two weeks and five more practices to feel comfortable with Damon.

Tommy, however, fit in from the first minute we met him. His shaggy brown curls and crooked smile appealed to me right away. He just looked like a nice guy. When we met with him, we talked about our journey and where we envisioned our path would take us. Tommy nodded and added his own dreams, which mirrored ours. His sense of humor and the way he bantered with Charlie made me laugh. He nicknamed her *Stan*, based on her last name. He said it fit her face better than *Charlie*. Someone needed to keep her in line, and Tommy fit the bill.

Most importantly, his morals meshed with Heaven Scent. It just felt right to have him in our presence. To be honest, over the next week of practices, I waited to see when our connection would falter, for some red flag to show itself. It didn't.

Iron turned out to be a tool, as the name would suggest. Right when we started to mesh, Aunt Kat called with the results of his background check. We had to know what we were getting ourselves tied up in—for safety reasons, of course. Imagine our surprise when we learned that Iron had a warrant in three states for assault, armed robbery, and domestic abuse. Yeah, bye.

One night during practice, Aunt Kat left a voicemail, asking us to call as soon as we could. She had already booked gigs for the next six months and needed to discuss the details. Before I returned her call, I spoke with Charlie and Sara. We agreed the timing had been perfect and invited Tommy to play with Heaven Scent on a permanent basis, to officially join the band.

We stayed at *Our Place* a little longer that night to have a couple drinks. Tommy grabbed a few beers from the fridge and sat on a stool at the bar.

“So, what do you think?” Charlie tilted her head and pointed her bottle toward Tommy. “Wanna join our family?”

He paused, took a pull on his beer, and frowned. “Kinda thought I already did.”

Charlie’s mouth dropped open, and Tommy laughed. “Just kidding, Stan.” He rushed to Charlie and picked her up in a bear hug. “I thought you’d never ask.” An infectious smile spread across his face, and we all joined in the Heaven Scent family hug.

Aunt Kat congratulated us on finding Tommy and recited the dates and locations of our next month of gigs. “You need to check your email and print the list I’m sending you. Oh, there’s a contract for all of you to sign. Not only does it protect you girls but Tommy as well.”

Known bands filled the bars on weekends, while we worked our way into the spotlight during the week. It was quite different being the new guy in LA. Silence must have tipped off Kat to our emotions; she always could read our minds.

"My first piece of advice is this: don't get discouraged. You're used to being on top of the world, and you will be again, I promise. But, for now, it's kind of like starting over. This time, though, you already have a working knowledge and a feel for what it's like to tour. Now you just have to go out there and make a name for yourself."

"Oh, that's all. No pressure." Charlie rolled her eyes.

Fallen Angel

Sara: October 31, 2010

"STOP FIDGETING," Charlie told me for the thousandth time. "You're stunning." Each time she reassured me how incredible or smokin' hot my costume had turned out, my confidence grew a little more.

The classic "little black dress" made the perfect sexy-kitten costume base. However, with every other step, I pulled on the hem, which didn't quite reach midthigh. Alli had loaned me her black stilettos, and I almost twisted my ankle with the first step.

The long, stuffed tail and perky ears attached to a headband completed the look. I colored the tip of my nose and drew on whiskers with eyeliner just before we left the RV.

Charlie dressed up as Elvira so she could show off her ample cleavage without feeling quite so trashy. Instead of spending money on a wig she would only wear once, she bought black hair spray and used the entire can. The phenomenal outfit mixed with her natural beauty created an entirely different persona.

Alli dressed as Dorothy from *The Wizard of Oz*,

complete with a blue plaid dress and red sparkly shoes. Always prepared for every situation, she had packed an old Halloween costume from high school for this very reason. Ingenious.

One of the regulars from *Our Place* mentioned that the Whisky a Go Go threw the best Halloween parties in LA. They said we should go. So, we did. Tommy had already committed to attending another party, so he and his best friend agreed to meet up with us later.

Without knowing what to expect, we arrived super early—ten o'clock. In Michigan, when we played, we had already completed half of our set by ten. In California, the first band wouldn't be on stage for another hour, at least.

The temperature fell below sixty degrees, and I shivered. This almost-balmy weather should be pretty comfortable, but because I hadn't covered much of my skin with clothing, I wasn't warm. Lucky for us, we wouldn't have to wait outside for long. The line only stretched about two blocks, you know, because it was so early.

Each time one of us leaned out of line to check why it hadn't moved, the large man collecting money at the door lifted his chin and winked. His slicked back hair and sleeves of tattoos emphasized the level of his ability to offer protection. He didn't hide the fact that he had his eye on our little group. I shivered and rubbed my arms, not sure if the cold air or creepy guy gave me chills.

Charlie paid the cover charge for all of us; she and Alli walked through the door with no problem. The bouncer outstretched his arm and stopped me. "Honey, I been watching you all night. Been waiting 'til you reached the door." His eyes drifted from mine to my feet, then he whistled as he gaped at my chest. "You're absolutely gorgeous in that costume. We hookin' up after the show or what?"

When he licked his lips, I shuddered and crossed my arms. Creeper. "Um, no thanks. I'm here with my friends." The crowd pushed Alli and Charlie through the small room toward the bar and out of sight. I offered a shy smile, unaware of the expectations of this Hollywood lifestyle. Apparently refusing a bouncer's advances is a no-no. If I wanted access to the bar, I needed to agree.

A frown dimmed his eyes, and he gripped my biceps, lifted me off the ground, and set me to the side.

Dismissed, I grew stronger. "I paid my cover, and my friends are inside. Let me in."

He tossed a ten-dollar bill at me and turned his back.

The man behind me in line didn't hesitate to come to my rescue. "Lyle, I think you forgot your purpose here, *friend*." He stood tall and stared at the large man—Lyle, as he had called him—until the bouncer relaxed his shoulders. It had been obvious that the bouncer knew him.

With a huff, Lyle opened the door and let us both pass.

At first, I didn't know what to do. What if the guy who had just saved me was just as dangerous as the bouncer? What if he tried to manhandle me and demand I do questionable things? My cheeks warmed at the thought. This tall drink of water was the first guy I had been attracted to since Jeff and I split. Shoulder-length black hair accentuated his dark eyes and sly smile. Standing taller than me, I found his thin frame and crooked smile oddly sexy.

To my surprise, the man put his hand in the middle of my back and escorted me inside. His warmth eased my worry. Polo reached my nose and reminded me of home. Once I spotted Charlie and Alli, I tossed a *Thank you* over my shoulder and pushed through the crowd.

"What the hell?" I was a little miffed that my friends had left me alone. "Where did you go? Why didn't you wait for me?"

It was difficult for them to hug me with my hands on my hips. When they grabbed me tight, Alli strained her voice to be louder than the crowd. "Oh my God. We thought we lost you."

I relaxed. They hadn't left me, after all.

"Where were you?" Charlie added. "We've been looking everywhere for you. This crowd is so thick that it was impossible to get back to the door."

The bar filled so fast that it was like a tidal wave. Loud voices made it impossible to explain the super-weird situation, so I shrugged and mouthed, *I'll tell you later*.

Before moving across the country, we had agreed to keep an open mind but be cautious about everything. And everyone. Taking in the surroundings, which had been so far removed from smalltown Michigan, gave us pause.

This strange world housed all sorts of strange people. Although we understood we would need to take risks and make changes, we had promised not to lose ourselves along the way.

Aunt Kat had explained the Whisky's reputation with a wide array of narratives: seedy, impressive, intense, classic, a legacy. Excited to experience one of the legendary venues for up-and-coming bands, we were not disappointed.

At the bar, we had to yell our orders to the bartender over the roar of the crowd: Sex on the beach, Long Island iced tea, and tequila sunrise.

"What?" The bartender's face squished in disgust.

After I repeated the order, he smirked and shook his head. "I heard you the first time. You do realize that fruit and rock and roll don't mix. Don't you?"

We had just been schooled. Our goofy girly drinks had not been an acceptable order at the Whisky.

"Girls," he patronized, "we don't have any juice or funky-ass-flavored vodkas behind the bar. I think what y'all really want is a Jagerbomb."

We exchanged glances, shrugged, and watched the bartender make our drinks.

When he placed them in front of us, he winked. "Extra Jager."

Charlie nodded to the stairs opposite the bar and led the way. We pushed our way through people dressed in sexier costumes than we donned and more elaborate than I could have imagined. I felt a little childish in my cat getup and pulled at the hem of my dress between steps.

A nurse, who showed most of her breasts and a lot of her cheeks, stood so close to a vampire that I thought he would actually bite her; his teeth appeared all too real. This was Hollywood though, so I shouldn't have been surprised.

From the balcony, we could behold the entire bar. Many reports have described the venue as *intimate*. They weren't wrong.

On the small stage, roadies prepared instruments for the band. It wasn't long before the emcee climbed on stage and screamed into the microphone, "*Hellooooo, Whiskyyyyyy*! People, people, people." He waited for the crowd to calm a bit. "Put your hands together for Rhinestone!"

Applause, whoops, and whistles made it difficult to hear the rest of the introduction. It didn't matter, though.

The group of four found their places beside and behind their instruments and played.

Startled by their immediate loud, fast, heavy guitar, we all laughed. We hadn't yet become accustomed to the harsh, wild style of bands who played at the Whisky. Not quite the scene you would find in the kinds of places we frequented back home.

Something about the lead guitarist seemed familiar. I touched Alli's arm when I realized what it was. "That's him. Oh my God, Alli. That's the guy who saved me from the bouncer."

Confused, she searched the crowd below us. "What? Who?" Because I hadn't told them about the incident at the door due to the volume inside the venue, I understood the confusion.

I pointed to the stage. "Him. Lead Guitar Guy. That's the guy who saved me."

The song ended, and the lead singer screamed a *hello*, and the crowd applauded louder this time.

Lead Guitar Guy locked eyes with me, smiled, and pointed back.

Embarrassed and surprised, I gasped and lowered my arm. I couldn't believe that out of hundreds of people in the crowd, he had found me. Again. For the rest of their set, I stayed glued to my spot at the railing. Watching.

He couldn't take his gaze off me either. The way he

stared at me was sexy as hell. His smile was infectious, to say the least. It impressed me how he played without missing a note.

After the show, one of the staff approached us and asked if we would follow him. At first, we hesitated, but because he had summoned all of us, we decided it would be safe to go with him. Maybe we would find ourselves in an adventure.

The lead guitarist of Rhinestone introduced himself as Chad McGentry. He reached for my hand and didn't let it go once we shook. Inching toward each other, our mutual attraction was obvious to everyone.

While Chad remained focused on me, the lead singer laughed and introduced the rest of the band.

We found our first band friends that night at the Whisky a Go Go. Who would have thought?

Party in the USA

The Interview: January 8, 2015

"AH, THAT'S how you met Chad." Addressing Sara, Jenni smiles. "I wasn't sure how you met the man who continues to make you happy. What a great story."

Without missing a beat, Sara says, "The best thing that ever happened to me."

Charlie clears her throat and glares.

"Whatever." An eyeroll emphasizes Sara's passive response. "I know, now I have to say it in full. The best thing that ever happened to me, besides Heaven Scent."

Amused, Alli shakes her head at the game her bandmates play.

"Not only is he my perfect match but he also had tons of connections from being in the music scene for so long. He arranged the meeting with Mike."

"Yes, Mike Allen. What was it like to get noticed by him?" Jenni asks. "He's a superstar in his own right. What's he like, for real?"

"Getting noticed by him was, in a word, surreal." Charlie smiles at the memory. "From the day we formed Heaven Scent, the direction of our dreams had been a paved road—straight from start to finish. I never thought the fork in the road would have so many proverbial tines. There are so many possible directions to go depending on what your group decides to do and when. So many bands make choices that affect every member without realizing the totality of their decisions."

Sara notices the confusion on Jenni's blank face and explains in simpler terms. "If we chose to do drugs, the direction of our original path would have changed. If we chose to dress differently, be negative, sleep with a bunch of people to get ahead, our path would have changed. You have no idea how many groups have a well-laid-out plan when they get here and totally let the glam and glitz take over their priorities. So many great musicians have lost their way once they play at the Whisky, the Rainbow, or the Roxy. Us three kept our end-goal in mind and have enough love and respect for each other to discuss what we were feeling and what we should do about it—or shouldn't, for that matter. After all, we chose this life together, added Tommy, and chose to behave a certain way."

"Because of that, Heaven Scent succeeded," Tommy agrees. "One of the stops on the paved road, the reason the girls came out here, was to meet Mike Allen. The next stop on the success train was to play at Lisa's."

Leaning back, Charlie crosses her legs and, with a glass of wine in hand, makes a toast. "To Mike. Our reason for having a future, for making it possible to fulfill our dreams."

Charlie: April 3, 2011

CHAD HELPED us find our way around the city. After their initial meeting at the Whisky, he became a regular at *Our Place* to watch Sara. It would have been impossible to avoid her, and, instead of trying to deny their mutual attraction, they gave in and quickly became a couple.

Lisa's was, obviously, one of the first places we wanted to see for ourselves. Chad knew exactly where it was and introduced us to the band scheduler, Rowdy Phillips. Rowdy decided who went on stage and when. If.

We needed an appointment to simply have a full conversation with Rowdy, so we added our names to his list. He said he would let us know when to come in for an interview, and we hoped it would be sooner than the six-month wait.

Between gigs and practices, we had plenty of time to explore our new hometown. We liked to hang out on Sunset and hoped to meet more up-and-coming bands. Making friends in this industry, like Chad and the rest of the guys in Rhinestone, was the best way to get an introduction to the right people.

After a night on the town, I woke up and powered on my phone. The voice mail icon blinked, and I ignored it, because no one ever called me. Alli had been the one with family who constantly checked in, so I hadn't been in a hurry to check the message.

When I finally did listen to it, my mouth fell open. "Hey. Guys?" Sara and Alli assumed my gaping mouth meant something awful. They hopped up from the couch and rushed to my side.

"What? Charlie—what is it? What's wrong?"

A smile spread across my face as I said, "We got the call."

"Okay …" Alli raised her eyebrows. "What call?"

"From Lisa's."

"Jesus, Charlie. You scared the shit out of me. Don't do that." Sara poured a glass of orange juice and slumped onto the couch.

"Lisa who?" Alli opened the plastic bag from inside a box of cereal that was sitting on the table and poured herself a bowl.

"*Lisa's*, Lisa's." I tried to find the words that they would understand. "Mike Allen's Lisa's."

That got their attention. They both rushed me again.

Sara almost spilled her juice she had popped up so fast. "Lisa's? Oh my God. You're shitting me?"

My sly smile threw them both off. I hugged Sara. "I wouldn't shit you. You're my favorite turd."

She grimaced at my juvenile sense of humor.

Alli grabbed my arms. "Why didn't you say something sooner?"

"I don't know why you gave Rowdy my phone number. You all know the battery hits zero before the end of the night. Anyway, he wants to meet to talk about playing at Lisa's."

"I thought it was a six-month wait?" Sara tilted her head.

"Well, my dear," I raised one eyebrow. "Seems that your lover boy has more connections than he admitted. He and Rowdy went to school together, and he talked him into calling us. We have an appointment tomorrow afternoon at two."

Within such a confined area, it wasn't easy to jump up and down in a circle, but we managed.

Charlie: April 6, 2011

KAT INSISTED we call her the moment we got the call from Lisa's, so an hour before our meeting, we met up with Tommy at a diner and put her on speakerphone. Scared shitless wouldn't even come close to describing the emotions pulsing through each of us.

As she always did, Kat calmed us with reassurance. Suggestions like, *Just be yourself* and *Play like you love Heaven Scent more than anything on Earth*, weren't difficult to follow; that's how we always carried ourselves. Reminded of how Kat had a special way to make us believe everything she said made us miss her.

Lisa's wouldn't open for hours, so Rowdy met us at the door. During our conversation earlier, he had insisted that we didn't need to bring our equipment. He just wanted to meet us and have a conversation.

Dim lighting made it difficult to see, until our eyes adjusted. Once they did, a warm, classy, modern honky-tonk welcomed us. An empty, shiny, large dance floor, with a surrounding wooden split-rail fence, spread out before the stage. Elevated booths lined two walls with wood high-top tables between them and the dancefloor. A bar stretched the entire length of another.

Seven Springs Saloon and Lisa's could have been sisters; their allure and ambiance mirrored one another.

The five of us sat around a random table on the edge of the venue. Rowdy asked questions about our history and why we wanted to play at Lisa's. We told him how our manager had heard through her connections that this was the place to be. If we were serious about making a career out of performing on stage, Mike Allen was the one person who could help us achieve our goals.

After we gave him our backstory, Rowdy made a phone call from behind the bar. We chattered among ourselves until he returned with four glasses of water. "What do you think about playing a couple songs?"

Not expecting to play without our instruments but

open to anything, we exchanged looks and shrugged. "Sure," Alli and I said at the same time, sharing a smile. "But we don't have any equipment," I added.

"No worries. We've got a stock set ready for you on stage." Rowdy nodded toward the other side of the dancefloor. "Go ahead and play any two songs for me."

Our own instruments were an extension of ourselves, but we weren't strangers to an impromptu performance. We moseyed toward the stage, and Alli leaned toward me to ask why she didn't feel as nervous as she thought she should? I shrugged.

It went without saying that "Summertime" had always been our go-to original. We knew it better than any cover and played it as if we had just been messing around. We enjoyed each other and the new venue so much that I longed to come back and play to a full crowd.

For the cover, we played "Miss Independent" by Kelly Clarkson. The female lead and strength of Alli's voice emulated Kelly's. The lyrics about keeping our independence resonated with each of us—so did the lyrics about letting go and falling in love. Our emotions pushed us to play our hearts out. As they always did.

After we played two songs, as requested, I strummed the intro to Miley's "Party in the USA". We had so much fun on stage that once we got going, it was hard to stop. Besides, this song pretty much explained our current situation.

During the second cover, two men dressed in jeans and concert t-shirts appeared at the bar beside Rowdy. I nodded to Sara. She followed my gaze and shrugged. They applauded when we finished our short but powerful set.

"Heaven Scent." The taller of the two approached the stage. "I'm Mike Allen. I own this place. It's a pleasure." He nodded; his shoulder-length shaggy light-brown hair, square jaw, and trim waist reminded me of Brad Pitt in his younger days. "This here is my best friend, Danny."

A sly grin turned into a warm smile, and I could tell Danny liked to have fun. "We watched you walk in. You don't see many bands with such confidence and poise. It's usually as if someone had won the lottery—girls all giggly and guys stumbling over their words." Not lowering his voice or disguising his pleasure, he addressed Mike. "Dude, these girls got something special." He chuckled, then pointed to Tommy. "You, too, my friend."

Of course, my head ballooned, and I couldn't help but watch Alli's smile widen. We kept our cool and proved Danny right; our poise was one of our strong suits.

Mike put an arm around his friend's shoulders. "His ear is even better than mine. Couldn't run my business as well as I do without him."

Danny bowed his head as if embarrassed, then laughed and scuffed the ground with his cowboy boot. "Awe, shucks."

After a playful shove, Mike refocused on us. "You write your own songs. I didn't recognize the first one you played. I like it. A lot."

"We do. We made a record last year, all our own originals. We still play covers to bond with the crowd. Once we hook 'em, we play our stuff. We're always writing something. Alli just wrote one on her own yesterday, as a matter of fact. This girl"—I pointed a thumb over my shoulder toward Alli and smiled—"has an incredible imagination. Once something touches her, she writes about it."

"Can I hear it?" Intrigued, a grin accompanied the tilt of his head.

"That one's not quite ready yet," Alli told him. Although she hated to turn down the one person who could make or break Heaven Scent, she felt strongly about not sharing a song until she was certain it would be phenomenal.

"Play a different one for me, then," Mike suggested, respectful of our craft.

I strummed the first chords of "Stupid Love." Sara and Tommy followed my lead. Alli danced and, when the time came, sang like an angel.

Can't find my socks,
I just put them down
Why did I walk into the kitchen
again?
Where are my keys?
Oh, they're in my hand.

Walkin' around here like a clown
Thoughts of you cloud my brain
Stupid love, stupid love, stupid love
My love for you makes me stupid

Before we finished playing, Danny and Mike exchanged a glance and nodded to the beat.

"I love it." Mike applauded as a wry smile twisted his lips. "Your sound is so unique. I had no idea what to expect. I just love it. I need to hear more. Play me something else."

Who were we to deny the great Mike Allen from listening to another one of our songs? Happy to oblige, we went to another of our most recent creations. We had written "Believe" the same way we had written most of our others—on the fly. When we brainstormed after an event that meant something special to us, we birthed another song.

Now it's time, time to believe
Believe, believe, believe Marie

She won't settle, won't give up
She's finally, finally, finally free

Persistence will pave the road
Lead to joy, love, and success
She has to do this on her own
Push away feelings of distress

Hold your head up, don't back down
She repeats the mantra every day
Determined to follow all her dreams
One day she'll live in Monterrey

Mike and Danny invited us to have a drink so they could get to know us better. They didn't need to spend this kind of time with some unknown smalltown band, and, at the time, I kind of wondered why they did. Discussing our previous life, how we got started, and our journey to California felt natural. We laughed about our time in Michigan, which seemed like a million years ago. Then we impressed them with our stories from touring in Florida and Texas and cried a little when explaining why Kevin wasn't with the band anymore.

They laughed with us and empathized about losing a bandmember to drug use. The more we talked with them, the more our connection grew. Without a doubt, the men's intentions were genuinely good.

Once we finished with our short history, Mike shared stories about his experiences. Since moving to LA, he had opened two bars: Gene's and Lisa's. "When I bought my first bar last year, it had a stage, and I had an epiphany. We always had to travel so far to hear good music back home, so I decided to bring music to my customers. Good music. Great music. I told Danny my idea of opening these bars, and he was the first one to throw suggestions at me. Good ones. Gene's is located on the other side of town and focuses more on rock bands. I named the place after my friend who made it all possible. Gene, God rest his soul, left me his entire estate after he died in a car accident. Like you, I'm from a small town, where everyone knows everybody. I was born and raised in Oakdale, Tennessee. Danny was my best friend growing up. I see a lot of us in you."

As we listened to the cadence of Mike's voice, mixed with the banter of Danny's, I recognized our similarities. The dynamic duo found it easy to connect with those they wanted to help.

The help Mike offered didn't come in the form of a handout or charity. On the contrary, it was fueled by pure generosity and the goodness of his heart. It was hard to comprehend that Mike was worth millions; his demeanor made it easy to talk to him. He and Danny reminded me of home.

"I don't book huge names. I promote up-and-coming stars. After Gene's got so busy and I could hardly keep up, I opened Lisa's. There's a need to separate country music from our typical genre at Gene's, so this place will focus on country. We've only been here long enough to renovate and book a few gigs. We just had our grand opening two weeks ago. We anticipate Lisa's will grow faster than Gene's. When that happens, I'll open Sam's. Maybe next year."

Mike had named Lisa's, as Danny told the story, in honor of Mike's one and only true love. "Sure, he has a wife now, but it will always be Lisa who makes his ticker tick." Danny winked, and Mike shrugged.

"It's true. Even though we split eons ago, she inspired me to help great bands find their way." He cleared his throat. "I want to let you know that I absolutely understand what you're going through with Kevin. My brother Sam is in the middle of his own crisis. His demons have caused him to lose his wife, his son, and his home." He reached across the table and squeezed Alli's hand. "I'm really sorry."

Tears came to the surface, but Alli blinked them away. Unable to speak, she nodded her appreciation.

It went without saying that Mike didn't need to open up to strangers like he had, but we felt honored that he did. Our conversation had been smooth and relaxed, like long-lost friends. Mike invited us to play at his bars, exclusively, until something better came along. We signed our first contract with him after consulting with

Kat.

Girls Just Want to Have Fun

Alli: April 23, 2011

WE COULDN'T have asked for better timing. Aunt Kat had us booked at other local bars through mid-April, so she only needed to cancel one show to eliminate any overlap with our new Mike Allen contract.

We finished our fourth gig at Lisa's, pleased with our new surroundings. Chameleons had been our spirit animal until that point; we could adjust to fit in just about anywhere. The crowd really enjoyed our sets, even though Lisa's focused on country music. While marketing our shows, we made it clear our genre was rock and roll, but we gained a following at Lisa's anyway.

Most of the patrons left after we finished our last song, but we regularly stayed for a few drinks while the staff closed up. Seated at the farthest booth beyond the bar, the oversized circular one we had claimed as ours, sat a gorgeous lady with long dark curls. I nodded a greeting, smiled, and motioned for the band to sit in the open booth beside it.

Charlie muttered to herself, displeased that someone had taken our booth.

Danny approached and stood beside the elevated booth. "Why are y'all sitting here?"

With a frown and a slight tip of her head, Charlie signaled that someone occupied our usual spot.

Danny picked up on her signal and laughed. He herded us into our booth despite the confusion.

The classy lady, dressed all in black, didn't protest. Instead, she smiled and scootched. Her smooth curls swished with each movement.

"Brooke Mason, may I present to you Heaven Scent?" Danny introduced us individually, recited a background line for us each, then moved aside so the waitress could serve the drinks we had ordered after coming off stage.

We all shook hands with Brooke and anticipated the reason for Danny's sly actions.

"Heaven Scent." A smile tweaked at the corner of his lips, showing he had been proud to keep this secret. "This nice lady here is Brooke Mason. She hails from Tyler, Texas. I think you've heard of it?" He raised his eyebrows and chuckled. "She's the best manager I've ever had the pleasure of working with, and she asked for an introduction to Lisa's hottest new band. Mike has been talking about you. I think all y'all are going to be great friends."

"It's nice to meet you, Ms. Mason, but we already

have a manager," I blurted without thinking.

Charlie attempted to pull me aside to discuss how we should handle this. Although my intent was not to be rude, I guess I did sound a bit protective.

"I've heard about your aunt Kat." Brooke smiled and spoke with respect. "Mike mentioned that she's been instrumental in your growth and flat-out great for your career thus far. However, it may be time for the band to expand to a point where she can't sustain it on her own." This obvious Hollywood player certainly knew the right words to use.

We had the best support from Aunt Kat, but with her in Michigan, it would be close to impossible for her to represent us the way we needed.

"That's where I come in."

Charlie stood, grabbed my arm, and nodded to Sara and Tommy. "Let's go have a little chat." The side door led to an area of the parking lot that only bands used. Once securely out of earshot, she said, "Listen." Understanding that she needed my attention most of all, Charlie faced me and touched my arm. "We all love Kat with everything in our being." She paused when I frowned and crossed my arms.

"But?" Pursed lips explained my semi-hurt feelings.

"But she's not here." Charlie's voice softened. "She has a family, a husband and kids who need her attention. She's a fantastic human, momma figure, protector, and supporter."

"But?" With less gusto, I focused on the clouds passing above us in the dark sky. She began to get my point.

"But it may be time to make a change."

"She's given more of herself than anyone ever expected." Sara agreed with me, but she also agreed with Charlie. "She has been our biggest fan since day one. It's time to let her rest."

Tommy understood how much Aunt Kat meant to all of us and realized the need to tread lightly. "Kat will always be number one in my book."

Outnumbered, I hung my head and nodded. "You're right." I wiped a tear from my cheek and sighed. "How do I tell Aunt Kat?"

Charlie wrapped an arm around my shoulders, squeezed, and led me back through the door.

An older lady had joined Brooke in the booth. The back of her short spiky blond hair was visible from the door.

As we approached the table, the lady stood. "Girls!" Aunt Kat hugged me, then Charlie, Sara, and Tommy. We were all shocked to see her. Then she hugged me a second time, held me around the waist, and nodded sideways toward Tommy. "So, who's the hunk?"

When the laughter died down, I had a chance to address my favorite aunt. "When did you get here? Oh my God, it's so great to see you. I missed you so much."

We all piled into the circular booth and peppered Aunt Kat with questions. "How long can you stay? Did you come here alone? How is everyone back home?"

Hesitant, I lowered my voice and raised my eyebrows. I almost winced, not sure if I wanted to know the answer. "How's Kevin? Think he'll ever forgive us?"

Aunt Kat answered the last question first. "Kevin is doing better. It took your parents a lot of time and energy to convince him to get help. He's currently at an in-patient facility in Chelsea."

An audible sigh joined more tears. My day had been more emotional than the rest of the bandmembers', but they all absorbed a little of my pain. Times like this were when Heaven Scent was the tightest; we each supported every member of the band, as if they were family. Because we are.

Charlie held my hand, and Sara offered words of encouragement. "He'll be fine. One day, when we get back to Brooklyn, he and Tommy will hit it off, and we'll all be back together again—just one extra. Who couldn't use an extra drummer?"

Aunt Kat cut through the somber mood with her bubbly nature. "Girls, let's get back to today, shall we?" Always knowing when to change the subject at the perfect time, she continued, "I will be here for a week. I wanted to be here when you discussed your future with Brooke. We've gone over what I designed in the past and how she can move the success of Heaven Scent forward."

Confused, Sara and Charlie exchanged glances, and Tommy chuckled. My jaw dropped. "What? You knew about this?"

"Of course, my dear. I know all." Her squinted eyes relieved my mind. "I'm thrilled that Brooke will be representing you. She's fantastic. We've been talking for the past month or so since you started playing here. I wouldn't trust just anyone with my girls. And my Tommy."

"We haven't made that decision yet." I shook my head and tried my best to hold on to my comfort zone.

"No need, Allison. I made it for you." She took my hand in hers. "I'm passing the baton. Your career is getting too big for me to handle from Michigan, so Brooke will take over. No worries, she'll take good care of you. I promise." Aunt Kat nodded to Brooke, who, until that point, had only observed.

"The lovely Ms. McIntosh has made it abundantly clear how much she loves not only you but the band. I promise you all that I won't let you down." Our new manager paused, then announced, "I have taken it upon myself to book your first gig."

We stared and waited for her to elaborate.

Brooke let a twitch tug at the corner of her mouth. "You're playing Gene's next weekend."

"B-but." Stunned, Charlie stuttered, "We … they …

Isn't there a huge wait list at Gene's?"

"Yes!" Sara and I exchanged smiles.

"Sweet." Tommy drummed the table with his index fingers, just like Kevin used to. "Wonder if anyone from here will follow us over?"

In manager mode, Brooke picked up where she had left off. "Your energy is unparalleled. Y'all are certainly naturals. I don't say this often, but I truly think all y'all have a gift. The way you complement one another and obviously enjoy being on stage together, it's nothing short of spectacular. With that being said, you can always work to improve your gift, to make yourself better. The more you know, the more confident you will be in your craft. That confidence will show on stage. This is one area where I can help you grow." While she had our attention, Brooke leaned forward and clasped her hands. "It couldn't hurt to take some classes. Very specific classes." She peered at me. "Voice lessons for Alli. Even though you sing like an angel, classes with a close friend of mine will help you improve."

I shrugged. "Why not. Couldn't hurt."

"Guitar and drumming sessions with the three of you, individually, will be worth every minute. I promise." Brooke smiled and nodded. "Learn why what you're doing works and what won't work for you, moving forward. Learn why you sound so good together. Hone it in and perfect it." She pursed her lips and squinted at each of us. “I can picture you in five years. You’ll be headlining all over the world. You’re going to be stars.”

“I bet you say that to everyone,” Sara teased.

Aunt Kat laughed. “I think these are grand ideas. Thank you, Brooke, for picking up where I left off. I know this partnership will be plentiful.”

We signed some documents, toasted to our new manager, and watched Brooke Mason walk out the door.

“What the fuck just happened?” Charlie stood and asked the universe. With her arms stretched to her sides, she tilted her head back and twirled, as if dancing in the rain. Dizzy, she grabbed the table and laughed. She reached for her drink and raised it in a toast. “To us. To our future.” She smiled at Aunt Kat. “To our past. To Heaven Scent.”

We cheered and drank, reminisced with Aunt Kat, and enjoyed our time with our shared momma bear.

“Hey, Charlie?” I pursed my lips. “Think I should take some dance lessons? If my sorry ass is going to keep performing, I can’t use my current moves. I dance like Elaine.”

Caught off guard, Tommy spit out his drink, and the rest of us laughed out loud.

“Ain’t that the truth.” A familiar voice reached our booth from across the room.

Charlie tweaked her head like a dog, listening intently, turned, and stood. “Well, I’ll be damned. Look what the cat dragged in."

Eddie Francis stood in the middle of the dancefloor with arms wide open. He caught Charlie midjump and swung her in a circle.

"My hero," she teased, and he set her down. "Can this day get any better? What the fuck are you doing here?" Charlie signaled to the bartender for another round and led Eddie to our booth.

"Patti said y'all might need some protection now that you're making a name for yourself here. Thought I might as well hop on the Heaven Scent train before you get too big and forget about your old friends."

"You moved here?"

"Yes, ma'am."

Alli: April 30, 2011

ELATED. Overjoyed, unworthy, exhilarated, complete. Playing at Gene's brought a new level of emotions to our group.

Bands who play at Mike Allen's bars are on their path to success. As long as the members are strong enough to deny their peers offering any drug, girl, or guy you could dream about, that is. With each level of fame and recognition comes a higher level of temptation.

I thought playing with Nickelback had been a

high—good lord, the energy at Gene's was indescribable. Our stage presence flowed, as if we had played a thousand years together. Everyone in the crowd sang every word of every song we played—even our originals. Talk about surreal.

Fans we acquired during the nights we performed at Lisa's had followed us to our new home venue—Gene's. More people packed the bar each time we played. We had sold out a few nights, forcing the bouncer to turn away paying guests.

At one performance, Eddie pushed a couple guys away from the stage: one hot and one creepy as hell. Having him protect us was the best way for us to be totally at ease on stage. Not having to worry about freaky people allowed our craft to flow without obstruction.

Our tenure at Lisa's and Gene's will all be a distant memory one day, but at that time, we were on top of the world. Nothing could be better, and nothing could derail the feel-good train. Until Brooke delivered good news.

After our last set, she held open our dressing room door for a waitress holding a tray of drinks. She followed her to the small table, tipped her, and turned to greet us. "Y'all rocked this place! I'm so proud of you." A smile as wide as the Grand Canyon spread across her face as she embraced us all. "The crowd loved you, couldn't get enough. Each and every one of you are stars in your own right."

A flood of friends followed. Mike and Danny entered the small room and dished out hugs. They had arrived in time to see our set and were delighted to watch one of their discoveries play at their packed venue. Chad arrived a minute later and found his spot beside Sara.

Once we all held our respective usual drinks, Brooke cleared her throat. “May I have your attention please? Heaven Scent, I have some great news.” She paused; we stared. “I have booked an official tour. A real tour with a pre-arranged set of dates that will include transportation, hotels, a rider, and a nice little paycheck.”

“Get *out*!” I jumped out of my chair, sloshing some of my drink over the edge of the glass. “Shit.” I stopped my personal celebration to mop it up with a napkin.

The perfect ending to a perfect night. *This is it; it's happening*, I thought as I looked at the ceiling, imagining clouds and a burst of sunlight. *Thank you, God.*

“That's fucking awesome.” Unable, or unwilling, to stop drumming, Tommy thrummed his fingers on the table.

“Deets, please.” Charlie's face lit up the room.

We all waited impatiently.

Always gauging our reaction before handing us news, good or bad, Brooke paused. Satisfied with our anxiousness, she said, “You're opening for the Journey/Foreigner tour in October. Just the California leg, from San Diego to Seattle. Oh, and Vegas."

"Vegas!" A jumping circle-hug had become our go-to celebratory reaction. We needed to congregate in larger rooms if we wanted to continue this routine. We bumped into chairs and people in our expression of excitement.

"It's only ten shows, but the experience alone will be worth every second." Brooke grinned and faced Mike. "They're going to be so great."

"They already are." Eddie winked.

"Let me know the dates you're in Vegas, and Mike and I will come see you," Danny offered his support.

Don't Stop Believin'

Charlie: October 8, 2011

"THANK YOU, *Las Vegaaaaassss*." Alli placed the microphone into the holder atop the stand. The walk to the front of the stage to take our bow had become second nature, almost as familiar as our pre-stage routine.

Applause and chants from the crowd followed us backstage. Nothing could ever match the electric buzz and contentment of pleasing our fans. Not only were we having the time of our lives, but we also were making money doing it. From the sales of our CDs and shirts during this tour alone, we had made more than playing at any bar.

A concert at MGM Grand had never been a fantasy. Never did I expect to play in Vegas, even though we had dreamed about it in Brooklyn. I also couldn't have imagined Heaven Scent opening for two of the best bands in history. But there we were.

All the guys in each of the bands were super supportive of us, if not a little hesitant. They wanted to see if we were really any good, so they all watched us perform the first three nights. We learned a lot from watching their set the first three nights, as well. Repetition created a sense of comfort, which our band had figured out from the start.

Because they didn't seem to feel obligated to continue to watch us, we didn't feel obligated either. There hadn't been a real need to experience the same setlist again.

Vegas proved to be unlike any other city which we had toured. Not only did the venue staff ensure that they met all our basic needs, along with a few one-offs, but strangers also waited for us backstage.

Beautiful women and men so gorgeous they must have been models stood around, making small talk, until we entered the room. Once we stepped through the door, all attention turned to us.

Swarms of men surrounded us girls in seconds, and honestly, it made me uncomfortable. It was like swimming with sharks. I didn't want anyone to put their arm over my shoulders or hug me unless I knew them. I didn't know those people.

One guy wrapped an arm around my waist and pulled me close. He tried to kiss me on the lips, but I turned away fast enough for the peck to land on my cheek. Call me a prude or whatever, but I had my standards.

My face most likely gave me away, because one of the men handed me a drink and lifted his chin. "Go ahead. It will help you loosen up a little. Looks like you could use it." A line of coke stretched across a mirror on the table in front of him. Offended, I pushed him and the drink away.

One of the roadies asked for help with the fans who lingered, so Eddie said he would stay. If he'd been backstage with us, he would have certainly kicked the creep's ass without questioning his intent. Besides, Chad was with us, so he had been put in charge of our safety.

I pulled Alli from a guy who had gotten too close, and together, we went to find Sara. Luckily Chad had already rescued her and made it clear that she was with him.

Tommy didn't look like he minded having hot girls all over him, but when he noticed my gaze, he stood and frowned. One of the girls glanced at him from under her eyelashes, and he smirked. She wrote her name and number on a napkin and blew a kiss as he turned away.

"This is just fucking weird. Let's get out of here." I pushed through the back door and stopped short, as if engulfed by Jell-O.

The city, illuminated to the point of daylight, struck me as odd. As we stepped into the night, all my senses received an overload. First, bright neon lights flashed in all the colors of the rainbow, then traffic—horns honked, sirens wailed in the distance—and people talked, yelled, and cheered.

It was impossible to walk a straight path, because so

many bodies lined the streets. We zigged and zagged through the crowd. Scents mixed, and my stomach rolled. Between loud perfume, body odor, fried food, and stale beer, I thought I might lose it.

Walkways stretched across the main road, and I thought it would be smart to get a sense of where we were and where we should go, from a higher vantage point.

"Where we goin,' Stan?" Tommy's voice came from somewhere behind me.

"No idea. Never been here before."

"Come here." Tommy caught up with me, offered his hand, and led me through the maze of people to the edge of the walkway.

"Check out this view." Sara gaped as she stood beside me.

"Holy shit," Alli hissed. "I had no idea. *Vegas Vacation* didn't make it look this big." From the MGM Grand, we faced north, most of the strip laying in front of us.

Buildings, concrete, neon lights, cars, and people spread out as far as the eye could see. So many possibilities, so many options, I wasn't sure we had enough time to properly explore the city.

Tommy suggested, "What one thing do you want to see the most? Let's do that."

"Bellagio," Sara, Alli, and I said in unison. It had been one of our dreams to watch the dancing water since we were kids. Kids—like that was so long ago.

SLOT MACHINES buzzed and dinged, clinked and clanked, chimed and rang all around us. Tommy strolled toward the craps tables, and Alli went in search of a roulette game. We agreed to meet in an hour out front; the fountain ballet performance began each hour, on the hour, and we didn't want to miss it. Again.

Sara sat in front of a penny slot machine depicting a rock star, slid a dollar into the slot, and pulled the lever. A song by Guns N' Roses played from the speakers as the split-display rolled. Not much of a gambler, I hung out with Sara and Chad instead of wandering.

Three rectangular segments aligned to form a picture of an electric guitar—Sara had won! A red light atop the machine flashed, and buzzers rang loud enough to startle us both. Because of the commotion, people gathered to watch the amount of winnings displayed atop the screen grow.

"No way is this thing going over two hundred." Sara relaxed in the chair. The counter rolled, passing one thousand, and climbed. Sara's jaw dropped.

"Since we're in Vegas, I bet it stops at five thousand," Chad guessed.

In the end, Sara had won the largest payout from that machine in history. With ten thousand dollars deposited directly into her bank account, we sauntered to the front of the casino to meet the others.

"Hey," Sara said, oozing nonchalance. "Guess what happened at the penny slots?"

"You look like you won," Alli guessed.

"Yup."

"Sweet. How much?" Tommy's eyebrows lifted.

"Eh ..." Sara shrugged. "Enough."

Chad promised to let Sara share the good news with Tommy and Alli. He shook his head and put his arm around her.

"Come on." I nudged Sara. "It's killing me not to yell it to the world. Tell them."

That got Alli and Tommy's attention. They focused on Sara and waited for her to speak.

"Ten K."

"What? No fucking way!" Alli almost jumped into Sara's arms.

"Sweet," Tommy repeated with more enthusiasm this time.

MIKE AND DANNY found us at the Bellagio as the fountains had begun to dance. Set to music with lights illuminated under the surface, water danced through the air in hypnotizing fashion. I found it impossible to look away. Each time the water moved, my heart expanded. I loved it there.

The rest of the band talked with Danny as Mike

sidled up beside me. We stood in front of the crowd, along the concrete barrier, and followed the graceful water in astonishment.

"Amazing, isn't it?"

"Yes," I agreed. "And so many other things. Peaceful, magnificent, beautiful, soothing, exciting. I've never experienced such contradictions from looking at water."

After a long silence, Mike's soft voice reached my ears. "Penny for your thoughts."

"Cheapskate," I said, smirking.

With his arm resting over my shoulders, Mike laughed. "Yeah, I guess so."

"We're well on our way, aren't we?" I faced the man who had given us our big break and had introduced us to the people who would make our career successful.

He nodded.

"Thank you so much for all you've done for us. We wouldn't be here without you and Danny."

"Don't mention it." He covered his humility with a shrug. "You and the band have done all the hard work. I'm just glad you fell into Lisa's when you did. Perfect timing. Serendipity, if you believe in that kind of thing."

Touched, tears pooled in my eyes. That was thanks enough for Mike. I never imagined a person as humble and giving could actually exist. Didn't everyone have some agenda? Something they needed or wanted from every connection they made?

Oh, well, I guess not. Heaven Scent doesn't ask anything of anyone—another of our promises to each other: never take without giving. But figuring out a way to give back to Mike escaped me.

"Let's go meet up with Eddie. He should be on his way to the Excalibur by now." Excited to see the one man who treasured me and treated me like a queen, I headed toward our meeting place.

On the way, we threw out lyrics, like we usually did when something exciting had touched us. Writing organic songs in this way had proved to be our most effective style. Words took so much longer to reveal themselves on days we spent around a table or if we made it a point to focus on writing.

Ready for a night on the town?
Listen, now, I ain't messin' around
Let's get this party started
Let's show this place what we're
made of

Rollin' down the Vegas strip
Rockin' out at the MGM
Kickin' ass and takin' names
Watchin' boys tryin' to light our
flame

Chowin' buffet food at Excalibur
Gimmie some crab legs and
pancakes

"Wait. Pancakes? That doesn't rhyme with Excalibur."

"What the fuck does rhyme with Excalibur?" I spurted out some examples. "Fur, purr, sir."

"Are you rhyming, Stan, or naming your cat?" Tommy teased, and Sara giggled.

Mike appreciated our way of brainstorming, nodded, and smiled at Danny. "We're witnessing history in the making."

I may have a little country in my
heart
And I ain't gonna let you tear it
apart
You can clean me up for a night on
the town
But I'll never give up my hillbilly
crown

"I love it!" I danced in the middle of the sidewalk, spun around, grabbed Sara's hands, and led her in a square dance.

Not when we're in Vegas, baby!
Vegas, Vegas, Vegas
Clean me up for a night on the town

You better believe I'm wearin'
My hillbilly crown

Charlie: October 31, 2011

SUNSHINE HIT me in the face like the beam of a cop's flashlight. It seemed like California's sun was brighter than in Michigan; weird, but the thought often crossed my mind. The warmth, though, was what I loved the most. To think it was not unusual to wear snowmobile pants to go trick or treating like we did back home made me giggle.

"I can't even get over how warm it is on Halloween. I'm never moving back to Michigan. Like, ever."

"There is nothing I could agree with more than that statement." Alli pulled her sunglasses from her purse and squinted until they covered her eyes.

Sara motioned for us to stop when we reached the restaurant's parking lot. "Listen. I've been thinking about this since Vegas. I want to use my winnings to pay for the studio time."

"Not a chance," Alli interrupted before Sara could explain more. "We're all in this together. We've all saved some money. I say we split it evenly."

"Agree," Tommy stated.

"Agree, agree." I wasn't about to let her spend all

her money on the band. Alli had a point; we all had an obligation to pay our fair share.

"Guys."

"Nope. Let's plan on a thousand each and go from there. Shouldn't be much more than that for the entire album. If it is, we split it."

To push back, Sara opened her mouth but closed it when Alli held up her hand.

"Period," she emphasized.

"Okay. I hear you." Sara nodded and changed the subject. "Can you believe it was one year ago today when we went to the Whisky Halloween party?"

"And you met Chad," Alli remembered.

Sara smiled and squeezed her boyfriend's hand. "What time do you go on?" Rhinestone had played at the Whisky on Halloween for the past four years, one of their first traditions as a band.

Chad checked his watch. "In about two hours. I should go." He kissed Sara and walked to his car. "See you in a bit."

"In a bit," Sara waved and walked on air beside the rest of us.

"Stupid love," I said, envying their relationship. Even though I was happy for Sara and Chad, I tried hard not to be jealous. I missed experiencing the kind of connection I once had with Tony.

"*Walkin' around here like a clown*," Sara quoted our song and smirked. "Tonight is our first-meeting anniversary, and Chad said we can't miss any of their set. I think he's got something up his sleeve."

"Well, we better hurry up and get dressed, then."

In the past year, the Whisky has been more than just a place to go drinking. We played gigs, made friends, supported other bands, made connections we otherwise may not have made, and, ah, who am I kidding? A place we definitely went to drink.

Halfway through Rhinestone's set, Chad grabbed the mic and introduced his girl to the entire bar. Sara blushed and waved to the guests. "Babe, I'm going to need you to come on stage."

Sara tilted her head and shook it while she mouthed, *No*.

Rhinestone's bassist faux-coughed into the mic. "Uh, I'm not feelin' so good. I'm gonna need someone to fill in on this next song. Anyone in the crowd play bass?"

Laughing, Sara climbed the stairs and accepted the guitar.

"Nothing says, *I love you*, like putting your girl on the spot," Chad said, grinning. "Ready?"

Sara nodded and began one of Rhinestone's songs.

Sara and Chad had played together for the first time a few months ago, and they really jelled. Their styles fit together like pieces of a puzzle. That night, being their one-year date-iversary, made it all the more likely that it wasn't just a one-time thing. It scared me that she might leave us for them. She had fallen hard for Chad, and I know how stupid love can make you.

We had spent plenty of nights talking, drinking, and laughing with friends in one of or all the dressing rooms. Once the crowd dissipated, we would all hang out in the bar. That night had been no different from the rest.

Some of the bands had impromptu jam sessions for shits and giggles; any number of Heaven Scent members would join at one time or another.

Chad and Sara repeated the song they had played earlier in the night, and the friend-crowd went wild. Not everyone had been in the bar the first time they'd played, and several people made it a point to tell them that they should play together.

One night, I mentioned the possibility of Chad stealing her from us, but Sara reassured me that she would never leave. "Not only do I love you, Alli, and Tommy, I love Heaven Scent, what we're about, and who we support."

Relieved but needing to secure our future, I asked, "Would you be willing to sign an updated contract?"

To ease my anxiety, she rolled her eyes, stuck out her tongue, and walked away.

THE NEXT WEEK, during our band meeting with Brooke, I brought up the subject of updating our contracts. "Listen. We've been through a lot in our short lifetime. We're so young, as people and as a band. We've done some great things together, from tours all over the US, to studio work and putting our own spin on production. We've learned the ropes and grown up. We're on our way to selling a bazillion records and becoming seventeen times platinum. We are Heaven Scent."

"*Whoo-hooo*," the band cheered in unison.

Their excitement filled my heart. "This is more than a pep talk and an appreciation meeting—it's both of those things, too. I need to know for sure that nothing would happen to split us up. Again."

"Charlie ..." Alli frowned and tilted her head. "We aren't going to do what Kevin did." Her face relaxed; I knew she got it. "But I'm willing to do whatever it takes to make everyone at this table feel secure."

"Me, too," Sara said, smiling.

"Me, three." Tommy nodded.

Uptown Funk

The Interview: January 8, 2015

"VEGAS SOUNDS incredible. I can't wait to go someday. How awesome is it that you won so much money, and even more awesome how you offered to pay for the studio. It's obvious that you all absolutely love what you do. I'm honestly a little jealous." Jenni sighs.

"You've had your share of meeting some celebrities now. Everyone is curious if their favorite celebrity is a normal person, like them. They want to know if they should love the real person behind the famous allure. Who, would you say, is the most down-to-earth?"

"You know, it's funny." Alli taps her finger to her lips. "When we got into this scene, the popular trend was boy bands, and if a female lead was on stage, everyone expected them to dance like Britney or Christina. We haven't had the pleasure of meeting Britany, but Christina's pretty cool. Nick and Justin are equally as cool. We tend to gravitate toward people who mirror our own style and genre but find some of the nicest people, the most down-to-earth people, are the old-school country bands."

"It makes sense, I guess. Loretta and Dolly came from nothing, so they know what it's like to struggle. They didn't change who they are just because they made tons of money."

"The guys in Nickelback took us under their wing after we got to LA," Sara continues. "They found us at the Whisky one night, welcomed us, and we've been good friends since. Showing us the ropes and keeping us safe from creepy fans made them seem like real people. They're completely humble and don't expect special treatment."

Charlie agrees, "They've been downright fantastic. Without their advice and showing us around the life of a rock star, we probably wouldn't be where we are today."

"Keep in mind, these girls were pretty uneducated about the ways of rock life when they landed on the strip." Tommy flashes a loving smile. "Even after touring with Nickelback. They've admitted to everyone how they didn't know the first thing about how to act in Hollywood."

"Didn't take us too long though, did it?" Allie lifts one eyebrow.

An unplanned question pops into Jenni's mind. "What motivates you to push for more?"

"Our fans, for sure," Tommy admits. "They're the reason we do it all. Stay healthy, make good choices, respect each other. If any of our morals slip and it affects the rest of the band, it also affects our fans."

"We have so much fun on stage that I can't imagine a life when we aren't entertaining. It's in our blood now," Sara adds.

"Landing our own tour, though. The. Best. The absolute best feeling in the world. We didn't have to depend on anyone else's manager to communicate with our manager," Charlie explains.

"Brooke didn't need to have every little thing on our rider pre-approved, like she had in the past," Sara says. "I could understand if we demanded caviar or Dom Perignon. Seriously, was it really a problem to have extra bottles of water or hair dryers in the hotel room? I'll never forget the day she made the announcement and what it meant for the band."

Sara: November 2, 2011

BEFORE OUR tour with Journey, we understood the importance of recording our second album. Brooke booked some time at the studio where she sent all her clients.

Our first record had taken so much out of us as a band that we studied the process before we tried again.

We spent quite a few nights at Studio 42, observing other bands as they recorded and the producers as they worked their magic. It helped us understand what we should expect of recording on a larger scale and what the engineers would expect of us.

Although we sat back and observed each move, everyone who worked there treated us like family, like we belonged.

Time passed faster than I had expected, and I was surprised when the day arrived. It was our turn inside the studio. Again. I hoped and prayed for success. We couldn't fail. I wouldn't let us fail.

Already accepted as part of the family, it allowed us to relax. In addition, money wasn't as much of a hindrance this time around, so we could spend a little more time to allow the process to organically complete itself.

We followed the producer, Jeremy LeMaster, through the door and watched him flip switches on all the equipment. He grabbed a fresh two-inch reel master tape from the storage closet and wound it between the posts on the soundboard. He plugged in all the equipment, including video cameras and microphones, before setting a few levers and buttons to a base starting position.

The first time we had visited this studio, Tommy had noticed the state-of-the-art equipment right away. "Badass! This is a fucking NEVE board. Do you have any idea what this means?"

At first, us girls did not. The recording console had master controls, buttons, and knobs.

"Ancient," Tommy explained. "This shit was the real way to record before all the synthesizers came out. Dude, we're rolling back to the seventies."

Time spent educating ourselves paid off. Immersed in the process, we appreciated each step of making this record.

Jeremy explained how laying down separate portions of the song worked, even though we had been watching other bands. I was glad he had, because the personal experience had been different than I'd expected.

Tommy went first.

"Drums are the heartbeat of the song. Let's start there," Jeremy explained. The drum room was separate from the instruments room. The engineers placed microphones all over the room, while Tommy arranged the equipment to his specifications.

Watching him jam alone reminded me of being at practice. He would warm up before the rest of the band joined, so this didn't seem much different.

Once he had completed a few songs, it was my turn. I sat in front of the mic, tuned my bass, and donned my headphones.

The producer's voice echoed in my ears, "You ready?"

I nodded and closed my eyes.

He flipped a switch. "We're rolling."

Here we go. This is it.

I followed along with Tommy's drumbeat as they flowed through my headset to my fingers. When we had recorded in Boots's barn, I didn't have a chance to play without the others, so I had been especially nervous for this day. Each time we practiced recently, I would envision this moment. It helped to mentally prepare me for the odd sensation of playing alone.

Charlie went after me, jamming out like she always does. Perfection came to her as naturally as breathing.

Alli prepared for her turn by performing her *fives*, as we now referred to her preparation with love. She stood in front of the mic and closed her eyes. Glass separated her from the producer and gave her a sense of disconnect. Her hands covered the headphones, which covered her ears. We talked Jeremy into playing "Kiss" to loosen her up. The minute he pumped the song to her, she smiled and bobbed her head to the music.

Alli sang along with the song and laughed, as she always did. Her smile grew radiant when she reached the last lyrics. Had she only known what we had up our sleeve, she might have stayed nervous.

It came time for her to sing while listening to our previous recording through the headphones. Flawless, she completed her portion and joined the rest of us in the control room.

While we waited for Jeremy to do his thing, we grabbed beers and chatted about how cool it was to finally be there. Together.

"What does this do?" Tommy reached for a knob.

Jeremy slapped his hand. "Don't touch that!"

Alli admitted, "There's such a different energy when you're singing there alone without the band behind you. Still, without instruments surrounding me, it's as weird as the first time. The heavy songs just don't feel the same when they're not recorded live. If we're doing something slow, we can piece it together, but it just doesn't have the same effect when completely getting into a fast jam."

"Well, then"—Jeremy turned to face us—"let's do some live tracks instead of overdubs and see what you think."

Excited to play together, we rushed to our places in the second studio and waited for our cue. We must have played "Summertime" a hundred times before we got it completely right.

During one of the attempts, I stopped in the middle of the song. "Did that sound just come out of your face?"

Alli's eyes widened, and Tommy cracked up.

"I fucking hate this song," Charlie confessed after rubbing her fingers together to ease the burn. "But man, I fucking love this room. It's like we're jamming during practice."

At one point, we all played different pieces, brainstorming ideas: "Hey, what if we do this?" and

"Let's try this beat," and "What about this riff?"

"Oh!" I stopped after one off-the-wall jam of "Stupid Love," my eyes wide. "What the hell just happened? Did we just find our sound? Jesus God, I hope it's recorded."

Every second spent finding our sound and getting it on tape had been worth all the petty bickering and frustration. Nothing done or said here would be a dealbreaker. It was more of a safe space to let go and be free with our craft. It was a time that will live in each of our hearts forever.

"Okay, team, that's all for today." Jeremy clicked off the speaker and gave us a thumbs-up.

We replaced the headsets on their respective stands and joined him in the control room. Gathered around the board, we checked our progress.

"Jesus, do we really suck this bad?" Tommy expressed what we all thought.

"Nope," Jeremy reassured us. "Check this out." After he clicked the mouse and turned some knobs, he hit Play. To our delight and surprise, the track sounded much better than before.

Alli was worried it might not sound quite right. "Don't overproduce this. We still have to be true to ourselves and give our fans what we truly are and what we honestly sound like. We can't be perfect on tape because we're not perfect."

I agreed. "We need to keep our integrity."

"How cool would it have been to record at Sound City, like the legends did?"

"Yeah, but this equipment is just like what they used there, right?"

"Honestly it may be the same exact board."

We all laughed, then wondered if it could be.

"Well, I would call our studio time today a success." I slung my backpack over one shoulder and led the band toward the exit.

"Coming organized definitely helped. Compared to last time, finishing this record will be a piece of cake."

DISTRACTED by hoping the little details would get mixed right by Jeremy, I heard murmurs from Brooke float over my head. Tommy stood beside me near the stage at *Our Place* and asked a question about his solo on "Beer Tears". He worried that a section of the song might be a little off beat. I chuckled and eased his worry; he loved that song.

Charlie whispered to Alli about a mistake she thought might throw off the flow of "All Right". Usually, we weren't this disrespectful of Brooke, but in our defense, we had just finished recording our second album, and all sorts of energy pumped through us.

"The schedule is solid; contracts are signed. We've been paid deposits, and I have feelers out for roadies."

Squinted eyes burned through my soul as Brooke spoke.

Her words didn't register. I heard what she said, but it didn't make sense. "I'm sorry, Brooke. I didn't catch that."

"I need to book hotels and take care of the little stuff. I've reached out to a designer and marketing company for promotional material. New t-shirt designs and other merch will need to be approved in the next thirty days."

"What hotels? Brooke, what are you talking about?" Charlie hadn't registered her comments either.

"Your first show is June fifteenth. Guys!" Brooke demanded our full attention. "Did you hear me? Are you paying attention? You're going on the road for nine months. This is it. You're headlining. We've done it. You made it."

Grins stretched across our faces as we absorbed our manager's words.

"Nine months?" Alli tilted her head. "What about the RV?"

"Oh, God," Tommy teased. "Would you forget about the damn RV?" His voice raised almost to a yell. "We're going on tour!" He picked up Charlie and twirled her in a circle.

Alli looked at me. "We need to call Aunt Kat. She won't believe this."

"Yes. She will. She started us on this path, remember?"

Alli and I sat across from Brooke at the big table in the middle of *Our Place* and waited for the others to join us. She had done it. With her communication and dedication, Brooke had made our band famous.

"Here. You've earned this."

Envelopes with each of our names sat before us. I opened mine and gasped. A check with more zeros than I'd ever seen had my name typed on the *Pay to the Order of* line.

"Each bandmember received the same check. This is only your initial payout. Once we promote your records, you'll receive royalties from each one sold. Every time your song is played on the radio, you'll get paid. You're all going to be very busy, starting next week. I've scheduled interviews with radio stations and magazines. I suggest you start talking about *Our Place* and invite fans to watch you practice. Just for now. After y'all get on the road, maybe you can sublet it or turn it into a bar. Talk to Mike—I bet he'll have some ideas."

"Can we see that?" I pointed to a piece of paper with dates and cities listed.

Brooke grinned and pushed it across the table.

Alli and Charlie sat on either side of me. Tommy stood behind us and looked over our shoulders. We took turns speaking the names of cities across the United States.

I focused on the list, starting at the top. "Can you

believe we're playing in Brooklyn?" Nothing could have made me happier. I glanced at Brooke, smirked, and nodded my approval. "I want to donate some of what we make at MIS to a homeless shelter in Jackson. I'll get you their name."

"That's a great idea, Sara. I never imagined playing at MIS. Who knew they booked concerts?" Charlie shrugged.

"How about the rehab where Kevin went?" Alli squinted. "Can we donate to them, too?"

"Of course. Anything you want. It's your money. Although, I highly suggest not spending it all in one place." Proud of each of us, Brooke winked. "I wanted to book Callaghan's, but they just don't have a large enough space. What I was able to do, though, was arrange an intimate concert there the night before MIS. Invite your closest hundred friends to see you for free. I've arranged to cover the normal entrance fees for everyone that night. My homecoming gift to you."

When we got to the RV, each of us simmered in our own emotions. Thoughts of the beginning, our tours to Florida and Texas, how we had gotten to LA, meeting Mike and Brooke, all proved too much for my heart to hold. I crossed the highway to the beach, found a picnic table, and removed my shoes. Sitting with my toes in the sand, I allowed the tears to fall.

In the past, I had learned to fight back tears. Through my entire life, my mom had reminded me again and again of how only weak people cry. She had lied about so much in my past that I found it hard to believe anything she had ever told me. Despite her, or maybe because of her, I let myself cry.

Heaven Scent had reached the next level: a headlining tour across the United States. All our dreams were coming true.

Releasing positive emotions differed in comparison to all the times in my youth when I had cried out of anger; happiness had alluded me for so long. Holes in my bedroom walls were the result of holding in the tears. If I had only let them out, back then, I might have been less resistant to criticism.

Or maybe if I didn't believe my mom every time she had told me how much of a fat ass I was, I might have found it easier to believe in myself. Allowing the tears to flow that night helped rid negative thoughts. Since then, it has been easy to convince myself how I had always been good enough.

My best girls followed me to the beach, let me sit alone for a while, then sat on either side of me. Alli handed me a Coors Light, and we held hands, laughing like we were back in high school. We understood how our nights of juvenile sleepovers would soon be over. Our childhood friendship had morphed into an adult form of love, respect, and appreciation.

"Remember when we would sit like this at

Vineyard?"

Alli hummed, then released her angelic voice.

Remember me?
Yeah, it's been a long time, too long
It's so good to see your face
I've seen you so many times in my
dreams

When the words to another impromptu song reached my heart, I added my own lyrics.

I remember you like it was yesterday
Carved our names in that old oak
tree

Charlie sang,

Threw me into the water off your
dad's brand-new pontoon boat

Then Alli:

Made love beside the river at dawn

Together, we harmonized.

Remember me?

Who Says You Can't Go Home

The Interview: January 8, 2015

THE CLOCK chimes twice, and Jenni checks her watch. "Goodness, we've been at this for a while. I am enjoying your story so much. I hope you don't mind me taking up so much of your time."

"Don't be silly." A swish of Sara's hand dismisses the thought. "This is the most fun we've had reminiscing in, well, forever. What's next?"

"Good. I'll wrap up here soon. Do you have a special practice to keep you centered? Something that reminds you where you came from?"

"I'm glad you asked. That's a great question." Alli scoots forward in her chair. "We make it a point during all our concerts to do something special for one of our attendees. Whether it's giving him or her something that's signed or having our manager write them or their parents a check for a college scholarship or bringing them backstage to meet the band. We know how hard it is to do normal everyday things in life, and we want to pay it forward. We want to do something good with the fortune that we have been lucky enough to attain."

"I love that. How selfless of you." Jenni scribbles on the notepad in her lap and smiles. "Okay, I have a question about the meaning of "Set Me Free" .It's been pretty controversial over the past couple of years. Some people think it means it's about a breakup, other people think it's a family issue, and still others think it is just a bunch of words thrown together. The lyrics match the music; maybe they don't mean anything."

"It was inspired by watching Alli's dog chase a stick that someone threw into the lake." Charlie leans back in her chair and strums her guitar. "He didn't care if he got wet, he didn't care if his owner didn't want him to run after that stick, he didn't care if he looked like a fool trying to swim his way back to shore. All he cared about was having fun doing his thing, having his own experiences, no matter what everyone thought about him. If he was silly or tripped or so happy, he trotted in circles, he was free. This song is about that—being free."

As if signaled by Charlie, Alli sings,

Like an eagle flying high
Like a dog running across a field
Nothing in this crazy life
Should hold you back from things
you love

Nothing in this crazy life
Should keep you from being healed
Set me free, set me free
Let me live my best life
Just because it's different doesn't
make it wrong

Set me free, set me free
You be you, and I'll be me

"That's what life should be like. No one should hold you down; no one should make you feel stupid for doing things differently than they do. And no one should have such power over you to make you change your mind about things you feel so strongly about. It's about making your own choices and being free."

"You can find inspiration in almost anything, can't you? So many people have talked about the uplifting message from Heaven Scent, of what you stand for, and how you've stayed true to yourselves. I'm proud to say I'm from the same small town, and now I can be proud to say we've met."

"I'm proud to call you a friend, Jenni." Charlie offers a genuine smile. "You know just as much about our lives as we do each other. I'm so glad we took this opportunity to tell our story, and I know you'll do it justice in your book."

Touched, Jenni places a hand over her heart and

smiles. Tears gloss her eyes. "Thank you so much. That means so much to me." She blinks a few times and takes a deep breath. "If you had a real job, what would it be?"

Charlie lightens the mood. "Wait, this isn't a real job? Shit ..." The strum of her guitar emits a dismal energy that surrounds the group of friends, and they laugh at her humor.

"My bank account says it is." Alli lifts her drink in a cheers.

"Okay, let me rephrase." Jenni takes a drink to hide her smirk. "What did you want to be when you grew up before you decided to be rock stars? And what is the first thing you bought with your newfound riches?"

"I wanted to be a photographer and take pictures of all the pretty things," Alli's gaze lands on the over-sized framed photo of a longhorn in a field of bluebonnets along the far wall. "I wanted to travel and experience places that were totally off the beaten path. I make it a point to venture to see something weird during most every stop of our tours. The first thing I bought was my own car. Don't get me wrong; Sara's mom's Accord was great, but, man, I needed something with a little more oomph."

"How much more oomph?" Jenni lifts an eyebrow.

"A little over five-hundred horsepower. My dream car was always a Corvette, so I got one. Then I paid off my parent's house and bought a place for Kevin."

"Where is Kevin these days? What's he doing? Is

he recovered?"

"He's good, sober. He owns a construction company in Jackson that works with concrete. Pours basements and driveways."

"What happened between you and Tex?"

Lost in a memory, Alli smiles and closes her eyes. When she answers the question, relief and joy are apparent in her voice. "You'll remember how Tex and I mutually broke up when Heaven Scent left for California. He had already enrolled for the spring semester at Michigan State, so it made sense to take a break. We both understood the extent of temptation and didn't want to hinder our choices. We promised to live a full life apart, like we had never been together, but neither of us could fight the love we shared. We made it a point to not stay in touch but never lost what we had. It killed me to not tell him about everything in real time. With the band, touring, LA. But we both kept our promise. After he finished with his engineering program, he heard we would be back in Brooklyn. We both wanted to be sure we still had the same connection, so we met up before I even saw my parents. From the minute I stepped off the plane in Detroit, we have been inseparable. At first, it was supposed to be a test to see if we could pick up where we left off—if we still had it. Boy, did we ever. Now we are happily together and planning our future."

"What about you, Charlie?"

"I wanted to be a rock star. But when that idea had been beat out of me because of how utterly ridiculous and unachievable it was, I decided to be a veterinarian." Charlie smirks at her own smart remark. "Because I proved my mother wrong, I dropped the vet idea and spent my money on things other than family. My first large purchase was a gorgeous horse farm outside LA. I've loved horses my whole life and dreamed of breeding them one day. Now, with Eddie as my stable boy, my dreams have come true."

"When is the wedding? Have you started planning yet?"

A huge diamond weighs down Charlie's left hand. She lifts it, smiling as she jokes about how big it is. "I didn't want something so flashy, but we all know how Eddie likes his bling. Sometime in the spring."

"I think we should have a double wedding," Sara says, giggling. "We want the same colors and people to stand up, so why do it twice?" She focuses on Jenni. "I bought Chad a Harley and our house in Malibu, not far from the RV park, and began my lifelong dream of starting a unique line of fitness clubs. Chad's band broke up soon after Heaven Scent landed our US tour, so he manages the clubs. He comes with us to certain shows but is happy just running our business. Going home for me is a mix of happiness and sadness. My parents spent a lot of time away when I was little, but they refused to let me spend much time with my grandmother—still not sure why. She grew up with nothing and can't understand why I want to spend so much money on her."

"Tommy?" Turning in her chair for a better view of the drummer, Jenni grins and anticipates his response.

"Donna and I met during our first show in Vegas—that girl who wrote her number on a napkin—and we got married on Valentine's Day. I bought her a diamond ring, a house with a pool, and a Mustang." He shifts, embarrassed. "When I was little, I wanted to be a train driver. Didn't know then that they were called engineers. My dad always talked about taking a train to see the world, to go to Florida, where the most beautiful people in the world lived. We didn't have much money, and I thought if I learned how to drive that train, I could help him get to where he wanted to go. Turns out, he just wanted to get away from my mom. He had a secret family across the country. That's where all his money went. And that's where his stripper wife and gorgeous kids lived."

"Does he know about your life now?" Interested, Jenni tilts her head.

"I changed my name when I got to LA, and I don't talk to anyone in my family, so I doubt it." He ponders for a moment, then adds, "Maybe I should look him up. Just for shits and giggles."

Jenni nods. "Maybe. I bet Donna would be super supportive, and it would bring closure." With her warm smile reciprocated, Jenni moves to the next subject.

"Which city has the best fans? I know coming home to Detroit is always a big draw for the locals, and no one knows how to throw a party like a hometown crowd."

"You're right. There's nothing like playing in your hometown. And Detroit does have fantastic fans, but"—Tommy rubbed his chin—"I'm from a town outside of Topeka. Not many tours go through Topeka, so it's hard to gauge their level of coolness. I would definitely say when we tour in Detroit, the crowd is freaking insane. Maybe it's because it's the closest venue to Brooklyn that we play. Maybe it's simply because Detroit fans are crazy. Maybe both." He laughs.

"What's it like when you go back home now?" Jenni adds from her own knowledge, "The biggest celeb before y'all was Vivian Kellogg. The first base All American Girls Professional Baseball League player put Brooklyn on the map. Of course, MIS was built in the sixties and still brings tens of thousands of tourists twice a year. But what's changed, emotionally, for you?"

Raising her hand, Sara answers, "It's almost like we've just been on a really long vacation. Only now, wherever we go, someone says hello or I overhear a girl tell her mom who I am, and I wonder how they know me. Honestly, it's kinda weird." She almost didn't take a breath before changing subjects. "Hey, remember those guys on Lake Columbia who raced cars? I went to see them run around a local circle track a hundred times with my dad."

"Yeah," I added. "One car was the *Pink Pant*her and another one was a red Earnhardt-style car. Number three, I'll never forget watching him race in Lansing. I went with his daughter a few times. Super cool. Wonder where they are now?"

Tommy brings the subject back on track. "It's bizarre and fantastic to witness the transformation from stars to smalltown girls. Once they enter a restaurant, bar, any store, and someone *oohs* and *ahhs*, these three turn into shy teenage-like girls who can hardly believe they're doing better than anyone else in their hometown. They're so humble and gracious. I don't know how much money they individually donate to local shelters and charities, but I think everyone they care about is doing well."

"Ah, Tommy, you're so sweet." Alli blows him a kiss.

"Things came to us quickly, and we made it look like there's nothing to it, but it wasn't always this easy." Alli admits, "We had some pretty trying times on this path to get where we are. Something you can learn from this band is, if you try your hardest, stay true to yourself, make smart choices, and follow your heart, you can do anything you set your mind to."

Alli: June 29, 2012

CALLAGHAN'S hadn't changed much in the six years since we had first played a set there. Hell, it hadn't changed much since it had first opened as a bar called Harvey House in the 1930s.

Most of us have always known it as Callaghan's; the icon in downtown Brooklyn has kept the same name since 1988. Everyone's parents, sisters, brothers, aunts, uncles, and cousins had the honor of spending their twenty-first birthday in this fine drinking establishment. It had almost been a tradition. Most of us had begun drinking there a year or two before that. Not only did regulars hang out to socialize, but the bar provided an avenue to play billiards and videogames and enjoy live music—some good, some not so much.

Darkness impaired my ability to focus for an elongated beat. The undeniable scent of spilled beer and stale cigarette smoke reminded me how I had stepped over a threshold to my previous life.

I was glad we had decided to arrive a day early so I could catch up with Tex. I didn't want to be all googly in front of family or share some much-needed private time. He led me into the bar and greeted friends on the other side of the door.

As if she had been waiting forever, Aunt Kat jumped off her bar stool and rushed me when light filtered through the entrance door. I hadn't even made it two steps inside the building before she wrapped her arms around me so tightly that I thought I might suffocate. She practically pushed Tex out of the way so she could reach me. Her contagious laugh brought a smile to my lips and warmth to my heart.

"I can't believe how much I missed you." A tear slid down my cheek, and I pulled her close to continue our embrace.

The waitress pushed four tables together near the dancefloor so the rest of the band and our families could join us. My parents and the rest of Kat's family had arrived early so they could spend some time with us before we took the stage.

Sara had decided to invite her mom as a goodwill gesture. She had worked hard to reach the point in which she forgave her mom for the way she had treated her in her youth. She didn't think I noticed her looking around for her; it broke my heart that she didn't have the support of her family. She had ours to share though, and she knew it.

Even if Charlie had tried to call her mom, she wouldn't have come. She hoped her dad would make it, though. She had Eddie for support, and he fit in well with the rest of the family members.

Once we had dished out all the hugs and hellos, we sat sipping our drinks. Enjoying these few minutes before setting up our equipment proved to be special; memories of our first show in 2006 flooded back.

"I was so frickin' nervous." I placed my hands on my stomach and leaned back in my chair. "Thought I would throw up."

"What's changed?" Charlie nudged me with her shoulder, and Eddie laughed.

"Dick," I growled and stuck out my tongue.

Tommy set his beer on the table and leaned forward. "My first gig was in a place a lot like this. Smaller, though. My hometown dive has been open since before Scranton had been founded."

Aunt Kat always asked the best questions, and she lived up to my expectations while getting to know Tommy, Eddie, and Chad better.

Tony and his twin brother, Steve, Terry, and Jill, Joey, Boots, and Aaron Loomis walked through the door at the same time. Hugs and greetings flew around the bar for the next thirty minutes. Tony shook Eddie's hand and welcomed him to Brooklyn.

Through the grapevine, we had heard Jeff had moved to Nebraska to follow an internship after college. Sara had been more than a little relieved that she wouldn't have to face him.

Chatter among these people who meant more to me than I ever imagined filled my ears and made my heart sing. A sense of calm spread over me, like a thin veil, and that was when I knew. It hit me out of nowhere. Not only was I good enough but deserving of success, I was worthy of this life.

As a band, the four of us continually preached this to our fans and each other. When you start to believe it yourself, though, that's powerful.

"Welp …" I pushed the chair back and stood. "Let's do this, y'all." Leading the way to set up the stage, I could say for certain that I was happy. Truly joyful.

At precisely eight o'clock, Callaghan's owner tapped the microphone. "Can I please have your attention? I would like to welcome back to the stage, after a long few years of drifting around California, our hometown stars: Brooklyn's very own—Heaven Scent!"

Just as we had six years ago, we waited in the background until Bud Wright introduced us. We sauntered on stage like it was the first time. I had butterflies in my stomach and hoped I wouldn't fuck up. Charlie nailed it; nothing had changed.

"To all the haters or people who thought we couldn't do it, how do you like me now?" Charlie shouted into the microphone and strummed her guitar.

Many of our Brooklyn and Jackson fans hadn't heard us play the songs that we had written about our Midwest roots. Because Kevin hadn't shown up to Callaghan's, it felt a little weird to sing his song, "NASCAR", but we powered through.

Around, around, around they go
Turn left
Then turn left
Smoking tires
Hold on tight

Earnhardt drives so frickin fast
Lap after lap, he's right on Gordan's ass

That line made everyone celebrate. I laughed because my parents had raised me as an Earnhardt fan. The next line eluded me as I watched my brother walk through the door.

Charlie noticed and played an impromptu solo. Once I regained my composure, I nodded to her and finished the song.

Brooklyn kids cheer while their dad's
down beer after beer after beer
Here they come around turn four
Past the fans, the stands in a roar
Checkered flag waves
Cars stretch four wide
Jeff Kasey Matt and Dale
Who's got the most drive?

When we played "Home", the four of us shared a knowing look of accomplishment. We were, in fact, home.

Whoever said there's no place like home
Knew about being on the road

About missing their friends and
family
About being lonely and tired

Whoever dreamed about the land
over the rainbow
Never knew what it meant
To work your ass off to get what you
want
Boy, I bet they do now
I know I do

For the first time in years, Charlie missed a chord. We would all make mistakes during practice but never during a show. Not Charlie. It didn't interrupt us, but I noticed. I followed the direction of her stare and understood the minute I saw him.

Her dad leaned against the back wall with a smile that literally spread from ear to ear. I didn't think one's face could sustain a smile so wide. I sent a silent, *Thank you, God*, to the heavens and sang.

All I want to do now is go home
Home, home, home, home
Where my dad flies RC airplanes
And my mom relives memories while
scrapbooking
Where my friends build their families

And miss me when I'm gone

Home, home, home, home
I can't wait to get home to hug my
aunt Kat and uncle Dan
Our visits are always too short
To drive the streets of Brooklyn
Where we used to play at Supersport

After playing our hearts out—as we did at every concert, be it in a bar or a stadium—we ended with "No Sleep Till Brooklyn". The fans' energy lifted our emotions and reminded us of how lucky we were to live a fully fruitful life.

After all, three of us were girls from this small town in the Midwest. We had grown up with strong morals and had ended up answering a calling. We never imagined this kind of success was possible. It had all started with Charlie's Christmas gift, a dream, and great friends.

As I always do, I addressed our fans to close the show. "Thank you, *Brookllyyyyynn*!"

This day had truly become our homecoming. Charlie ran directly to her dad and got lost in his embrace. She motioned for Eddie to follow, and they walked outside for some privacy.

Kevin approached me with open arms, as well.

Thrilled that he had overcome his addiction, I

hugged him hard. "I didn't know if you could ever forgive us for …" My voice trailed off, and my brother punched my arm, like old times.

"Of course, I forgive you. I completely understand why the band decided to kick me out. I deserved it. You were right; I needed help."

"How long have you been sober?"

"Since about six months after you left. Mom and Aunt Kat pushed so hard that I almost took off, myself. I know, now, that I was headed down a dark path. It could have been so much worse. I could have never recovered and ended up a fifty-year-old man living in my parents' garage."

We shared a much-needed laugh at just how absurd the notion sounded.

"I want you to meet someone." I stood to pull Tommy from a conversation with Tony. He reluctantly followed me to the table where Kevin chatted with my parents.

"Tommy, meet my brother Kevin."

They gaped at one another for a couple seconds before Tommy offered his hand in greeting.

Kevin stood and pulled him into a bro-hug. "Thanks, man."

"For what?"

"Taking care of my sister. I know she can be a pill. You need to remember; I taught her everything she knows. But not everything I know." He winked.

She's a Big Star

January 8, 2015

"HELLO, *DALLAAAAS*!"

Charlie followed Alli on stage, her fingers strumming the notes of their most-recent number-one hit, "Lemonade".

Fireworks exploded before multicolored lights flashed in sync with the drumbeat.

"Are you ready for a party?" Alli asked the crowd of twenty thousand plus.

Always on key, she sang in what critics had described as her signature unique steely tone. A slight twang snuck through from their days touring in Texas.

All my teachers said I would fail, that
I had no future
They thought they knew me, but they
were so wrong
Just because I came from nowhere
didn't mean I wasn't strong
I was a little shit with a bad attitude
But those days are all a blur

Only a few feet from the stage, Mike Allen's group enjoyed being fully immersed in the Heaven Scent experience. Speakers positioned at the corners of the stage blared a guitar solo which no band could match, men or women.

Mike's teenaged nephew, Steve hadn't blinked since Charlie strutted in front of him. He found it impossible to take his gaze off her. He nodded to the beat and sang along.

Life gave me lemons, lemons, lemons
And I made lemonade
Sun shining on my face, sunglasses
give me shade

My girls swimming in the pool,
getting a chlorine marinade
We'll all be smokin' hot, ready to set
this town ablaze
While I make my lemon, lemon,
lemonade

Honest lyrics, written by young girls breaking through into a man's world, touched the crowd. Each song, uplifting and positive, fulfilled a promise that Charlie, Alli, and Sara had made the day they founded Heaven Scent. They had agreed to use their platform to help people through hard times. Hard work and persistence had paid off with fame and success.

"This next song is special to us in so many ways. It was our first single and one of the songs we played the night when Mike Allen discovered us. Mike saw something unique in us and believed we had what it took to make it. For those of you who know our story, you know about Mike. Super cool thing is, he flew out here tonight to enjoy the show. Thanks, Mike. We love ya, man. This one's for you."

While Mike's friends belted out the beloved words of their first hit, Steve sang along with the chorus.

Now it's time, time to believe
Believe, believe, believe Marie
She won't settle, won't give up
She's finally, finally, finally free

Persistence will pave the road
Lead to joy, love, and success
She has to do this on her own
Push away feelings of distress

Hold your head up, don't back down
She repeats the mantra every day
Determined to follow all her dreams
One day she'll live in Monterrey

Charlie ripped the guitar riff as she strutted across the stage. She stopped in front of Steve, pointed at him, and mouthed, *for you*. Her eyes closed, and she leaned her head back, long blond hair moving to the beat of the background drums.

Steve stared without blinking the entire length of the solo.

At the end of the concert, when all of us had met our goal of pleasing the crowd, Alli closed the show. "Thank you, Dallaaaasss!"

Thank you for reading!

Please consider writing a short review wherever you purchased, rented, or borrowed this book. Your social media pages and Goodreads are also great places for you to express how much you loved this book!

Reviews help readers find their new favorite stories and authors improve their craft.

Also by Kristi Copeland

TEXAS SUMMER NIGHTS

Somewhere Outside of Sunset - Book 1

Home in Paradise - Book 2

The Art of Loving - Book 3

OTHER WORKS

Oakdale

COMING SOON

Uncle Eli

Scan the QR Code to be directed to Kristi's author page:

About the Author

KRISTI COPELAND is the author of contemporary and book club fiction. She lives in Texas with her husband and multiple critters on their ranch. When she's not writing, Kristi enjoys spending time with close friends, wine tasting, and cat collecting.

www.kristicopelandwriter.com

Let's get social :

Kristi Copeland (Instagram)
Kristi Copeland - Writer (Facebook)
Kristi Copeland (Goodreads)

Made in the USA
Monee, IL
11 September 2023

42503980R00184